ɹherz

Introduction

As someone interested in history books, what always caught my attention was the kind of actions and decisions taken by world leaders and what these decisions meant in terms of moral standards.

To navigate through history, from the beginning of the 13th century to the present days (822 years), the Vivone dynasty establishes "moral codes", travels to different countries, contacts authorities and analyses their behavior.

The large amount of information obtained throughout the entire period was essential for the classification of the most important leaders. They were listed as either VIRTUOUS or NON-VIRTUOUS, based upon the concepts contained in the famous book written by Francesco, the family's patriarch, an Italian linguist whose life was dedicated to teaching principles of moral integrity.

Obviously, the combination of a real and an imaginary story would have to comply with certain rules, i.e., the historical facts should be trustworthy and based on reliable sources, and the activities of the imaginary family should not affect the course of history.

This first volume comprises a period of four hundred years, from 1200 and 1600. It was indeed a very thrilling and diversified phase of history, filled with wars, political disputes, crises, epidemics, and important innovations, especially in the shipbuilding industry and in the manufacture of improved navigation equipment which gave incentive to new land discoveries. In addition, progress in medicine, art, and literature were also significant.

A list of classified personalities is presented at the end of this first volume. The second contains similar research in two hundred years, from 1600 to 1800. The third encompasses the events starting in the year 1800 and ending in our present days.

The author

Chapter 1

Francesco Vivone, the family´s patriarch, was born In Rome, Italy, in the year 1201 right after the beginning of the 13th. century (in the Middle Ages) when the Roman Catholic Church instituted the Inquisition[1]. Francesco pertained to the Roman nobility and became a famous writer specialized in linguistics, a man with an enviable culture and extremely religious. In addition to his dedication to letters, he was considered one of the most honest citizens of his community.

In 1231, Francesco authored the book considered his masterpiece, by the name **"Morality and Ethics"**. With unshakable persistence, he produced four copies, (all written by hand) one of which he offered to Frederick II (1197-1250), Emperor of the Holy Roman Empire[2].He kept the second in a chest of his wife and donated the last two to the Vatican Library.

Impressed by the author´s generosity, as well as his honesty and public prestige, Frederick II named him "Absolute Herald of the Vatican Letters and Symbol of the Perfection of the Roman Empire."

Occupied by his royal obligations, Frederik did not give due importance to the present and simply added it to his collection of private books. He did not even have the curiosity to open it to see what it was about.

Regrettably, due to Francesco´s inexperience in political matters, he forgot to reserve one of his books for Pope Gregory IX (1148-1241) a flaw that was easily discovered by His Eminence. Disgusted with such a disregard, he sent his emissaries to the Vivone residence, demanding that he hand over one of the copies of "Morality and Ethics."

Frederik learned of the invasion of the author´s privacy, which contributed to further stir up the mood between him and Pope Gregory. Both were enemies since the Sixth Crusade, because the pope disagreed with Frederik´s strategy of giving preference to dialogue with the Muslims rather than attacking them[3].Co

---

[1]https://www.britannica.com/topic/inquisition.
[2]http://www.britannica.com/EBchecked/topic/217800/Frederick-II and Holy Roman Empire | Map, Definition, History, Capital, & Significance | Britannica.
[3]https://www.britannica.com/event/Crusades/The-Crusade-of-Frederick-II#ref1184384

nsequently, the Pope decided to excommunicate the emperor. Despite this climate of confrontation, Gregory finally accepted the terms of Frederick's Constitution of 1224 which imposed the death penalty on heretics and in 1231 created the Inquisition Court to investigate people accused of heresy, defined as those who did not follow the precepts of the Catholic Religion[4].

That same year of 1231, Francesco married Larissa Fracti, a former Nun of the Order of the Holy Souls who had had serious disagreements with the Mother Superior of the Convent. Despite her age, close to 30 years, her greatest wish was to marry and bear children as most other women.

Male triplets were born out of the marriage, something unusual in the 13th. century. The birth, which occurred in 1232, was normal and none of the children had any malformation at birth. The only problem at the time was the disagreement between the couple because Francesco was a staunch religious believer, respecting all the axioms of the Catholic church, while his wife refused to continue practicing these commandments.

The conflict quickly escalated to a point where the separation became inevitable. The divorce took place in the year 1240, especially affecting her husband, who went on to live in a state of severe depression, while Larissa, with the children, returned to her hometown near Rome.

Unaware of the donation made to the Vatican Library, Pope Gregory IX, still unhappy with Francesco's disregard, convicted him for a year of isolation in one of the Vatican dungeons. Terrified by the threat of being beheaded if he did not comply with the pope´s demand for the book, Francesco decided to write another copy especially for His Eminence.

After a year of exclusive dedication to this task, he finished the fifth. copy in 1241, two days before the death of Gregory IX. Before his passing, although showing clear symptoms of dementia, Gregory magnanimously decided to absolve the author of his confinement. Gregory did not have the strength to read any part of the book that had been offered to him. The work, however, was carefully kept in a case in the crypt next to his remains.

---

[4] https://www.britannica.com/topic/heresy.

Chapter 2

Historical records show that both Frederick II and Gregory IX, acted according to the spirit of the age in which the punishment of heretics was considered as something normal, obeying the strict rules of the Catholic religion.

Released from the prison thanks to one of the last acts of Gregory IX, Francesco stopped writing until 1250. Without news from his children, Francesco decided to travel to the rural town where they lived. The three young boys, Godofredo, Sinibaldo and, Rolando, were 8 years old and resented the father's absence.

With the arrival of Francesco, the three brothers were able to take advantage of his immense culture. Sinibaldo heard the words "inquisition" and "crusades" and asked his father what they meant. He also wanted to know things about the Catholic Church and other religions.

Francesco´s teaching ability had a definite influence on their youthful dreams. He started talking about religion:

"Many people believe that the world was created by God. Although nobody has seen Him, the Catholic Religion says he lives in heaven. God had a son called Jesus Christ who came down to earth, helped people, and told them that they should be good to each other, be honest and love everyone. These are the main rules adopted by the church and, if you believe in God and respect these rules, you are called a catholic. There is a man who represents God on earth called the Pope and he is the chief of the Catholic Church and lives in a city called Rome where I was born."

"And what was the Inquisition?" asked Rolando.

"Now imagine if someone does not believe in the rules of the church, or believes in something else, said Francesco. According to the Catholic Religion, this attitude is considered a sin and therefore he or her must be punished." Those who commit this sin are called "heretics."

"Daddy, what is this punishment?" inquired Rolando.

"It is horrible. Sometimes they are tortured, killed, burned alive, strangled, or hanged. Those who refuse to admit their guilt are considered criminals. The Church created the so-called Court of the Inquisition, responsible for judging the gravity of each sin and choose the type of punishment," said Francesco.

"Who is the chief of this Court? asked Rolando.

"The Pope is the chief, but also kings, princes, bishops and other civil authorities can persecute heretics," explained Francesco.

"Now I will talk about the Crusades. Around the end of the 11th. century, the Christians (those who are faithful to the Catholic religion) organized military expeditions to fight against the expansion of the Muslims. Later I will explain who they are. The Christians used to travel to the holy city of Jerusalem to pray. However, the Muslims hampered the pilgrimage to the city and began to capture and murder those who visited the place solely for their faith. The first crusade failed and so many were killed in the battles. After the defeat, the Christians created the Order of the Knights Templars who played an important part in the fighting. Later, another western army, commanded by the French, invaded the east to fight for the same cause. The soldiers used as an emblem the sign of the cross stitched on their battle uniforms. Under the leadership of Godfrey of Bouillon[5], these warriors massacred the Muslims during the combat and took Jerusalem, again allowing free access for pilgrims (those who travel for religious reasons). The fighting attracted great kings like Richard I, also called Richard the Lion Heart, and Louis IX. The Crusades increased tensions and hostilities between Christians and Muslims in the Middle Ages. Even after the end of the Crusades, this tense atmosphere between members of both religions continued" [6].

"Are you going to explain who the Muslims are?" asked Rolando.

Aside from the Catholic Religion there is another religion called Islamism which was founded by the Prophet Muhammad in Arabia in the 7th century CE (CE meaning Common Era, which started in year 1 after Jesus Christ was born). The believers of this religion are the Muslims, and their God is called Allah.

---

[5] https://www.britannica.com/biography/Godfrey-of-Bouillon.
[6] https://www.britannica.com/event/Crusades.

Muslims say that Allah is the only God that exists. As you know, the Catholics also say that their God is the only one.

Increasingly interested in the subject, the children asked about the quantity of crusades that existed. For our readers we added a table with all the crusades and the respective periods:

CRUSADES	PERIOD
1st Crusade	1096-1099
2nd Crusade	1147-1149
3rd Crusade	1189-1192
4th Crusade	1202-1204
5th Crusade	1217-1221
6th Crusade	1228-1229
Albigensian Crusade	1209-1229
Children's Crusade	1212
7th Crusade	1248-1254
Shepherds Crusade	First in 1251 Second in 1320
8th Crusade	1270
9th Crusade	1271-1272
Northern Crusade	1193-1316

R

olando was the son most connected to sporting events and loved to hear stories of battles and heroes. Impressed with his father's story, he decided to join the army commanded by the French king Louis IX who was induced by Pope Innocent IV (1195-1254)[7] to lead the uprising against Muslims.

Rolando was known for his skill with the sword and his extraordinary physical strength, and, despite his father's opposition, he joined the troops of Louis IX and, in 1248 left with the Seventh Crusade, made up of 35,000 men who reached Egypt. Louis IX obtained important victories and the domination of territories. Unfortunately, a flood of the river Nile surprised the Christians, and the Muslims took the opportunity to plunder their food supplies, generating hunger and diseases like typhus and scurvy to plague Louis IX's troops. The king ended up falling prisoner of the Muslims.

Rolando was one of the few not to contract typhus, thanks to his physical vigor. But he was imprisoned by the enemies until the release of Louis IX. As evidence of the king's gratitude, Rolando was promoted to Officer of his troops

---

[7] https://www.britannica.com/biography/Innocent-IV.

and accompanied the king to Palestine in the negotiations for the release of Christian prisoners. In 1254, he returned to his native home and accompanied the king, later canonized as St. Louis. His Majesty died years later during a plague.

Disappointed with the successive defeats and with the violent deaths in the battles of the crusades, Rolando gave up his military life and returned to the company of his parents.

Meanwhile, Godofredo and Sinibaldo followed different paths. The first became a painter and sculptor while Sinibaldo dedicated himself to letters, following his father's footsteps. He became interested in the book "Morality and Ethics" which he discovered in his mother's trunk. The subject of the book impressed him considerably and aroused his curiosity to investigate the dogmas of the Catholic Church and the actions of its members. The purpose was to find out to what extent the prelates of the Catholic Church respected the moral attributes defined by his father. Therefore, he considered that a visit to the Vatican would be important. The final objective was to interview the priests at their various levels.

In 1256, at the age of about twenty-five, he asked his father for advice on how to reach members of the clergy and wanted his opinion on the type of questions he should ask.

"Father, I'm very curious to know what the prelates think about some controversial issues like, for example, the relationship with the pope, celibacy, heretics, contact with nuns, homosexuality, pedophilia, marriage of priests, the crusades and the inquisition," said Godofredo.

"Wait a minute, argued Francesco. In the first place, it is not easy to get permission for such a survey, but I may be able to get an order from my dear friend Alexander IV (1199-1261) elected in 1254, for a visit such as you described. Second, it is an extremely challenging task, as each person considers himself honest and has high feelings of morality. It would be like asking any emperor or the Pope himself if they consider themselves honest. The answer would be obvious."

Francesco, very well connected with the pope, obtained authorization for Sinibaldo to visit the Vatican to interview ecclesiastical dignitaries, from the beginners to the most qualified. It would be a challenging task, as there would certainly be resistance in revealing secrets about what happens inside the Holy See. But, authorized by the Pope, his subordinates were under the obligation to attend him. Through the hierarchy of the Catholic Church (Pope, Cardinal, Archbishop, Bishop, Priest), one can imagine the work that Sinibaldo was willing to face.

With modesty and diplomacy, he obtained information that no one else could imagine. The conclusions were interesting.

Reporting the results of his research to his father, Sinibaldo tried to be prudent, as he knew about Francesco's religiosity and in no way wanted to influence his faith in the Catholic Church. However, he was forced to be consistent with what he heard from the various hierarchical levels.

"Father, forgive me if what I have to say may surprise you, but I need to keep the information in line with what I heard from the different dignitaries."

"Speak, my son, said Francesco."

"We discussed several extremely controversial issues. First, I was able to conclude that the majority do not admire Pope Alexander IV. Cardinals and archbishops are envious of his high and distant position, complaining about the little prestige he gave his subordinates. The decisions were his alone and no one else's. Father, according to your teachings, envy is a sign of bad character, so anyone who lets himself be influenced by it cannot be virtuous."

"I also noticed that there are groups within the different levels. Each group meets to combine certain actions and aims to obtain advantages from their superiors who, in turn, also form groups of power. For me, the formation of such groups with similar intentions was not very surprising, as this is one of the forms of survival in any society. It is difficult to assess whether this habit can be considered amoral. Whoever forms a team to obtain advantages over others, should not be considered virtuous."

"Some archbishops and cardinals have declared themselves against any kind of torture, strangulation or death of heretics, punishments adopted regularly in the inquisition. They also considered it legitimate for people to have beliefs other than the Catholic religion. It is an encouraging fact that the church members adopt this approach. If they had no other defects, they could certainly be considered virtuous. Unfortunately, this is not the general rule among them, as many fully supported the punishment of heretics and infidels."

Francesco listened attentively to Sinibaldo's report, feeling slightly disappointed by what he had assimilated so far. He asked his son to continue the report.

"Father, as you know, celibacy is mandatory in the Catholic Church. The Bible teaches that celibacy is a state of honor. St. Paul the Apostle, original name Saul of Tarsus (4 BCE-62-64 CE)[8] writes in 1 Corinthians 7:

It is good for a man not to have sex with a woman. But due to the temptation to sexual immorality, each man must have his own wife and each woman her own husband. (Verses 1-2). I wish everyone to be as I am. But each has his own gift of God, one of a kind and another of another. For singles and widows I say it is good for them to remain as I am. But if they cannot exercise self-control, they should be married. That is why it is better to get married than to burn with passion[9]."

"I discussed at length with the priests about this passage by Paul of Tarsus. I argued that it seems strange that they contain themselves or that they do not have the same desires as everyone else, whether men or women. The response of almost everyone was as follows":

"We are certainly people like everyone else, but we took the vow of chastity; therefore, we have a commitment signed with Jesus and we accept the determinations of St. Paul the Apostle."

"Well, Sinibaldo, added the father, your argument is very plausible. In fact, I have always wondered how a priest or a nun who adopt these practices (or abstains from these practices) can survive without having contact with the other sex. I have the impression that your mother did not agree with this imposition."

---

[8] https://www.britannica.com/biography/Saint-Paul-the-Apostle.
[9] https://www.biblestudytools.com/1-corinthians/7.html.

"Then I asked everyone if the celibacy did not have a direct relationship with the wealth of land owned by the Catholic Church, continued Sinibaldo. If marriages were allowed, the lands would certainly also belong to the priests and their children as heirs. This multiplication would cause further division of this immense wealth, which in turn would not be of interest to the Holy See. Would this perhaps be the main reason for the institution of the celibacy of the priests?"

"Most of the interviewees declared that they never heard anything of the sort. They never thought that the Popes continued to prohibit marriage for that reason, but they admitted that the idea had a certain logic."

Before proceeding with his account, his son Godofredo suddenly appeared with news of his trip to Rome. Nervous and with the appearance of happiness stamped on his face, he communicated enthusiastically:

"Dad, imagine who I met today."

"I can't imagine it, but because of your enthusiasm, this person must be very important."

"I was with Nicola, can you imagine?"

"And who might this Nicola be"?

"Nicola Pisano (1220-1278/1284?)[10], the greatest pulpit sculptor in the Catholic Church. He was the founder of Italian sculpture. He has just built a marble pulpit in the Cathedral of Siena and invited me to participate in his work and he will teach me how to build pulpits and engineering and I will be able to make pulpits with him in other churches. Then I will be able to teach these wonderful skills to my children."

"Congratulations, you are starting to stand out with your work. But at this moment Sinibaldo reported his work at the Vatican. Would you like to participate in our conversation?"

"Sure, I'm really curious."

---

[10]https://www.britannica.com/art/Western-sculpture/Italian-Gothic.

"Well, going back to the interviews, I touched on another sensitive topic. Contact between priests and nuns. Most hinted that there is a great deal of respect between the two parties. It is evident that there are cases of attraction between the two sexes, but the limits are apparently well respected."

"Next, I had to be extremely careful when talking about the issue of same-sex attraction. All the priests I spoke with reaffirmed their belief that there is no homosexuality in the Vatican. I argued that this statement must be at least biased, a consequence of the indoctrination to which all members of the church are subjected. Considering the world's population, there is a certain proportion of people with attraction for the same sex, therefore one could assume that in the ecclesiastical environment this proportion is also valid. Even so, everyone declared to be unaware of any act of this nature that took place in the Holy See. I received the same answer regarding pedophilia, something they consider to be a mortal sin. I must admit that I was not very convinced of the honesty of the answers. But because they were unanimous, we have to give them some credit."

"Regarding the marriage of priests of the Catholic Church, I had the impression that some were in doubt. The majority confessed that if this strict rule would change, marriage would be beneficial and would not harm their work. However, any modification from their superiors is far away."

"Then I touched on the subject of the crusades. I asked what they thought of the deaths caused by the troops on their way to the holy city. The murders of Muslims by soldiers of the Catholic Church were approved as they prevented pilgrims from arriving in Jerusalem. They thought that victory would only be possible through heroic struggles, especially by the Templar knights."

"Anyway, I think that my visit to the Holy See was extremely enlightening, and I want to thank you for your interference with Pope Alexander IV who made it possible."

"The result of your work with church members was interesting. I confess that I was unaware of various opinions of the clergy. I must retire to meditate on them," said Francesco.

12

Chapter 3

Francesco, despite remaining separated from his wife Larissa, returned to live with his children in the same house where they moved in the countryside. She proposed a truce to her ex-husband and was happy to have him at home. Sinibaldo told her about the results of his stay at the Vatican, which they happily celebrated with a barbecue and wine.

During dinner, the family heard a loud knock on the door. Three emissaries of Pope Alexander IV were standing outside and without any further delay delivered a written order of the Pope demanding Francesco´s and Sinibaldo´s presence at the Vatican.

Surprised by the convocation, they immediately went to the Vatican.

As soon as they entered the Audience Room, the Pope Alexander IV immediately addressed Francesco. His face showed his extreme dissatisfaction.

"How could you disrespect me after I authorized your son to visit the Holy See? How dare you to authorize him to invade the privacy of my priests, with unreasonable and biased questions? Didn't you imagine that the clergy would be offended by this boldness? From now on, I will never allow anything like this. I only did it out of respect for you because you are the Absolute Herald of the Vatican Letters and Symbol of the Perfection of the Roman Empire! All my cardinals looked at me with reproaching eyes and I heard that marriage between the members of the Holy See was discussed. The absurdity was even greater when the theme of same-sex attraction among us came up, something totally unacceptable and nonexistent."

"Furthermore, it came to my attention that you, Francesco, presented one of my predecessors, His Eminence Gregory IX with a book of your authorship, under the name "Morality and Ethics," a work that should have been donated to the Vatican library. Where is this book? I order you to bring it to me."

"Allow me to assure Your Eminence that my son Sinibaldo never intended to offend the priests with whom he had the honor of speaking, said Francesco. His objective was merely to better understand the high sanctity of those who live for the grace of God and Jesus Christ. If he committed a sin, he shall ask for your forgiveness and will never again try to offend the clergy in their humility with the Lord."

"You may leave now and only come back after my emissaries find out where your book is located," shouted the Pope.

Relieved for having been spared of major punishments by order of Alexander IV, they returned home with innovative ideas about the visit to the Pope.

Chapter 4

Francesco thought about the interview at the Vatican. He found that Sinibaldo did not touch on the subject considered the most important, that is, the existence or not of God and Jesus Christ. Obviously, such a question would be ridiculous, since all the clergy was there because of their commitment to the Almighty and his son Jesus Christ. He was also convinced that all the information Sinibaldo managed to obtain from his visit, did not invalidate his dedication to the Catholic Church. He thought that everyone has faults and, therefore, his faith in God would not be affected.

Ronaldo and Godofredo, however, thought differently. They did not accept the fact that priests are in favor of torture and other punishments, including the killing of heretics. How could they agree with something so cruel and ignore that God condemned such acts? They communicated this idea to their father.

Francesco was seriously worried by the episode and again went into a deep depression, certainly because he felt that his feelings towards God had been shaken. Struggling with his conscience, and unable to bear his doubts, he suddenly felt a severe pain in his chest. The children tried to help him, but despite the efforts of the doctor called urgently, Francesco did not resist and died in 1257 at the age of fifty-six.

The sorrow for Francesco's death deeply affected the family, his friends, and colleagues. Francesco represented honesty, culture, and dedication to his art of writing and was buried with honor. Pope Alexander IV felt personally responsible for the unfriendly treatment with which he had received him at the Vatican. As a result, he ordered his subordinates to abandon the search for the book and announced the complete forgiveness of Francesco.

On his headstone, the children wrote a tribute to their father, summarizing his life with the following sentence:

IN LOVING MEMORY OF FRANCESCO VIVONE
1201-1257

Francesco's death seriously affected his wife. Larissa´s love for her husband was so strong that life completely lost its meaning. She practically stopped eating. The worried children did everything to comfort her, but it was useless. The serious food deficiency was the cause of her death. She died in her sleep in 1258, with the certainty that she would find Francesco in heaven. Her grave was next to her husband.

Chapter 5

Godofredo became great friends with Nicola Pisano and was praised for his work with the illustrious artist. He had the hope of being able to pass on to his future children the notions learned from his master. In 1273 he married Matilda, a French lady from Marseille born in 1240. They had two children, a girl and a boy Michele and Luigi, born in 1274, and 1275, respectively. His work as a pulpit sculptor earned him a real fortune, all of which came from the Vatican Treasury. He received his remuneration in gold coins.

Rolando preferred to dedicate his time to raise sheep. Because of his extraordinary strength, there was no need to hire employees for shearing the animals. He sold wool, used in the production of winter clothes and blankets. In the same year as Godofredo, in 1273, he married Giovanna born in 1234, who lived in a cattle farm. They had two children, Alfredo, and Salvatore. Due to the high quality of his wool, Rolando was able to sell his production to the wealthiest merchants who came from distant countries.

Sinibaldo also got married in 1273. His wife Anabella, born in 1236, was his childhood friend, with whom he had twins, Alina, and Bianca, both born in 1274. Continuing in his father's footsteps, Sinibaldo went deeper into the study of the book "Morality and Ethics" and began to take the first action towards the formation of a school, one of Francesco´s dreams. He called it "Istituzioni di Moralitá" (Institution of Morality). At the same time, he promised his brothers that in time he would write the Code of Conduct of the institution. He took advantage of the fact that he was the only member of the family to read the book. He knew how to preserve his secrets as a treasure. However, for a matter of justice, he handed over the only copy to his brothers who took the oath to never reveal its contents. He also told them his plan. Unlike his brothers, Sinibaldo was not able to have the same financial success and earned his livelihood by writing children's stories.

The formation of the school would be difficult due to the need to keep it as a secret. By his emissaries, Pope Honorius IV (1210-1287) learned that a society with that name was being formed. The three brothers knew that it could lead to conflicts with the Catholic Church. Honorius ordered a thorough investigation, but his emissaries were unable to obtain any consistent information. For 17 years, the society remained in obscurity.

Finally, in 1290, after the death of Honorius IV, the institution was founded. The children of the three brothers were already about seventeen and were instructed by their parents to keep the institution secret. Everyone fulfilled that request.

Pope Nicholas IV (1227-1292), elected in 1288, remained in the Holy See until 1292. After his death there was what the church called interregnum or vacancy, meaning an interval between two popes. The absence of an authority in the Vatican, Sinibaldo and his brothers started the constitution of the new society.

To hinder investigations by cardinals and archbishops, Sinibaldo established the headquarters at Rolando's property in Fiumicino, sixteen miles from Rome, close to the coast. The name painted on a sign at the entrance said:

ISTITUZIONE DI CARITÀ (IDC)

This name, meaning CHARITY INSTITUTE was a disguise to avoid being investigated by the Vatican authorities.

The construction followed the style of the Catholic Church, with columns and arches made by Godofredo and a design by Nicola Pisano. It resulted in a beautiful work of art that impressed all those who went to the IDC to find out what it was about. It was a novelty never seen in the region. The entire work was financed by Godofredo and Rolando, while Sinibaldo was in charge of managing its operation.

The family's children were enthusiastic about the plans outlined by Sinibaldo. In the year 1292, for strategic reasons, the daughters were enrolled in the School of the Virgin Mary and the sons in the School of Christ the Redeemer. The objective of the enrollment was to get acquainted with the dogmas of the church and the form of indoctrination in a catholic school.

The experience was frustrating. The students had to get up at 3:30 am for the first prayers, without any food until 7:00 am. Then everyone received bread, cheese, and goat milk. At 8:00 am, religion classes began and continued until 1:00 pm. With a diet based on beets, kale, spinach, nuts and hard-boiled eggs, students would be punished if they did not eat everything. The punishment consisted of blows to the hands and the back.

In the afternoon there were classes in sacred music, French, English and German and history of the Inquisition and Crusades. All references to the episodes that occurred during the inquisition and the crusades were in praiseworthy terms, highlighting the heroism of the soldiers who represented the Catholic Church. The barbarities committed by Muslims against the Templars were considered deadly offenses. Nobody, however, referred to the behavior of the soldiers of Christ in the battles to liberate Jerusalem. At 6 pm there was a class of the history of the Catholic religion and the constitution of the clergy at the Vatican and in other countries. At the end of the day, new religious songs were practiced until 8 pm. The six children were thus able to assess the type of education given to students at the time, which influenced their concept about religion.

After graduation in 1299, the six cousins decided to work exclusively for the institution founded by their parents. The positions were evenly distributed among them. Matilda, Giovanna, and Anabela were engaged as mentors and organizers of the flow of candidates. They determined that all clothing worn by the participants should be embroidered with the letters IDC.

Chapter 6

In 1300, to commemorate the passage from the 13th. to the 14th. century, Sinibaldo decided to detail the principles of the Code of Conduct of the institution. He divided it into four parts, as follows:

1-Objectives of the Institution:

a- Disseminate the concepts of morality in our society and in other countries.
b- Provide courses in foreign languages.
c- Learn major events of the History of Civilization.
d- Analise and qualify the acts of civil, military, and ecclesiastical authorities according to moral standards.
e- Develop Sports and Fitness.

2-Admission: Candidates for the course will be judged by a board of administrators.

3-Cost: The course is free.

4-Certificate of Completion: Approved students will receive a Certificate of Proficiency in Moral Standards and in all other courses.

Thereafter, Sinibaldo scheduled a party for the Vivone family to spread the IDC among the inhabitants of Fiumicino. The children have recently reached the age of twenty-six and twenty-seven and were eager to meet other young people. The party would serve for this purpose and for the dissemination of the ideas of the IDC. Posters hung strategically in the hall and said: "After the inauguration, we will be pleased to answer all your questions. A special invitation was sent to Bishop Cornelius Urbanus of Fiumicino.

Inexperienced in diplomacy and politics, the three girls responsible for the school's administration forgot to invite the mayor of the city. Informed about the inauguration, Mayor Armando Gallucci was disgusted by the omission and sent his assistant to the IDC headquarters and summoned those responsible for the party to attend the local city hall. Calmly, he mentioned to Sinibaldo that the inauguration came to the mayor's attention and that he wondered why he was not invited. Immediately Sinibaldo asked for an audience with Gallucci.

Sinibaldo confessed the mistake he made and apologized a thousand times to the Mayor and declared that it would be an honor for the IDC to have the presence of His Excellency on the specified date.

The party went as planned, with the presence of the authorities and attracted a considerable number of people interested in the Institution. One of the important authorities was Divo Grassi, commanding officer of the Municipality's militia, purposely brought by Gallucci. He toured the premises and sought to absorb details that, for the public, would not attract attention. But accustomed to investigations, he confided to Mayor Gallucci:

"I would like to respectfully inform Your Excellency that there is something strange about this institution. I do not know exactly where the mystery is, but I am sure that an association is being formed that does not comply with the rules of the Catholic Church. What would be the reason for inviting so many young people from all over Fiumicino? What is the real purpose of this institution? Is it something different from our Religion, a company that would protect heretics? Besides, what was Bishop Urbanus doing at the party? We know that the bishop does not exactly agree with the precepts of the Holy See. I humbly suggest that we deepen our investigation.

Chapter 7

"Dear brothers, dear wives and dear sons and daughters, I requested this meeting to analyze the presence of the Mayor and Commander Grassi at the party, warned Sinibaldo. He was obeying the mayor's orders to obtain information about our society. Although the name CHARITY INSTITUTE is a well-crafted name, the call for candidates must have aroused suspicion. What I am afraid of is that this call for participants may imply that we would be organizing a sect or forming a society that opposes the Catholic Church. If they can prove that we have other intentions, we will be immediately considered heretics and you know what that means."

"In addition, we have to recap where the five books written by our father are. I have a copy. As soon as he finished the first four copies, he presented Emperor Frederick II with one. I am also aware that the emperor did not give due importance to the book and sent it to his library. The other two were donated to the Vatican Library. Therefore, the fifth book remains to be found. I don't remember exactly its destiny."

"I am sure that our father, when he was arrested by order of Pope Gregory IX, wrote the fifth copy and offered it to the Pope in the year 1241, informed Rolando. However, Gregory died in the same year and did not have the strength to read it. From what I heard at the time the book was placed in a box in the crypt next to his remains."

"I think that we are going to have problems, whether they come from the Vatican, or the City Hall" said Godofredo. I have a suggestion to make. Due to my work with Nicola Pisano, I developed an excellent relationship with the main ecclesiastical authorities. If you all agree, I will take Michele and Luigi and visit one of the archbishops who must have information regarding the mayor's visit and its consequences. I'm sure that Mayor Gallucci (who studied at the same college as Pope Boniface VIII[11] (1235-1303)) has already sent information about the event and about the suspicions of commanding officer Divo Grassi."

After the unanimous approval, Godofredo went to the Vatican and sought his friend Archbishop Guillermo Filippo. He received him immediately.

---

[11]https://www.britannica.com/biography/Boniface-VIII.

"What a beautiful surprise, Master Godofredo Vivone. To what do I owe the honor of your visit? asked the archbishop."

"I am here to pay my respects to my beloved friend Don Filippo and to introduce my children Michele and Luigi to you, said Godofredo. They are planning to travel to France to study art and follow my footsteps, especially in the construction of pulpits. My brothers and cousins celebrated the plan at a party we had last month. At the same time, they want to visit the Vatican Library to look for books on their specialty."

"Well, feel free to visit the library. I am sure that your children will be as skilled professionals as their father, even better. As for the party, I am happy that you had a pleasant celebration and I wish I could have attended. The Mayor of Fiumicino was informed of the success of the meeting and learned about the new society you are organizing. Later, I would like to know a little more about it."

"I will be personally responsible for bringing you all the details of the organization. I would also like to thank the friendly reception and I will be happy to visit the library with my children. I wish you peace and health with my gratitude."

The visit to the library was a success. First, they were unable to find the two books donated by Francesco. Therefore, they went through the corridors to look in unusual places and found them among books beginning with the letter "P". Thus, it would certainly be difficult for potential interested parties to locate them, especially because "Morality and Ethics" starts with an "M."

The joy about the "disappearance" of the books vanished due to the information of Don Filippo, confirming that Pope Boniface VIII had already been made aware of what was happening in Fiumicino. It would only be a matter of time before all members of the Vivone family were qualified as heretics.

Sinibaldo proposed a new family meeting to analyze the future.

"We should leave Fiumicino immediately. We have to close the Institution, take what we can with us and look for a country where we can continue with our goal of publicizing our father and grandfather's dream."

"But what will we say to our friends and to all the candidates who wanted to participate? asked Luigi".

"We cannot take any risks. Our situation is serious, and you know how the Church treats infidels."

"I suggest that we move to Marseille in France where my parents lived. After his medical studies in Montpellier, my father started to produce wine in a huge winery that he inherited from his ancestors. The estate produces one of the best wines in France and he became the main supplier of the palace of Philip IV, king of France (1268-1314)[12]. I am sure that they would welcome us enthusiastically if they were still alive. Knowing our family was their greatest wish, informed Matilda."

"We must prepare to leave our residence and facilities within 24 hours. I know that such a decision is painful, especially after we have had so much success and so much joy in Fiumicino, added Sinibaldo."

---

[12]https://www.britannica.com/biography/Philip-IV-king-of-France.

Chapter 8

Each branch of the Vivone family is composed of four people (husband, wife and two children). Each group would travel independently for approximately 560 miles across unknown roads. Sinibaldo looked for three carriages that could travel the distance. They were going to travel along the west coast of Italy with rest breaks at inns along the way. They took part of the gold coins that Godofredo and Ronaldo had earned with their work to pay the coachmen.

The timely decision proposed by Sinibaldo was intelligent, as there was no time for the City Hall or the Vatican to discover the escape. In about ten days, the three carriages reached La Spezia, 250 miles to the north of Fiumicino. With another 20 days, stopping occasionally to catch their breath, they reached Marseille and the property of Dr. Pierre Bonimond and his wife Natalie, Matilda's parents, born in 1200 and, 1203, respectively. Matilda discovered the dates of the parents' deaths occurred in 1260 and 1264. The property was managed by a former employee of the vineyard, who was surprised by the number of people that formed the Vivone family. It would be impossible to host them all at the farm's headquarters. There was room only for Godofredo, his wife and children Michele and Luigi. Rolando and Sinibaldo and their children decided to look for inns for a short stay.

Sinibaldo had taken Francesco´s book and the code. He planned to disseminate his teachings in France. However, it would be necessary to evaluate the status of Pope Boniface VIII's relationship with King Philip IV of France (1285-1314)[13]. As Sinibaldo discovered, Boniface regarded the power of the papacy superior to any kingdom and demanded subservience from kings and emperors. Philip IV challenged this order, expelled the clergy of the administration, and demanded that the church pay taxes to finance his wars against other countries. Excess authority of Boniface was one of the reasons why the poet Dante Alighieri, in his book "The Divine Comedy", said that Boniface belonged to the "Eighth Circle of Hell."

This dispute would distract the attention of both leaders and favor the creation of a society in Marseille, like the one Sinibaldo implemented in

---

[13]https://www.britannica.com/biography/Philip-IV-king-of-France.

Fiumicino. More time would be necessary to complete research in the region, to assess the extent of the community's interest and approval. According to his calculation, they would need a period of two to four years to prepare the new project.

At the end of 1303, with the death of Boniface VIII, a new pope was elected with the name of Benedict XI (1240-1304) who died soon after his nomination. The next one elected was Clement V (1264-1314)[14]. Philip IV (Philip le Bel in French and Philip the Fair in English) used his power and influence to elect this pope, mainly because Clement could be convinced to remove the excommunication of the French royal family imposed by Pope Boniface VIII.

In 1303, the age of the three Vivone brothers was already over 70 years. Sinibaldo had suffered due to the trip from Fiumicino to Marseille. The permanent changes of weather reduced his immune system and caused a high fever that did not recede. Despite the efforts of the family and doctors in the region, he did not recover and died in the presence of his wife Anabela. Two hours earlier he called his wife, his two brothers, and all members of the family and informed them that Anabela would be the guardian of the book "Morality and Ethics" as well as its Code.

"I thank you all for having so enthusiastically embraced our father's ideas. I am sure that they will awaken in men the honor of accepting his precepts. It is our destiny to love our neighbor, be pure and honest, adopt the highest moral principles, reject lies and falsehood, fight corruption and envy. Anyway, all of you have assimilated these rules and I know you are going to promulgate them.

With these words, Sinibaldo asked Anabela to hide the book and the code in a place where only the family would be aware and to leave a note for each member about the location. It is not necessary to describe the sadness that affected the family with the death of Sinibaldo. He was their leader and the one who gave impetus to Francesco's thoughts.

Due to the number of negative episodes that affected the family, the members needed a break to rethink the strategy of implementing the

---

[14]https://www.britannica.com/biography/Clement-V.

school wherever possible. Everyone should have the opportunity to gain more experience to avoid the mistakes made in Fiumicino.

Thinking about destinations for the break, Godofredo wanted to go to Paris with his wife and children to continue his work in sculpture, architecture and engineering and learn new techniques. He knew that the French had specialized in this type of work and the exchange of experiences could be extremely valuable. Rolando decided to visit Scotland, as he wanted to know what the Scots adopted for their wool production. One of his main competitors was originally from Scotland and Rolando was astonished with the quality they achieved. The reason was a better breed of the flock of sheep. Anabela and her daughters Alina and Bianca intended to visit Spain, as they heard about the excellence of their artists, especially painters and sculptors.

The departure was planned for 1305. Everyone took notes with them about the location of the books. The notes were as follows:

1-Anabela has one book and the Code.

2-Two copies were at the Vatican Library, wrongly filed between books beginning with the letter "P".

3-A copy offered to Frederick II of Germania is among his books.

4-There is one copy offered to Pope Gregory IX, kept inside a case, in the crypt next to his remains.

Chapter 9

The distance between Paris, Spain and Scotland certainly did not make communications easy at the time. The family members have rarely heard from each other. At the end of 1312 they received news about the death of Rolando in 1310, his wife Giovanna in 1311 in Scotland, and Godofredo in 1312 in Paris.

The year 1312 was extremely sad for Matilda, due to the death of her husband Godofredo. According to her parents last will and testament, she learned that all assets of the Bonimond family now belong to her. For this reason, Matilda decided to return to Marseille to take definitive possession of the property. Shortly after arriving with Michele and Luigi, she still managed to pass the farm on to her children's name and, in 1313, she died due to a massive heart attack.

Anabela, Sinibaldo's wife, died in Barcelona in 1316.

After all these episodes, Matilda's children decided to stay at the winery to manage the wine production. The following tree summarizes the composition of the family members as of 1316:

Vivone's Family Tree in 1316

Francesco Vivone (1201-1257) and Larissa Vivone (1201-1258)
Rolando (1232-1310) and Giovanna (1234-1311)
    Alfredo (1273-
    Salvatore (1273-
Sinibaldo (1232-1303) and Anabela (1236-1316)
    Alina (1274-
    Bianca (1274-
Godofredo (1232-1312) and Matilda (1235-1313)
    Michele (1274-
    Luigi (1275-

According to the above tree, the family formed by Alfredo, Salvatore, Alina, Bianca, Michele, and Luigi. They were all born between 1273 and 1274. Alfredo and Salvatore, for not speaking English perfectly, were considered intruders and were unable to have a more friendly contact with the Scots.

Alina and Bianca, after the death of their parents in Spain, did not get used to the country and did not even understand Spanish or Catalan. They could not stand the typical type of food in Spain and were horrified by the unequal distribution of income among their inhabitants. The four cousins returned to the winery inherited by the brothers Michele and Luigi. Upon arriving in 1330, they learned that their cousins got married that same year. Michele with a French noble person named Robert Valois, born in 1273 and Luigi with a Norwegian girl named Sigrid Andersen, born in 1305. The joy of the gathering was extraordinary.

The cousins continued to live at the winery, again benefiting from excellent sales of wine to the French king and nobles. "Since you arrived, our wines have been consumed more and more since 1326", said Michele.

"I would like to tell you what is going on in the political arena, informed Michele. There has been a dispute between France and England in 1328 with the death of Charles IV, son of Philip IV. The confrontation took place between the English king Edward III (1312-1377)[15], nephew of the late Charles IV on the maternal side and Philip, Count of Valois, nephew of Philip IV. According to the family tree shown below, Edward III could not be crowned because he came from the maternal lineage, something prohibited by the Salic Law. Finally, in 1329, with the agreement of Edward III, Philip, Count of Valois, was acclaimed with the title of Philip VI (1293-1350)[16]"

Philip, Count of Valois was the nephew of Philip IV, and grandson of Philip III (grandson of a crowned King of France, through the younger son, male-line descent). Edward III was the grandson of Philip IV, through his mother Isabella (a direct grandson of a crowned King of France, but through a female-line descent). Edward III had a more direct descent from the more recent French king, BUT it was through his mother. French succession worked under the Salic Law, which meant that women could not inherit the throne. Philip VI was crowned under the assumption that the Salic Law also barred a woman from transmitting her claim to her male children. Edward III kept quiet on the matter until he had a big enough strength to enforce his claim through war[17].

[15] https://www.britannica.com/biography/Edward-III-king-of-England.
[16] https://www.britannica.com/biography/Philip-VI.
[17] https://www.quora.com/What-was-Philip-VI-s-claim-to-the-French-throne-How-was-it-compared-to-the-claim-held-by-Edward-III-of-England

Family Tree of Philip III of France

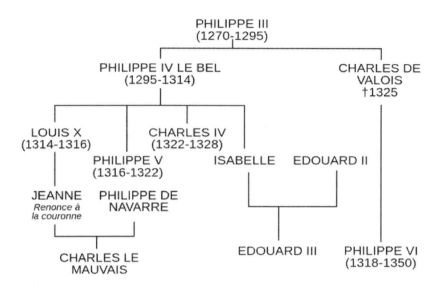

"Is Robert related to the king Philip VI? asked Bianca".

"That's right, said Michele, he is his uncle, can you imagine that?

"Do you think we should tell Robert and Sigrid about the book written by our grandfather Francesco?" inquired Alfredo.

"My husband is a man of integrity, argued Michele, so I would vote yes. We should even explain to them why we came to France and put the book at their disposal."

"If everyone agrees, let us do that tonight at dinner time."

In the evening, after a toast to everyone, Michele addressed Robert and Sigrid.

"I would like to take the opportunity to tell you why we came from Italy to France. In fact, I must confess that we were running away. You may ask what was so serious that motivated the escape of the whole family? Well, you must have heard of our grandfather Francesco. He wrote a book that was the cause of our trip."

"This book, a masterpiece written by the family's patriarch is a kind of manual of honesty, kindness, high moral principles, decency, and incorruptibility. He named it "Morality and Ethics". His great desire was to show the world that only through this behavior humanity would be a thousand times better than it is today. Francesco produced only five copies of the work. Fortunately, Anabela has the remaining original."

"Sinibaldo, father of Alina and Bianca, drew up a Code of Conduct based on the concepts emitted in the book and started to build a school in Fiumicino with the objective of implementing this philosophy among the citizens. He created a society which he called ISTITUZIONE DI CARITÀ (IDC), meaning CHARITY INSTITUTION. This name was chosen so that the Catholic Church would not think that it was a type of sect or doctrine to fight the rules of the Holy See."

"To inaugurate the new facilities, he organized a party attended by the people of Fiumicino with the presence of the Bishop and the Mayor of the city. Unfortunately, the mayor brought his military attaché who became suspicious about the real purpose of the society. My father found out that his doubts reached Pope Boniface VIII. Akin to what happened in Fiumicino, the principles of the book would certainly come under the pope's scrutiny and surely all family members would be considered heretics and executed. This was why Godofredo suggested our urgent escape."

"What an incredible story, said Robert. In fact, from what you told me, the society had beautiful goals and I admire your grandfather's idealism. I would very much like to read the book if I have the family's permission."

"Sure, added Salvatore. From what Michele told us, you have a reputation that proves your quality as a virtuous person. It would be an honor to have your opinion on the concepts contained in the book. In fact, I would also like to offer it to Sigrid, in case she is curious about the subject."

"I am very grateful for the trust placed in us and I am sure that we can implement this project here in France."

Chapter 10

"I want to report a very auspicious fact, Robert informed a week after receiving the book. Without your permission, I visited my nephew, and we had a lengthy conversation. You will remember that he is King Philip VI. Well, I did a summary of the excellent book that you have so generously lent me. I explained that the ideas presented by your ancestor are an innovation that will make a significant difference in the morale of our society. I exemplified that the killings we witness daily are condemnable, the tortures and murders of heretics are acts committed by barbarians who should be convicted."

"I showed him the qualities defined by Francesco Vivone so that a person can be considered virtuous. Philip is aware of the evils committed not only by the church, but also by kings, whether they were English, French or of another nationality. It seems to me that he appealed to his conscience and meditated on this type of warning from Francesco about what is good and what is bad. At the end of the meeting, he made a point of inviting the whole family for lunch at the castle in ten days."

The family's enthusiasm for the news was contagious. Everyone asked Robert about the type of protocol to be respected in a meeting with the King of France.

On the day of the awaited occasion, after all the greetings ceremony, Philip, extremely jovial and friendly, did not wait long to open the dialogue with the Vivone family.

"I loved my Uncle Robert's account of what Francesco elaborated in his book. Nowadays the premises defined by him must not have found too much echo, neither in the Catholic Church nor in the different kingdoms of the recent past. The struggles between the Crusaders and the Muslims are an indisputable proof of the disregard for the rules contained in "Morality and Ethics." As the book is considered secret, I ask you if the family could lend me a copy, if there is one more available."

Alina, daughter of the late Anabela Vivone received the book from her mother after Sinibaldo's death and immediately agreed with the King's request.

"In fact, we only have one more copy of the book, but we will have the greatest honor of placing it into your hands. My grandfather managed to make five copies and four of them were presented to ecclesiastical and royal authorities when he was still living in Italy. I am sure that the fifth book will be safe in Your Majesty's hands."

"I promise you that the book will stay with me, and I shall not allow anyone to examine it. Our lunch was extremely pleasant, and I would like to repeat it more often."

The year 1337 was active for Philip VI. After a successful campaign in Scotland, Edward III declared himself rightful heir to the French throne, disregarding the so-called Salic Law. With this claim, a conflict began between the French and English kingdoms, which later became known as the Hundred Years War.

A month passed after Philip VI received the book. He told Robert that he was delighted with the content and suggested that they should implement the project in France, starting in Marseille. He considered the name Sinibaldo invented in Italy was inappropriate and suggested the title ECOLE ROYALE FRANÇAISE DE MORALITÉ (French Royal School of Morality). Philip regretted not being able to dedicate himself more actively to the formation of the school, but he made available two of his best teachers to Robert, as he considered the participation of literate and highly prestigious men in the society of Marseille to be important. He appointed Robert as the spokesperson between the Vivone family and the teachers, and if urgent matters arose, he could be consulted.

The age of Francesco's grandchildren and of Robert in 1337 was around 65 years.

The youngest of the brothers was Luigi who was born in 1275 and was sixty-two. Sigrid, born in 1305 was thirty-two. How to set up the ECOLE ROYALE FRANÇAISE DE MORALITÉ with six elderly people and only one with sufficient energy to drive the entity? To make matters worse, Sigrid kept her pregnancy a secret, which would certainly prevent her from actively participating in His Majesty's plan. Therefore, it would be imprudent to start the project at this time, especially since France had just become definitively involved in the war against England.

Everyone agreed to leave the school's construction for another opportunity. The unanimous decision was to devote all the family´s efforts to the production and exports of wine. Robert explained the problem to His Majesty and made himself available to assist him in preparing for the war against the English.

"I'm in trouble in Flanders County, a wool-producing region for the Flemish textile industry, Philip confided to Robert. The bourgeois rebelled and I had to attack them. Fortunately, I neutralized them, and my troops took over the lands in the region. My support for David II of Scotland was a huge insult to Edward III. In response, he again raised his claim to my kingdom" [18].

The real conflict began in 1337, with victories and defeats on both sides. The French were wealthy and with a population of twelve million. They had the support of the courts of the kingdom of Naples and the kingdom of the Christians in Hungary, as well as allies in the Holy Roman Empire and in the Papacy of Avignon. Edward III, on the other hand, had a more cohesive kingdom and more advanced military strategy. The constant wars against the Scots ended up improving their military tactics, with emphasis on the use of the bow and arrow. The French, however, used technologically outdated feudal cavalry[19].

"Dear Philip, regarding the book we loaned you, I would like to know if you still need to have it, considering that we only have this copy, asked Robert."

"But Robert, almost a week ago I asked Professor Gerard Vigni to take it directly to the winery, I don't understand how they didn't receive it."

"Well, we'll wait a few more days, there must have been something unexpected, said Robert."

They waited another week and did not receive the book. Not wanting to disturb the king, they decided to contact the professor, who was also a high-ranking military officer. His wife reported that he was at the battlefront and had no idea of his whereabouts.

---

[18]https://www.britannica.com/biography/Edward-III-king-of-England.
[19]https://www.britannica.com/event/Hundred-Years-War.

Alina was terrified when she received the news. She regretted not having made a copy of the book and was afraid that it could have been lost or improperly disclosed. What if it ended up in the Papacy of Avignon? Pope Benedict XII (1280-1342) was certainly informed of the problems in Italy and of the frustrated investigation into the Vivone family due to their sudden escape. It would be a calamity, and everyone would be in danger again.

Therefore, in case of total loss, they would have to return to Italy to obtain one of the copies from the Vatican Library. But how to get it out of the place that only they knew (among the books of the letter "P")? Francesco's teachings prohibited any dishonest act, such as stealing the book! Sinibaldo was the only one who knew the Archbishop Guillermo Filippo who may have died. Even if he were still alive, he could not help them, otherwise he could be convicted of assisting fugitives.

In addition, they would have to undertake a trip that would take at least 20 days, with all the dangers they would be subject to due to the war. How to solve this dilemma?

"The only way would be to find Professor Vigni, said Robert. I can inquire at the castle about the fate of the detachment to which he belongs, and it is possible that the troops are still in the neighborhood. I will do that immediately."

Miraculously, Robert managed to discover Professor Gerard's location. He went to Toulon, about forty-five miles from Marseille.

"In a day's travel it would be possible to find him if he is still in the city. I will go personally, and I intend to take Michele with me."

The information they received was that the professor had been sent back to Marseille. Robert asked one of his subordinates if he left with a package with His Majesty's seal. Two of them remembered that Gerard was carrying a sealed volume when he returned from Toulon to Marseille. As a precaution, Robert obtained the names of both in case he needed more information. They were Ozires and Domecq.

Chapter 11

Finally, after a long search, Robert found Professor Vigni. The first question was: WHERE IS THE BOOK?

"I must confess a sad event that occurred during my trip from Marseille to Toulon. The sealed package with His Majesty's mark was stolen halfway. He was in the pouch on my horse and, one morning, I realized that it was gone. I apologize for not having communicated the fact earlier."

"From your account, I understood that the package was stolen before your arrival in Toulon, right?"

"Exactly."

"Did you conduct any kind of investigation to find the thief?" asked Robert.

"Yes, I instructed two of my subordinates for that, but it was useless."

"Well, I appreciate your kindness to inform me, and I wish you the best of luck in your campaign on behalf of His Majesty."

Robert and Michele immediately realized that Vigni was lying. If his subordinate in Toulon said he saw a sealed package in his commander's hand, it was because he was still in possession of the book when he left town. Therefore, it could not have been stolen before arriving in Toulon.

The dilemma now would be how to prove that he was lying. He was a professor and a high-ranking officer from Her Majesty. Vigni must have opened the package, found the book, and read its contents. Francesco's secret, so well kept, would be lost.

Robert and Michele asked Philip for an audience. Embarrassed and irritated by the lie, he immediately sent for Vigni. He also summoned Ozires and Domecq who confirmed Robert's story. Gerard failed to convince the king that the book had been stolen. Philip had him arrested and ordered his jailers to interrogate him to discover the book's whereabouts.

The result of the interrogation was terribly frustrating. Vigni confessed that he was instructed by King Edward III, who promised him a great deal of land should he reveal Philip´s strategy in his next attacks against England. Vigni wrongly believed that the package contained information that would be of the highest value to the English. The delivery was made to emissaries, especially sent to France by King Edward III.

Vigni was convicted for high treason and sentenced to life in prison. However, he refused to reveal to whom and where exactly he passed the package to the English, which further accentuated the desperation of the Vivone and Robert´s family.

Without any hope to recover the book, they turned their attention to the production and sale of wines. Everyone had enough money to enjoy life and that is what they decided to do. The family members were anxiously awaiting the birth of Luigi and Sigrid's son or daughter. She gave birth to male twins called Houston and Harold in the year 1338.

In 1340 the French fleet set out to invade England by sea, but unexpectedly faced the English navy consisting of 250 ships and more than 15,000 men, ahead of which was King Edward III[20]. The French were defeated in this confrontation called Sluys Naval Battle. Philip´s attempt failed completely and the British easily managed to invade France, which suffered great losses in terms of ships and men.

In 1346, the French lost once more, this time at the Battle of Crécy, south of Calais, in which the first cannons were used. With less soldiers (about 12,000 men) the English defeated a troop of more than 30,000 French warriors. The reason of the British success was the strategy used in the fighting. While the French lost almost 12,000 men, the number of deaths of Englishmen did not reach three hundred. In addition to the combatants, two nobles, Charles II of Alençon (born 1297), brother of Philip VI and John I of Bohemia died in the battle. It was imperative, therefore, that the obsolete French army would have to modernize, which required high expenses. Otherwise, they would be at risk of losing the war and the throne to England.

In addition to the scourge of war, an epidemic spread across Europe coming from Mongolia and other countries like China and Central Asia. It arrived in

---

[20]https://www.britannica.com/topic/Battle-of-Sluys.

Europe through the silk route in 1347 and spread to all European countries. It was the Black Death or Bubonic Plague[21] that relentlessly killed its victims. It also reached France and, what was worse, it arrived at the vineyard where the Vivone family and Robert de Valois and his wife lived. Robert was the first to feel the effects and succumbed in three days. Then, without any possibility of reacting against the disease, the plague hit Alfredo, Salvatore, Alina, Bianca, and Michele. The suffering was atrocious, with a high fever, swelling in their legs and groins, with tumors, black spots and bleeding that only ended with their death. The only survivors were Luigi, Sigrid and the two children, aged nine. Only in 1351 did the epidemic lose its strength.

The drama that unfolded after this sad episode, the fear of losing more loved ones, deeply affected the family. News reached the vineyard informing that the local population blamed the Jews for the plague and began to persecute them constantly, an absurdity that shows the ignorance of the population at the time. The Jews were mostly merchants blamed for spreading the plague during their journeys.

---

[21]https://www.britannica.com/event/Black-Death.

Chapter 12

In 1346, at the age of eight, the two boys (Harold and Houston) started in one of the best schools in France with the main purpose of perfecting their native language, and learn English, German, and Italian. They would also specialize in the fields of painting and sculpture. This goal coincided with the wishes of Luigi, who had accompanied his father, Godofredo to Paris where he learned new techniques of building pulpits and other engineering works. The art school would certainly serve for the two boys to follow their father's career and Luigi would teach them part of his experience.

The two sons were excellent students and learned much more than expected. In addition to architecture and engineering, they had immense success in mathematics, which gave them awards for solving problems of great complexity.

They graduated in 1356. After a period as interns in construction companies, they decided to visit England, still at war with France. It was a dangerous plan because they could be captured as enemies of the United Kingdom. As they spoke the language perfectly, they managed to board an English ship in Calais, a city conquered by the British in 1347. They landed in Southampton a port located in southern England.

Luckily, their names aroused no suspicion as they were common in the country. Soon they found work as teachers of elementary mathematics and of principles of architecture and engineering in London. Their skill in architectural design caught the attention of executives in the field.

Luigi had wisely passed on the techniques and art learned from his father, Godofredo who worked with Nicola Pisone for so many years. Curious about the advanced knowledge of Harold and Houston, the English engineers asked how and where they had acquired their experience, especially because they were so young.

"Our father and grandfather were Italians and had a long relationship with a great architect who built most of the pulpits and other engineering works in the main churches of the Vatican, informed Harold. Dad was the one who taught us his art during the time we spent in school. It was difficult for us because we were young, but we managed to assimilate the most important topics of his teachings."

Houston decided to tell their new friends about the flight from Italy to France and the trip via Calais to Southampton. Everyone admired the courage of the two boys and was eager to take advantage of their knowledge.

Two of the engineers worked with William of Wykeham (1324-1404)[22], responsible for the structural reforms of Windsor Castle. Knowing that the brothers could be useful in the construction of the new chapel in the Hall of St. George, they introduced them to Chief Wykeham. After undergoing various tests to assess their knowledge, they were hired in 1358. A year after actively participating in the construction of the chapel, they learned that the French were defeated in the battles of Sluys, Crécy, Calais and Poitiers and that Windsor Castle would keep French prisoners captured in these battles. They also learned that King Philip VI of France died in 1350 and that, after his death, his son John II took the throne. They also discovered that, in 1355, the English king resumed the war in France by sending his son Edward, Prince of Wales, the famous Black Prince, to devastate the central lands of France. The French army met the Black Prince's troops at Poitiers, where they suffered another overwhelming defeat. John II was captured and taken to England.

In recognition of their initial work in the chapel, King Edward III invited Harold and Houston to a party to celebrate the construction of the new São Jorge Wing. The celebration had an enormous impact on the lives of the brothers. During the ball, they met two young English girls, twin daughters of a deceased king's court lady. The passion was immediate. In the days that followed, Harold and Houston accidentally entered English high society as the twin sisters Grace and Audrey invited them to go horseback riding through the prairies of their widowed father, Lord Alfred Baltimore. The property was the famous Baltimore Estate.

Unfortunately, they had to politely refuse the invitation, confessing that they did not know how to ride a horse. Therefore, the girls decided to invite them for a picnic in one of the most picturesque places on the property. With two more weeks of almost daily contact with the two sisters, the two proposed to

---

[22]http://www.ancientfortresses.org/windsor-castle-timeline-important-dates.htm. See Years1357-1367.

the twins. The fact that it was a marriage of twins to twins caused the biggest sensation in the castle.

Chapter 13

In 1360 King Edward III negotiated a preliminary peace agreement with the French whereby he would receive large areas of land in northern France in exchange for the freedom of King John II[23]. It was at this time that John's son, the future Charles V negotiated peace with Edward III. That same year, the Treaty of Brétigny , ratified at Calais , gave Edward a considerable stretch of land in France (Calais and the entire French southwest) in exchange for abandoning his claims to the French throne.

On one of his visits to the São Jorge Hall and the chapel where the brothers worked, King Edward III's noticed the similarity between Harold and Houston. Admiring the beautiful work which they performed in the chapel, he wanted to know their names and where they came from. When he heard the name Vivone, he remembered having heard it earlier. He asked them to refresh his memory, as it was a name difficult to forget.

Houston, the most outgoing of the brothers took the initiative and clarified:

"Your Majesty, the name comes from our Italian great-grandfather Francesco Vivone. He was famous at the time for being one of the greatest linguistic experts. In 1231 he authored a book titled "Morality and Ethics" in which he specified the qualities that characterize a virtuous person which means someone who lives according to high moral values. His objective was to show the people how important it is to adopt these qualities. He managed to make five copies of the book. One was given to King Frederick II, another to Pope Gregory IX and two donated to the Vatican Library. The last one, that belonged to our uncle Sinibaldo Vivone, was stolen in Toulon, France. A soldier in the army of King Philip VI who became a traitor, managed to send the book to England, thinking it was a secret of war."

"Now I can remember where that name came from. What an incredible coincidence. I have good news for you. I have the book which I read many times. It was handed over to me by the emissary of the French military who stole it. I found the idea of your great-grandfather extraordinary and his

---

[23]https://www.britannica.com/biography/John-II-king-of-France.

courage to recommend these precepts so logical and almost never respected by kings, the church, and a large part of the population."

"In case you agree, I would like you to provide me with your family tree. That way I will learn more about your great-grandfather and the rest of your family. In fact, I remember now that my great friend Lord Baltimore informed me about his daughters' future marriage to two brothers who were also twins, something rare here in the castle. I just found out that you are the future husbands. As for the book, I am going to ask an emissary to deliver it to you and I think you should start that society you were going to organize in France."

To satisfy King Edward, the brothers drew up the following Family Tree:

Vivone´s Family Tree in 1360

Francesco Vivone (1201-1257) and Larissa Vivone (1201-1258)
    Rolando (1232-1310) and Giovanna (1234-1311)
      Alfredo (1273- 1338)
      Salvatore (1273- 1338)
    Sinibaldo (1232-1303) and Anabela (1236-1316)
      Alina (1274-1338)
      Bianca (1274-1338)
    Godofredo (1232-1312) and Matilda (1235-1313)
      Michele (1274-1338) and Robert Valois (1273-1338)
      Luigi (1295- and Sigrid Andersen (1305-
        Houston (1338- and Grace Baltimore (1346-
        Harold (1338- and Audrey Baltimore (1346-

After showing the wives the tree given to His Majesty, Grace's first question was:

"Where are your parents? Wouldn't you like them to come here? We want to meet them."

"As you know, they live in France and the country is at war with England. It would be difficult to bring them here and, besides, they are alone at the vineyard and there are few people who could replace them."

"I have an idea, said Lord Baltimore who overheard the conversation between the couples. I do not know if Grace or Audrey told you anything about my profession. For you to know a little about my life, since we are now relatives, I must clarify that I have a foreign trade company that operates with Spain and Morocco. I have a fleet of twenty-two ships for over fifteen years that are engaged in the trading of silk, salt, and pepper from China. As I have a trip planned for Tangier in Morocco, it would be possible to stop in Marseille and bring your parents."

"But England is at war with France and your ship would certainly be imprisoned in any French port, said Harold."

"It turns out that my ships travel with the flag of Scotland, so they can stop at Marseille without any problem. You should write to your parents to see if they are willing to face the rough sea at this time of year. But don't forget to ask them to bring "a few" bottles of wine."

As Lord Baltimore predicted, the trip was terrible. Luigi and Sigrid vowed never again to face storms like the one occurred in the Strait of Gibraltar. Finally, they arrived in England in 1363. The joy of Harold and Houston was formidable. Of course, they were eager to show their work in the chapel of São Jorge to their father.

Luigi's arrival was a success. The English engineers and their boss, William of Wykeham, upon hearing of the expert's presence, wanted to meet him. They were delighted with his comments regarding the work and felt they needed to learn more about the most advanced Italian specialty.

"Dear Master Luigi Vivone, said Wykeham, we know of your experience in architecture and engineering acquired from Italian specialists and mainly from your father, Godofredo. Based upon the information we received from your sons, we learned that he was a friend and disciple of the greatest pulpit builder of Italy, Nicola Pisani. If we have your permission, we would like to ask an audience for you with His Majesty Edward III who has a real passion for the chapel of Saint George. He would certainly be delighted to meet you to discuss other details of the project."

"I will be honored for this opportunity, but I do not know if I will be able to answer all your Majesty's questions."

It was not necessary to schedule the hearing. Upon learning of the presence of Master Luigi Vivone, the king requested his presence in the Hall of Saint George, along with Chief Wykeham and Luigi's sons. As His Majesty was not entirely satisfied with the shape of the chapel, Luigi volunteered to draw all the details of the pulpit of the Cathedral of Siena that had resemblance to the Italian chapel. The design had the immediate approval of Edward who asked Wykeham to include Luigi and his sons in his team of engineers to create the format in the style of Nicola Pisano.

"Can you imagine that I spent £ 51,000 to renovate Windsor, almost one and a half times my annual income? asked the king. I was lucky to pay a large part of the costs with the ransom money I received from the French after my victories in the battles of Crécy, Calais, and Poitiers".

Chapter 14

Luigi, assisted by his sons, dedicated himself to the chapel for another four years, until 1367. Unfortunately, when he was examining one of the arches in the dome of the chapel, he fell from a great height and had a severe concussion in his skull, eventually dying on the spot. The news did not reach his wife until hours later. The drama reverberated in the court of Edward III who sent for Simon Langham, Archbishop of Canterbury, for the funeral. With the death of Luigi, the children also ended their work in the chapel of Saint George.

Sigrid had already complained bitterly during the time she and her husband remained in England, claiming the abandonment to which she was subjected due to the intense work of Luigi and her children. She missed her native city in Norway where she was born. Without her husband, she decided it would be opportune to fulfill her dream and embarked for her homeland in 1367.

Invited by Lord Baltimore, Harold and Houston moved to the residence on the property that would be inherited by the sisters Grace and Audrey and by their husbands. When they arrived in Southampton, the two brothers could not imagine the transformation in their lives in England, as they moved from a family of winemakers to the English nobility. The specialty learned from Luigi had a profound influence in this change.

One day the two sisters discovered the book "Morality and Ethics" in one of Harold's suitcases and asked what it was.

"Would you like to read my great-grandfather's book"? asked Houston.

"Of course, we are curious to know details of what he wrote in Italy."

After reading Francesco's work, they wanted to discuss ideas about the whole theory of improving people´s behavior. Although they agreed that a person should adopt the principles outlined by the author, they argued that it would be hard to convince those who follow opposite principles to change their way of thinking. In this respect, Grace thought Francesco was a victim of the so-called "wishful thinking"[24].

---

[24]Wishful thinking: the attribution of reality to what one wishes to be true or the tenuous justification of what one wants to believe. In Merriam Webster

"There must be another way to implement his ideas and that is why I suggested to my sister to refine the philosophical question of his recommendations, said Grace. Let us think a little. One of the biggest doubts I have, for example, is the issue of wars. What would you say if a king invades foreign countries or promotes wars? He committed a crime. Now, what about the monarch who defends his nation against a foreign attack? It seems to me that in the first case it is an act of greed and in the second it is self-defense, but in both cases soldiers and innocent people will die."

"I would add, Audrey said, the case of criminals who kill innocent people and those who defend themselves to save their lives. What would be the difference between such an episode and the example you gave of the war? In my view, it is necessary to further discuss all these possibilities."

"I wanted to make a few more comments, Grace insisted. I think Francesco did not consider the differences in character between people in the world. I am sure it is difficult to convince a bandit that he must be honest, showing him how horrible it is to steal from his fellowmen. He will never be convinced of this easily, but there are other ways to convince people to be good too, and certainly all religions have this in principle, when preaching love. In addition, crimes committed in the past were considered as normal by kings and the people themselves, as they constituted rules accepted by all. An example is the death sentence for witches or heretics. The execution of these people is now condemned, but in the past, it was not considered a crime. How to assess whether, what is wrong today, could be right or acceptable in the past? I have one more question: all members of the Vivone family have adopted Francesco's principles, but do you really believe that, in their entire life, they would never commit an act that conflicts with these rules? It may be that the Vivone family respects these principles as much as possible, but someday they will make a mistake, even if it is small. Nobody is perfect."

"Grace, you are right, Houston replied, but Francesco tried to work out strict morality rules to show what he considered to be OPTIMAL. However, I am sure he knew human nature. On the other hand, imagine if he recommended the adoption of his moral principles, but that there are cultural issues that transcend what other societies consider right or wrong. With this he would be giving chance to a sinner who would use this argument to commit the sin. On the issue of wars, I agree that defending your country against invasions is not a crime. But everything has its limits and, in fact, not everything is so Cartesian. As for me, I will wholeheartedly try to respect my great-grandfather's concepts as the norm for my life and I know that everyone in the Vivone family will do everything possible to live according to these principles."

"I liked your arguments, my dear," added Grace.

In 1370, Harold and Houston were 32 years old, and Grace and Audrey were twenty-four. The girls' father fervently desired to live long enough to see his grandchildren who would inherit his properties, especially the shipping company. Finally, in 1374 the first heir was born, Anderson, son of Grace and Houston. Two years later, in 1376, Harold's wife, Audrey, gave birth to a baby girl named Lilian. In 1375, Jefferson, the second son of Grace was born and in 1377 Emily, Audrey's daughter unfortunately died during childbirth.

In view of the growth of the family and the need to take care of the children, the school opening was temporarily postponed. Harold kept the book for to his newborn children. He, in turn, looked forward to returning to the winery in Marseille and would love to take his family and Lord Baltimore to France.

After the death in 1376 of the Prince of Wales (the Black Prince) (1330-1376) and King Edward III in 1377, his grandson Richard II (1367-1413) took over the kingdom when he was only 10 years old. The beginning of his reign was tumultuous due to a tax of one shilling per adult, which had been introduced in 1377 as a way to finance military campaigns on the continent (a continuation of the Hundred Years' War) fought by Edward III. The peasants, in response, promoted a revolt that marked the end of serfdom in the country, with the struggle for reforms and for the rights of serfs. Richard finally agreed to introduce changes such as fair rents and the abolition of serfdom.

At the end of 1382, with the children a little older (and able to face the trip planned by Harold), Lord Baltimore took advantage of a silk export to Morocco so that the family could get to know the property in Marseille. This time there were no storms like the one suffered by Luigi and Sigrid. They arrived at the winery in 1383. Baltimore and his daughters admired the beauty of the place. They had never seen a property so well maintained.

The workers of the farm took care of production as if the owner had never left. All the money earned from the sale of grapes and wines was controlled. It was a surprise for the brothers who were not sure what they would find on arrival. In recognition of the exceptional honesty of the loyal employees, Houston hosted a party in their honor with pheasant and wine and other typical French foods.

"I would like to pay a sincere tribute to the four loyal friends who so well looked after the property of our dear parents Luigi and Sigrid in our absence, and I can categorically say that you reflect everything that my great-grandfather Francesco Vivone recommended in his book "Morality and Ethics." As a retribution for your loyalty, we decided to grant you a fifth of our property so that you can produce and enjoy the benefits that the land will offer."

Although Lord Baltimore had to return to England, the brothers decided to stay at the winery with their wives and children, to enjoy the local beauty and peace. At the same time, they would give the children a chance to understand the type of life in the countryside and improve the French language. Before embarking, Lord Baltimore struck a deal with Harold and Houston to export wines made at the winery to England, which would guarantee both families a considerable income.

Chapter 15

The latest news received from England informed that internal disputes were temporarily cooling the war against France. Richard II of England had to face rebellions by peasants and nobility, culminating with the rise of Henry of Lancaster (grandson of Edward III) to the throne in 1399, with the title of Henry IV (1367-1413).

In France, on the other hand, with the death of Charles V in 1380, Charles VI ascended the throne at the age of twelve and had the nickname "The Fool". In France, two groups of the nobility triggered a conflict for power, forming the so-called Armagnacs, and the Burgundians[25], starting a civil war between the two factions. Because they considered Charles VI to be incapable, the Burgundians sought to seize power, but were defeated, and then formed an alliance with the English.

At the beginning of the 15th century, the age of Harold and Houston was sixty-two and their children around 24 and 26. Grace and Audrey were fifty-four. Anderson, Jefferson, and Lilian became great entrepreneurs in the fine wine industry and had a considerable financial return. It was a year of great progress for the Vivone family. With the death of Lord Baltimore in 1399, the daughters inherited a huge property in England and their return was anxiously awaited by their old friends and employees. They learned on that occasion that Sigrid, mother of Harold and Houston, died in Oslo, Norway in 1369.

The updated family tree of the Vivone family as of the year 1400 is below:

---

[25]https://www.britannica.com/topic/Armagnac-party.

Vivone´s Family Tree in 1400

Francesco Vivone (1201-1257) and Larissa Vivone (1201-1258)

Rolando (1232-1310) and Giovanna (1234-1311)

Alfredo (1273- 1338)

Salvatore (1273- 1338)

Sinibaldo (1232-1303) and Anabela (1236-1316)

Alina (1274-1338)

Bianca (1274-1338)

Godofredo (1232-1312) and Matilda (1235-1313)

Michele (1274-1338) and Robert Valois (1273-1338)

Luigi (1295-1367 and Sigrid Andersen (1305-1369)

Houston (1338- and Grace Baltimore (1346-

Anderson (1374-

Jefferson (1375-

Harold (1338- and Audrey Baltimore (1346-

Lilian (1376-

Emily (1377-1377)

To give you an idea of the number of monarchs that reigned during the 13th. and 15th. centuries, the list provided below shows three different dates. The first is the date of birth of the kings, the second informs the date on which they took office and the third represents their death:

Kings of France and England from 13th to 15th Centuries

Kings of France	Kings of England
Louis IX (1214 - 1226 - 1270)	Henry III (1207 - 1216 - 1272)
Philip III (1245 - 1270 - 1285)	Edward I (1239 - 1272 - 1307)
Philip IV (1268 - 1285 - 1314)	Edward II (1284 - 1307 - 1327)
Louis X (1289 - 1314 - 1316)	Edward III (1312 - 1327 - 1377)
John I (1316 - 1316 - 1316) Five days	Richard II (1367 - 1377 - 1399) Neto
Philip V (1291 - 1316 - 1322) Uncle	Henry IV (1367 - 1399 - 1413) Edward III´s Grandson
Charles IV (1295 - 1322 - 1328) Brother	Henry V (1387 - 1413 - 1422)
Philip VI (1293 - 1328 - 1350) Philip´s Grandson	Henry VI (1421 - 1422 - 1471)
John II (1319 - 1350 - 1364)	Henry VII (1457 - 1485 - 1509)
Charles V (1337 - 1364 - 1380)	Henry VIII (1491 - 1509 - 1547)
Charles VI (1368 - 1380 - 1422)	
Charles VII (1403 - 1422 - 1461)	

The latest events have been surprising. With the income of the winery and the estate inherited in England, the Vivone family owns a considerable fortune and needed to decide what to do with their resources and the new property. At one of the family meetings, the countless possibilities for the future were analyzed. A possibility would be the sale of the winery and the return to England. Another would be to lease the property to other wine producers. In a third hypothesis, one of the couples with their sons or daughter could remain at the winery and manage the production while the others would move to the Baltimore Estate near Windsor Castle.

Grace, on the other hand, motivated by Francesco's book, thought that it would be opportune to invest part of the money in the school. Her suggestion was to start the project in France or England or in both countries. It was necessary, however, to check if the current Pope and the king would have something against a different kind of school like this.

"As you know, at this moment there is a dispute between the popes, claimed Audrey. Let me explain: Now there are two Popes. In Rome, the pope is Boniface IX (1345-1404)[26]while in Avignon it is the Antipope due to the Great Schism of the West[27](a religious crisis that began in 1378 between the two popes)".

"The French cardinals in Avignon elected Clement VII (1342-1394) and both he and Boniface IX claimed power over the Catholic Church. Each one promoted excommunication and accusations of heresy against the other.

"France, Aragon, Castile, León, Cyprus, Burgundy, County of Savoy, Naples, and, Scotland recognized the Avignon antipope, while Denmark, England, Flanders, the Holy Empire, Hungary, Northern Italy, Ireland, Norway, Poland, and Sweden supported the Pope of Rome. With the death of Clement VII, the antipope elected in Avignon was Benedict XIII (1328-1423)"[28].

"The current king of England is Henry IV, with whom we have no relationship as we did with his grandfather Edward III at the time of the construction of the Chapel de Saint George."

---

[26]https://www.britannica.com/biography/Boniface-IX.
[27]https://www.britannica.com/event/Western-Schism.
[28]https://www.britannica.com/biography/Benedict-XIII-antipope.

"Anyway, continued Audrey, despite this confusing situation, I see no reason we should not open the school here in Marseille. As to England, they support Pope Boniface IX of Rome, therefore I would also be in favor of creating a school near Windsor Castle. I think the case of the flight from Fiumicino has been forgotten."

"But it would cause our families to split up, said Harold. It would be more effective if everyone participated in one school and then, depending on its success, we could think about establishing another one in England."

"I do not agree with any of these ideas, Houston countered. I think our property here in Marseille is guaranteed mainly because we have our trusted employees taking care of production and sales. I think we must urgently look after our properties in England, because the nobles have always shown a strong envy of your father's estate and they could claim that it belongs to them too. Despite the absurdity of the claim, as the lands are being looked after only by employees, it would become an easy prey for invasions by these people. And after the crime has been committed, it would be difficult to expel them. In addition, you did not think about the shipping and foreign trade company of Lord Baltimore. Will the current managers have no other plans, maybe even take it from us?"

"My brother is right; I should have considered what he said. If everyone agrees, we should leave for England as soon as possible," suggested Harold.

Chapter16

With all the measures taken at the winery, in 1403 the Vivone family returned to England. The first step taken was to verify whether there was any invasion of the property. The second was to list all the assets of the deceased, to obtain the definitive title of the property and the legal possession of the other assets. The third consisted of checking on Lord Baltimore's company and whether he, as promised, wrote that the Vivone family would manage it, leaving the presidency with Grace and the financial administration with Audrey. Jefferson and Anderson would be responsible for the fleet and trade with Morocco, Spain, and other countries. Lilian, however, due to her extreme ability to deal with people of high social level, would be responsible for contacts with large customers. Harold and Houston, longing for their work as engineers, intended to visit Windsor Castle to see how the work on the chapel progressed.

Things resulted better than expected. There was no conflict about ownership, the firm's employees were instructed by Lord Baltimore before his death that the family would be responsible for the company.

William of Wykeham, chief engineer of Windsor Castle was delighted with the visit of the two brothers. He recorded the names of Luigi, Harold, and Houston in the hall at the entrance of the Saint George chapel in recognition of their work. It was a glory to have the family name in a place as famous as Windsor Castle. Wykeham suggested that the two should meet King Henry IV.

Two weeks later they learned from the king that he was present during the last ceremony for the completion of one part of the chapel. Henry had already heard about the contribution of Luigi Vivone and his twin sons. He proposed another tribute to the Vivone family consisting of the authorization for a permanent access to Windsor Castle. On that occasion, Houston took the opportunity to inform the king that they had moved permanently to the Baltimore Estate, inherited by their wives. He also told him about the huge shipping and foreign trade company that Lord Alfred left for his family, with a total of twenty-two ships for trade with Europe and Africa. He added that before his death, exports only included silk, salt and pepper to Morocco and Spain but now, under the administration of the children, they included wine produced in Marseille, considered one of the best in France. He further explained that the winery was inherited by his late mother who was married to Robert de Valois, uncle of Philip VI of France.

All this impressed Henry, who immediately saw an opportunity to develop England's foreign trade through the Vivone fleet, as the English resented the low exports of wool. On the other hand, French wine could be part of the English imports.

Anyway, Houston just opened a door to the kingdom of England. The next step would be to import boxes of wine for the king and his court, a faster way to develop an additional source of income for the family, as the quality of the wine is second to none and would be consumed by the country's nobility and all over England.

The news brought by the two brothers that all that remained was to receive permission from the king to set up the school so dreamed by Francesco. But that would be something to discuss in the future. The plan was set for early 1404.

To increase the family's joy, Harold and Houston received an invitation from William of Wykeham to return to Windsor Castle as soon as possible, as a column built by two of his assistants had collapsed. When they arrived, they found that they did not correctly calculate the amount of iron necessary to support the structure. Extremely irritated, Wykeham made a serious mistake by loudly blaming the assistant engineers in the presence of the two brothers.

"You can look for work somewhere else. At the Castle you will no longer be admitted. You should have learned your job from the Vivone brothers who are the real specialists."

One can imagine the shame the two engineers went through. They had already been furious because Wykeham decided to choose Harold and Houston to finish the Saint George chapel. Harold immediately realized that the hatred on both faces could have unpredictable consequences. Furthermore, they were two young ex-military, specialized in fencing and were descendants of one of the opposing families of Henry IV.

Houston informed the family and employees that he felt Wykeham's lack of diplomacy sparked the hatred of the engineers. He warned everyone to be vigilant in the coming days against any kind of threat to their homes. One of the signs that confirmed Houston's fears was the appearance, two days later, of 10 or 12 torches burning outside the property's border. Due to the distance, it was impossible to identify those responsible. The episode lasted only 15 minutes, but it was enough to terrify both employees and all members of the family.

"We have to bring this to the attention of the security of the castle, argued Lilian, because we are unable to defend ourselves against this intimidation by the engineers who are also trained army officers. I counted about twelve torches in all, and I know it is dangerous."

"I think it would be unreasonable to ask for help from the guard commander, as we cannot prove anything, said Audrey. There was no invasion, nobody was hurt, we just know that the experience was very frightening. Even so, we must keep the house locked on all sides and close the stables."

A month later the drama had already been forgotten. Anderson and Jefferson received the boxes of wine and were anxious to hear Henry IV's reaction. Eight boxes came with twelve bottles each, enough to satisfy the entire court. The delivery would be made by the employees, but Lilian decided to go along to get acquainted with the interior of Windsor Castle.

After her admission to the Castle thanks to Henry IV's offer authorizing the Vivone family to have permanent access, Lilian and the employees were lost within the immensity of the palace. By chance, she entered an immense hall where the king was having a meeting with his advisers.

Surprised by the intrusion, the king asked why such a beautiful girl invaded the room and how she dared to disturb him in one of his meetings with the War Council.

"I humbly apologize to Your Majesty. I was lost in the corridors and decided to enter this door to see if I could find my way. I am here with my employees to bring Your Majesty the eight cases of French wine from our property in Marseille as promised. My brothers who are responsible for our exports, informed that, fortunately, the ship that carried the wines managed to overcome the terrible storm in the Strait of Gibraltar."

"Well, you are forgiven, and I want you to convey my thanks to your brothers, and especially to Harold and Houston for their attention, knowing my preference for French wines. On the other hand, I would like to take the opportunity to inform your family that, within five days, there will be a ball to celebrate my military victories in the war against France and I would be honored with your presence and of your brothers."

Chapter17

Harold and Houston remained at home with their wives while Lilian, Anderson, and Jefferson went to the ball at the Castle. Recognized by the King, Lilian, the most outgoing of the family, had no difficulty in projecting herself as a charming, intelligent, and communicative person. On the other hand, Anderson and Jefferson found various merchants, English exporters eager to hear more about French wines and the Vivone family's export basket.

The harassment of the English young men to the beautiful Lilian was unforeseen. She did not know to whom she should concede the first dance, but she finally surrendered to a gentleman she considered the most elegant and attractive. The night was wonderful for the three brothers.

When they returned to the Baltimore Estate, they saw thick smoke coming from the property in the distance. Running as they could, they were horrified by a fire that had destroyed the stable and immediately noticed the absence of the six horses. Fearing that something more serious had happened, they quickly entered the residence and went up to their parents' rooms. It is impossible to describe the horrible scene they witnessed. The parents had been savagely murdered. They were unable to oppose any reaction, as they never got out of bed. They must have been stabbed in their sleep. Halfway between the bedrooms lay the bodies of two of the most faithful employees. Everyone burst into tears, trying desperately to see if there was still a mere breath of life, but it was useless.

They decided to return to the castle to alert the guards and receive help to prevent other killings. Furthermore, they had to request an investigation and take the necessary steps for the burial of the deceased. The three brothers immediately linked the episode to the two engineers who Wykeham censored about a month ago.

At dawn of the following day, soldiers from the castle, led by commander Jeffrey Wilson, came to the residence and witnessed the shocking scene. Friends of the family came to offer their condolences and king Henry IV, upon learning of the incident, came personally to the Baltimore Estate and promised that his security agents would do everything to convict those responsible.

Lilian informed commander Wilson that the assassins stole six horses with the brand mark "AB" (Alfred Baltimore) and certainly would be recognized and the capture of the killers could happen quickly.

The news gathered by the soldiers at the engineers' residence was vague. The information received was that the suspects left with four friends to hunt deer in the nearby forest. They also learned that the six horses, according to the residents, had been recently purchased.

Wilson immediately sent a platoon of soldiers and dogs into the forest to hunt for the killers. The investigation resulted negative, as they found no trace that could indicate the direction of the group. Therefore, the information turned out to be false.

The Holy Mass for the deceased was celebrated by the Archbishop of Canterbury, Thomas Arundel, with the presence of the nobility of Windsor and the old and faithful employees of Alfred Baltimore. The engineers of the Castle also attended in the absence of William of Wykeham who died weeks before the sad episode. Also present was the gentleman who met Lilian and his brothers at the ball. The parents were buried in the private cemetery located on the property, with the following words on the tombstone:

**IN LOVING MEMORY OF HAROLD, AUDREY, HOUSTON, AND GRACE VIVONE
CASTLE HILL COUNTY - OCTOBER 1404**

It was later discovered that the gentleman who danced with Lilian was the eldest son of Henry IV and his wife Maria de Bohun. Born by the name of Henry of Monmouth[29], Prince of Wales (1387-1422), he was knighted in 1399 and had to participate early in state affairs, including military campaigns where he proved to be brilliant. He managed to overcome popular insurrections, rendering valuable services to his father.

In the days that followed, Henry went on to visit Lilian, arguing that he wanted to console her for the loss of her parents, but in fact he was increasingly attracted to her. The obligations to his father, however, called him to reality, since England was at war with France. Lilian was sure that it would

---

[29]https://www.britannica.com/biography/Henry-V-king-of-England.

not be appropriate to have any loving involvement with a man who would be England's next king.

Henry was extremely shocked by the murder of Lilian's parents and promised to do everything to find the wrongdoers. In fact, he himself devised a plan to pursue them, but this time he decided to send the troops north, as they found no trace in the forest where they seemed to have entered with the horses.

The strategy paid off, as in all the villages visited by soldiers, they knew that six riders passed by the place just stopping to drink and eat, but no one had noticed the marks engraved on the horses' hips. From the indications obtained, it could have taken the direction of Watford, about twenty-five miles from Windsor Castle. The information was correct, as just before they reached Watford, there was an inn named Flanagan Inn where six horses were tied in front of the entrance, all with the brand "AB."

Without hesitating, the soldiers surrounded the place while eight of them entered the corridors where the cafeteria and bar were located. At least twenty people there drinking and playing cards. Among them they recognized the two engineers who had been disrespected by Wykeham. The other four were also ex-soldiers who participated in the slaughter. Seeing themselves surrounded by a much larger number, they surrendered without showing any resistance.

The prisoners were taken to Windsor Castle for the trial. Upon receiving the news, Lilian did not resist and hugged Henry effusively, realizing how she had been carried away by his charms. The same happened with Henry, but both knew that an involvement would be impossible due to his obligations in the war against France.

The six were sentenced to death by hanging. Lilian and her brothers asked Henry not to execute them at a public square, as the experiences in France with similar punishments were extremely traumatic. A week later they learned that the sentences were conducted inside the Castle.

Chapter 18

In 1404, Lilian was twenty-eight years old, Anderson the oldest was thirty and Jefferson twenty-nine. With a considerable amount of capital due to their success in exports, they finally decided to plan the establishment of the school their mothers had planned but did not live to fulfill the dream. Therefore, they decided to study the book "Morality and Ethics" in Lilian's possession. With so many places they went through, they acquired the necessary experience to manage such a venture. However, Anderson, in love with the export company, asked to be released from the project, since his relationship with the commercial world had been carefully planned. His objective was to continue to make full profits from English and French products. The war would have little influence on business, as his fleet under the flag of Scotland would have no difficulty landing in any city in France or other countries, thanks to the strategy of Alfred Baltimore. In addition, his trips would allow quick visits to the Marseille winery to control production and sales.

In 1405, Lilian found the love of her life on one of her trips to Windsor Castle as she prepared to deliver twenty cases of wine sold to the nobles of the court. In one of the halls was one of her admirers who tried to attract her attention during the ball at which she met the future King Henry V. He was a knight named Frederic Swinston, Henry's great friend, born in 1390, a little younger than Lilian. It did not take long before an uncontrollable passion emerged, resulting in a marriage proposal. The union was celebrated at Lilian's residence with the presence of only her two cousins.

The school, opened in 1410 at the Baltimore Estate, near Windsor Castle. The name "**THE ROYAL SCHOOL OF MORAL INTEGRITY**" was in honor of the family's patriarch Francesco Vivone. The inauguration party was attended by nobles of King Henry IV who sent his son Henry to honor the new institution and celebrate Lilian's wedding with Frederic.

Always guided by the principles contained in the book written by Francesco, Lilian, Jefferson, and Frederic managed to make the school famous. Children and adults from England and other countries were admitted, without any payment and all school supplies were provided free of charge. The teachers were paid with salaries in line with their specialization and all costs were borne by the Vivone family. In addition to other subjects, the study of the Basic Principles of Morality was the most important course in the curriculum. After two years, graduates would receive the **"Certificate of Morality."**

In 1412 the first group of students received their diplomas at the graduation party. Thanks to the invitation of King Henry IV, the prom was held in the main hall of the Castle. Henry was unable to attend because he resented a skin disorder that had plagued him for so long. All students were instructed during the ceremony to spread the principles of Morality in England, which would change the habits of the citizens.

In 1413, Henry IV died, succeeded by his son who took the name of Henry V[30]. A great strategist and military genius, he dedicated himself to the restoration of internal peace and English prestige in Europe. He engaged in an offensive against the continent and organized campaigns to conquer France, an action that had the full support of the English people for his war effort.

On one of his trips to Morocco in 1415, Anderson, aged forty-nine, met a beautiful 25-year-old Moroccan girl, born in Tangiers in 1390 by the name of Samira Amal. Both, hopelessly in love, decided to get married at the winery in Marseille. The ceremony was not attended by the family, as everyone was involved with the school. Anderson spent a few weeks in France managing not only the winery but also the flow of exports and returned to England with his wife. In the following year, in 1416 two twins named Zachary and Gordon were born and in 1418 Samira had another boy named Orson. Jefferson was not as fortunate to find an ideal wife as was the case with his brother. He preferred to dedicate himself body and soul to THE ROYAL SCHOOL OF MORAL INTEGRITY.

Henry V achieved two significant triumphs against the French in the battles of Harfleur and Azincourt. As a result, he signed an alliance treaty with Emperor Sigismund of the Holy Roman Empire (1368-1437)[31], which contributed to the end of the Great Papal Schism with the election of Pope Martin V (1368-1431) and the return of the Papacy to Rome. In 1420, Henry V signed the Treaty of Troyes with the French, becoming heir to the French throne and regent of France. He married Catherine, daughter of Charles VI, then reaching the height

---

[30] https://www.britannica.com/biography/Henry-V-king-of-England.
[31] https://www.britannica.com/biography/Sigismund-Holy-Roman-emperor.

of his power, but died shortly after, in 1422, in the castle of Vincennes, France. His body was transferred to London and is buried in Westminster Abbey.

Years passed and, in 1425, the family learned of an impressive episode in France about a young girl named Joan of Arc, 13 years old, born in Dom Rémy, in 1412[32]. She claimed to have received messages from Saint Michael, Saint Catherine, and Saint Margaret, asking her to save France under the reign of Charles VII[33]. Despite doubts about the veracity of her visions, in 1428 she claimed to be sure that she had heard insistent voices to help the king. The voices requested that she introduce herself to Robert Baudricourt, who commanded the neighboring city of Vaucouleur for the king.

Charles' military situation was becoming unbearable, with his defeat in Orleans expected at the end of the year. Joan managed to convince Baudricourt, because in 1429, predicting the defeat of Orleans at the Battle of Herrings (which was confirmed), Joan got an interview with the king at Chinon Castle. She was used to wear men's clothes and, after being subjected to various tests by bishops and doctors about their integrity, the king decided to provide her with a special sword, but she wanted her ancient sword saying that it was buried behind an altar in the Chapel of Saint Catherine of Fierbois. The sword, in fact, was found in the same place indicated by such voices, confirming Joan's power to predict events. But the most striking fact came when she promised to free Orleans. She further declared that she would be wounded but would not die and that the king would be crowned in Reims, telling yet other events that the king kept secret.

To the English she sent a message warning them that she would expel them from Orleans which made them furious with her audacity. In a quick maneuver, Joan entered the city and beat the English. On the seventh day, Joan was wounded in her chest by an arrow but did not die. With an additional number of battles, the victory was complete and finally Joan of Arc managed to have Carlos VII crowned in Reims while she stood at his side.

---

[32] https://www.britannica.com/biography/Saint-Joan-of-Arc.
[33] https://www.britannica.com/biography/Charles-VII-king-of-France.

After more battles including a failure to try to conquer Paris, Joan was wounded in her thigh by an arrow. Losing prestige increasingly, the Duke of Alençon withdrew her from military actions forcing her to lay down her weapons. Meanwhile, the French nobility feared that Joan would assemble the people against the king. It was Jean of Luxenbourg, vassal of the Duke of Burgundy who sold her to the English for 10,000 francs and, in 1430, she was arrested and chained in a secular prison in Rouen. Joan was subjected to a trial without having the right of defense. In 1431 she was burned at the stake by the English, based on accusations of witchcraft and heresy.

Despite being saved by Joan of Arc from the catastrophe that would have been the taking of Orleans by the English, Charles VII abandoned her when she was taken prisoner.

Chapter 19

Thanks to the military campaign by Joan of Arc and the coronation of Charles VII, the king's prestige increased significantly among the population. Soon afterwards, he conquered northern France, taking over Paris, Normandy, and Guyenne, leaving the city of Calais for the English. Charles also created a permanent army formed by the so-called compagnies D´ordonnance, an infantry formed by French archers[34].

Once again for the readers' clarification, we present below the Vivone family tree as of 1431.

Vivone´s Family Tree in 1431

Francesco Vivone (1201-1257) and Larissa Vivone (1201-1258)
  Rolando (1232-1310) and Giovanna (1234-1311)
   Alfredo (1273- 1338)
   Salvatore (1273- 1338)
  Sinibaldo (1232-1303) and Anabela (1236-1316)
   Alina (1274-1338)
   Bianca (1274-1338)
  Godofredo (1232-1312) and Matilda (1235-1313)
   Michele (1274-1338) and Robert Valois (1273-1338)
   Luigi (1295-1367 and Sigrid Andersen (1305-1369)
    Houston (1338- and Grace Baltimore (1346-
     Anderson (1374-
      Zachary (1416-
      Gordon (1416-
      Orson (1418-
     Jefferson (1375-
    Harold (1338-1404) and Audrey Baltimore (1346-1404)
     Lilian (1376- and Frederic Swinston (1390-
     Emily (1377-1377)

In 1431 the Vivone family was composed only of Anderson age 57, Samira 41, Jefferson 44, Lilian 55, Frederic 41, Zachary and Gordon 15, and Orson 13.

The dream of the three brothers was to listen to Anderson´s stories. One evening after dinner, Orson, the most curious, asked his father to tell the story of a man his teacher had mentioned. The teacher said that it would take two years from now to hear about this man in the history class.

---

[34] http://dictionary.sensagent.com/Compagnie%20d'ordonnance/en-en/.

"Who is this man that the teacher mentioned?" asked Anderson.

"She said that his name was Marcos Paul. Have you heard of him? According to what she said he was an adventurer who lived in 1254 and was born in Vaniza."

"I don't think you quite understood what she said. His name was Marco Polo, and he was born in a city in Italy called Venice in 1254 and died in 1324. I will tell his story, but first I will have to talk about two important leaders. One was called Genghis Khan and the other was Kublai Khan," said Anderson.

"Please tell us the story" asked Orson.

"Let me talk about Genghis Khan first. Then I'll tell you about Kublai and Marco Polo."

"Genghis Khan[35] was one of the greatest conquerors in the world. His name was Temujin, and he was born in a country called Mongolia in the year 1162 and he died in 1227. As Mongolia had tribes that were fighting each other, he ended the conflicts because he was a powerful leader, and everyone was afraid of him. He later expanded his kingdom from Asia to the Adriatic Sea and then he conquered China as a whole, forming what was called the Great Mongol Empire."

"He had a powerful army, and his orders were strictly obeyed. It is said that, while he was a barbarian, he was incredibly intelligent and was considered a military genius. His army was brutal with the people who lived in the invaded cities and his soldiers destroyed everything they found. Therefore, he was called a "devil from hell," by everyone. When he was born, they said he was the son of a gray fox."

"But Temujin (Genghis Khan) also had powerful enemies, called nomads who were people who had no fixed home. They did not stop anywhere; they were always moving but they needed the goods that Genghis Kahn possessed, and he needed the goods of the nomads. The two peoples were at war, but Genghis Khan was stronger, more courageous and always won."

[35] https://www.britannica.com/biography/Genghis-Khan.

"In 1206 Temujin set out to conquer the world with his well-trained army consisting of his sons and other loyal soldiers. First, he used horses in his invasions, but soon realized that horses were not adequate for invading cities. Then he started using other weapons such as catapults that threw huge rocks at a great distance, also stairs, boiling oil, and equipment to divert rivers."

"Almost all the people of countries invaded by Genghis Khan decided to join him. Despite killing all those who refused to cooperate, Temujin was a man who liked to hear advice, especially from his brother and his mother. He was also religious and worshiped a God he called the Eternal Blue Sky."

"Can you imagine that Genghis Khan had ten children? All of them had funny named. They were called Ögödei, Tolui, Jochi, Djaghatai, Checheikhen, Alakhai Bekhi, Tümelün, Alaltun, Khochen Beki, and Gelejian".

"Before he died in 1227, Temujin appointed his third son Ögödei (1186-1241)[36] as his successor and asked the other brothers to obey him and gave him a very well trained and equipped army. Ögödei was also an intelligent man and took advice, but he wanted to continue his father's dream of invading Europe and conquering the world"[37].

"But Dad, why did Genghis Khan choose Ögödei?" asked Gordon.

"Because he liked this son better than the other children. In addition, Ögödei was big, smart, and friendly and fulfilled his father's dream. When he needed it, he asked the generals for advice on what they thought was the right thing to do, but he also knew how to choose people he could trust. Ögödei conquered several countries after China. He invaded Korea, Persia, Russia, Hungary, Poland, and Transylvania. Had he not died before, he would have invaded Austria, Germany, Italy, France, and Spain, and was already on his way to the Atlantic Ocean which is further west. He also opened the Silk Road again, where traders passed with the silk shipments from China and the East (East) which would be sold to the countries located in the west."

"Ögödei was an important man. In fact, despite invading other countries and killing so many people, he changed made places wherever he went bringing the

---

[36]https://www.britannica.com/biography/Ogodei.
[37]https://www.newworldencyclopedia.org/entry/%C3%96gedei_Khan

customs of the Mongol Empire to all these invaded countries. He even showed Europeans that there were other countries on the east side of Europe that they had not heard of."

"Do you still want to hear the Kublai Khan story?" asked Anderson.

"Of course, please continue."

"Well, Kublai Khan (1215-1294)[38] was the grandson of Genghis Khan and he was the last of the Great Khans in Mongolia. He was a fantastic military leader and was the founder and first emperor of the so-called Chinese Yuan Dynasty. A Dynasty is a succession of rulers of the same line of descent, or a powerful group or family that maintains its position for a considerable time. For example, if a king dies, his son will become king and if he dies, his son continues to occupy his throne. According to Chinese tradition, Kublai was called "Tien-tse," which means "Son of Heaven." Kublai was the second son of Genghis Khan's second son and his mother's name was Sorghaghtani Beki."

"Kublai's life was not easy. In 1251, he fell in love with Chinese customs and, for that reason, won the respect of the Chinese population. Imagine that his fame reached Europe through Marco Polo who wrote about him. In that year, his older brother Mongke became Khan of the Mongol Empire and Kublai was appointed governor. In 1259, with Mongke' death, Kublai had to face his younger brother who wanted to become emperor. The funny thing is that the two brothers declared themselves kings and kept fighting until Kublai finally won. However, he had to face another dynasty, the Song Dynasty."

"After so much fighting he declared himself Emperor of the Yuan Dynasty and unified China, ultimately destroying the Song Dynasty completely. He performed important works in China, rebuilt the Grand Canal, built roads, and renovated buildings. In 1274, he planned to invade Japan in search for gold. He also tried to invade the Republic of the Union of Myanmar, Vietnam, and Java, but his efforts failed. He attacked Japan for the first time with nine hundred ships and was defeated by Japanese samurais, great warriors of Japan. In 1281, he tried again to invade Japan, this time with 1,170 ships (which had not been well built) and was again defeated. He died in 1294".

---

[38] https://www.britannica.com/biography/Kublai-Khan.

"As you are very sleepy, I will leave the Marco Polo story for tomorrow, right? It has been a long day for you and me."

The next morning the boys woke up early to hear the next story.

"Please tell the story of Marco Polo."

"Marco Polo (1254-1324)[39] was a very brave man. He learned to be a merchant and adventurer from his father Nicoló Polo and his uncle Maffeo who traveled from Europe to Asia to sell and buy goods which did not exist in Europe. The father and uncle became rich with these trips, especially with those made to the Middle East for so many years. They soon learned about the Silk Road from China to Europe where they bought silk, an expensive fabric."

"In the years 1260 and 1261 Nicoló and Maffeo lived in a city called Constantinople. As they were very smart, they suspected that the situation in the city was getting dangerous. Consequently, they took all their goods, exchanged everything for jewelry and fled the city to the Volga River and continued towards the east."

"Dad, you didn't explain the meaning of the word east, and you didn't explain where the Volga River is, asked Orson."

"Yes, I will explain. The Volga River is the longest river in Europe and has an extension of 3,688 km. The river starts in northern Russia. For you to know where Russia is, keep your back to me and extend your arm to the right. There you are pointing to the east. So east is a direction, ok?"

"We understand."

"But first I will tell you that Russia is a country like England, full of people. And it is far away. Can you imagine a river that is 2,200 miles long? If you put a boat in the river where it starts, you would stay in the boat for six months until you reach the end of the river."

"Well, arriving in Mongolia, Nicoló and Maffeo became friends with the Great Kublai Khan. Kublai trusted foreigners more than his own people and ended up naming the two as his ambassadors. In 1268, he gave an order for

---

[39]https://www.britannica.com/biography/Marco-Polo.

them to take a letter to Pope Clement IV, asking him to send a hundred intelligent and educated men to Mongolia to teach the Seven Arts to his people. The seven arts were architecture, sculpture, painting, music, dance, poetry, and theater. Furthermore, Kublai, who was very fond of studying, wanted foreigners to teach Christianity and European customs to his people. Unfortunately, that year Pope Clement IV died and so the two brothers were unable to fulfill Kublai's wish. In 1269, they returned to Venice and waited for the appointment of the new Pope who was only elected in 1271. The Pope elected that year was Gregory X. It was in that year that Nicoló and Maffeo invited Marco Polo to accompany them on their travels. The boy was only 17 years old in 1271".

"Marco traveled throughout Europe and Asia between 1271 and 1295 and stayed in China for seventeen years during that period. The effort of his father and uncle made Marco Polo's life much easier. With his travels and experience with so many people, Marco brought the customs of many different nations and can be considered one of the great ambassadors of culture in history."

"Due to the Polo family's courage to travel through such remote regions and peacefully maintain a great relationship with people who have completely different religions and customs, they were able to captivate the Mongolian kings who had the title of Khan, as they were impressed by the generosity and frankness of these foreigners who came from distant Europe."

"Dad, what is culture? asked Gordon."

"A person who studies a lot and knows many things is a person who has a lot of culture. For example, the teacher at my school when I was your age, was a man of great culture because he had studied and taught so many things. I thought he knew everything. That is the meaning of culture, OK?"

"We understand."

"Marco became the favorite of the Kublai Khan court and stayed in the kingdom for the seventeen years he spent in China. Kublai authorized him to travel freely around the country. In 1291, Kublai made another request to Marco. He wanted him to take the Mongolian Koekecin princess to find her husband, called Arghun Khan. Marco took a fleet of fourteen ships from

Quanzhou across the China Sea, through Vietnam to Java, Sumatra, Sri Lanka, and India before bringing the princess to Persia for her wedding[40]. In 1294 the Princess was "delivered", and the Polo family returned to Venice in 1295".

"When Marco Polo arrived in Venice, his compatriots did not recognize him, as he had left Venice 24 years ago. Marco, his father, and uncle arrived as pilgrims dressed in tattered clothes. Everyone thought they were dead. The relatives celebrated the return and organized a party in honor of the three travelers and when they arrived at the party, they were dressed in wonderful clothes made of satin and silk. When they untied the old clothes full of rags, a huge amount of jewelry of incredible value fell out. They were rubies, sapphires, garnets, diamonds, and emeralds."

"Now you have heard a lot of stories and I am tired. Tomorrow we will talk about the Royal School."

The school continued to grow, with more candidates, which came to the attention of the Windsor Castle authorities. They thought that the ideas taught at the Royal School could conflict with other educational institutions attended by children in England.

At the end of 1431, the 15th.graduation took place, and the celebration was attended by parents of students, teachers, and guests from different social classes, considering that there was no discrimination of any kind by race or social status. It was decided that at the graduation party, after the distribution of the certificates, only two speakers would speak as the board recognized that too many speeches would be boring for the audience.

Jefferson was chosen by the board as a speaker representing the school and the best student was invited to speak at the end. A Dublin-born Irishman named Sean Dwayne stood out.

"Today we are celebrating the graduation of forty-four young people who obtained the certificate of Moral Integrity, Jefferson began. You deserved and honored this title for having assimilated and used all the principles contained in the book written by our dear ancestor Francesco Vivone. Each of you already lives according to these principles and has agreed to spread them wherever

---

[40]https://www.britannica.com/biography/Marco-Polo/Sojourn-in-China.

you go in your future lives. We are proud of the success of this group that I classify among the best that have passed through our institution. We have been told that the success of our Moral Integrity courses has reached the ears of our governors and other educational institutions and should be copied in cities in England. Congratulations and thanks to everyone."

Sean's words touched not only his colleagues but also the audience. These were his words:

"When I entered the Royal School of Moral Integrity, I thought I was going to waste my precious time and have to give up the ball games with my friends. I refused to understand why my parents chose a school with that pretentious name. In the first few weeks, however, I realized that I was totally mistaken."

"In fact, I did not lose my youth, I gained maturity. They taught us to think, to analyze what happens around us, what we can do to convince others to see with new eyes what we did not see before. They also taught us how it is possible to change our habits without any trauma or regret. I will exemplify and ask you to think with me."

"Why do the Church and monarchs kill or torture those who profess different kinds of beliefs? What would it be like if, on the other hand, heretics could kill or torture church members or monarchs? Both profess different beliefs. Couldn't there be tolerance instead of expressions of hate? Would a drastic change in habits be possible?"

"Since 1337 England has been at war with France. Territories are conquered, territories are lost. In each battle thousands of people die. A surprising episode in this war was the sacrilege to which Joan of Arc was subjected, a French hero, burned at the stake by the English under the allegation of witchcraft and heresy. But let us think a bit about the war. England and France have enough land to house all their inhabitants. The yearning for power, which makes one king want to subdue the other, is the main reason for these conquests. Wouldn't it be possible to have a glass of wine together and enjoy the good times in life? If France produces something that England longs for, it is enough to propose an exchange with what exists in England and not in France. There is no need to kill so many people for this or to sacrifice women like Joan of Arc.

"I fought a lot with my colleagues at the other school where I studied. I wanted desperately the toys they had, and my mom could not buy. But I had other toys they did not have; what is the advantage of these fights? In fact, children still do not have that insight to understand what to do, but if I had attended our school, I would have acted differently."

"For this reason, I would like to thank the privilege that my colleagues and I had to attend the Royal School of Moral Integrity and the honor of being one of the new graduates. Thank you very much".

Sean Dwayne received a standing ovation.

Chapter 20

The next day Sean Dwayne and Jefferson were arrested by the order of King Henry VI (1421-1471). Without understanding the reasons for the arrest, they were brought before the king for a quick trial. Lilian and her husband Frederic were also summoned. Anderson was absent from England because he took Samira to France.

Upon being admitted to His Majesty's presence, the king recognized Frederic, a friend of his father, Henry V.

"I always respected you as a great friend of my father and, taking this into account, I would like you to explain the reason for the offenses contained in the speeches of the principal and of that Irishman at your school's graduation party, started His Majesty. I was offended, and the integrity of Pope Eugene IV (1383-1447) was questioned under the argument that we are two murderers! How could you get involved in something so shameful?"

"Your Majesty must have heard rumors that the two spoke of moral integrity and argued that the Church and kings killed or tortured heretics, said Frederic. That is true. However, we believe that Your Majesty would never practice such actions. I say the same of Pope Eugenius IV. We will immediately inform our school directors to avoid this kind of childish mistake and assure Your Majesty that this will never happen again. As kindness and magnanimity is the main subject of our courses, the Irishman was a little enthusiastic to highlight our teachings. The subjects taught at the Royal School of Moral Integrity do not allow any offense of this nature."

"Evidently, myself and the Holy Pope would never commit such atrocities. Well, in view of these explanations and your long friendship with my father, I absolve you this time with the promise that your school will never touch this subject again."

"Frederic, my beloved husband, you are a genius. In a second, you were able to put your words into His Majesty's mouth to the point that he considered himself magnanimous with his people! It is even possible that he could think more deeply about ending these human sacrileges, said Lilian. As for the Pope, we hope that the speeches do not reach his ears, because we know that he is a dangerous man."

When Anderson returned from France, they happily celebrated the episode, mainly because they were acquitted by Henry, an insecure and indecisive king, different from his father. Anderson brought another good news.

"I have a surprise for you. During the last trip to France, we came across traders we met at Windsor Castle, said Anderson. You will remember that during the ball when Lilian met Henry, Jefferson and I were introduced to English merchants who were curious to know what we are exporting. At that time, we told them that our fleet of twenty-two ships gave us a very satisfactory financial return."

"Our products are known among the English, the French, but also and mainly among the Portuguese, Anderson continued. I do not know if you heard that Portugal imported goods from England. At various times, the country suffered from a shortage of bread and the Portuguese were forced to import British wheat to meet their needs. Therefore, trade between France and Portugal was growing steadily. Portugal gave such importance to this trade that it exempted the French from any taxes and, on top of that, gave protection to English ships against privateers who acted in Portuguese waters."

"To shorten the conversation, in 1435, the French merchants decided to join the Portuguese and formed a company with a huge capital contribution under the name of **FRENCH-PORTUGUESE COMPANY OF INTERNATIONAL TRADE**. Now come the good news: The directors of the association want to make an offer for our twenty-two ships. I still have not figured out how much they are worth, but I think we should keep two of them for our wine exports."

"I'm looking forward to submit a somewhat different proposal, said Anderson. What would you think if I asked them to load our ships with goods that would be delivered to Southampton? I heard that the Portuguese are selling Persian rugs, pepper, oriental silk, and other products to the English. Well, instead of receiving money from the Portuguese for the ships, we could receive money from the English for the deliveries to be made and so the Portuguese would receive the twenty ships from our fleet, and we would be paid for the goods. Obviously, the new company would have to authorize the English to pay us. The exchange of ships for cargo would be a kind of "barter," with only one difference: the exchange would be between us and the Portuguese, but the English would make the payment. In the barter system there is a simple exchange of goods for goods, but in our case, although there is an exchange, we would end up with the money."

"What do you think of the idea?"

"Anderson, you forgot something important. What is the value of the goods? argued Frederic. How are you going to evaluate everything they have aboard the twenty ships?"

"I received the Bills of Lading of the whole shipment, and the price is convenient for us. We are delivering ships of a certain age and with outdated technology which would certainly require an expensive overhaul. In fact, we are keeping the best two and they will last for many years to come."

There were no arguments against Anderson's reasoning, and everyone agreed with the plan. The Portuguese approved the transaction after negotiations that took almost three months. Payment for the goods delivered in Southampton was done by the British, with the transfer of the amount to the account of the Vivone family. Anderson was overjoyed when he received payment in gold coins. With twenty ships less, the work could be concentrated on the wine trade.

Chapter 21

Zachary, Gordon, and Orson were enrolled at the Royal School in 1436, to assimilate the morality concepts and learn French and Italian and improve their English. Anderson and Jefferson thought it was important to speak different languages, because in the absence of other children, they would inherit all the wealth of the Vivone family, and the knowledge of other languages would be a precious asset. The family's fortune consisted of the two merchant ships, Lord Baltimore's enormous estate, and the winery in Marseille.

The brothers' graduation took place in 1438. It was a difficult phase, as everyone had to give up the good things of their youth to dedicate exclusively to their studies. However, the effort would pay off in the future when they would be proficient to manage all those assets. At this point, however, the brothers were looking forward to a break.

Samira, aged forty-eight, still full of life, captured this desire of her children and proposed a trip to her homeland and a visit to the vineyard in Marseille. Anderson felt a little old and tired to undertake a trip to Morocco, since he was sixty-four years old, as well as Jefferson who was the mainstay of the school, with sixty-three. Lilian at sixty-two already felt the symptoms of a deforming arthritis in her hands, which prevented her from writing. The three brothers had already passed the life expectancy of the Middle Ages, which was much lower.

"We are going to prepare for a slightly longer trip, said Samira. I propose that we take advantage of the cargo of Persian rugs that we must deliver to Tangiers, that is, we will stop in Lisbon and then go to my home. Your father will be responsible for the second ship to sell wine to England."

They finally left in 1444 and stayed in Portugal much longer than planned. The ship was anchored in Lisbon, waiting for the trip to Morocco. The charms of Lisbon, however, had too great a fascination for them. Especially women. Beautiful, captivating and cordial. The three brothers bowed to their beauty and did not know how to proceed, as they had never had more intimate contacts with the female sex. Understanding the boys' desire, Samira decided to dispatch the cargo to Morocco.

However, before the ship left, a total turnaround took place shortly after arriving in Portugal. In a random encounter with the buyers of the fleet sold by Anderson, they learned that the group formed by the Portuguese had had enormous success with the purchase and wanted to acquire the two that remained with the family. By coincidence, one of them was still docked in the harbor.

The Portuguese proposed to buy the cargo of Persian carpets that should be delivered in Morocco to later negotiate the price of the ship.

"It is impossible to sell the cargo to you, Orson argued, as we have to supply the carpets to our customers in Tangiers and that is a commitment of honor."

The Portuguese traders insisted and used every means to convince the family to sell the ship and suggested another kind of deal. They would pay in advance twice the value of the goods and deliver them to Morocco, maintaining the crew to avoid unemployment for the sailors. Thus, one part would represent the value of the goods and the other would correspond the value of the ship.

"Without a doubt, Samira argued, it will be convenient for us if you deliver the order, but we have to think about whether the value of the carpets matches the value of the ship. We will study your offer tonight and give you the definitive answer tomorrow afternoon."

"Well, my children, your father is not with us, but I think he would accept this proposal, especially because of his age. The price of the carpets seems to me much higher than the value of the ship. Therefore, I have the impression that we will do a good business. I do not know if your father would like to sell the last ship as well, since the Portuguese want to buy it. As for the future transportation of our wine to England, we could hire the Portuguese themselves to deliver. But the decision on the current sale has to be made tonight."

"Mother, we are in full agreement, said Gordon. There could be no better deal for our family. We would decrease the assets to be managed and save unnecessary costs. And we could stay longer in Lisbon and meet other wonderful creatures that exist in this country."

Once the deal was concluded, the Portuguese invited the family to celebrate with cod fish and white wine in one of the most famous restaurants of Lisbon.

"I am concerned about the winery that has not been visited for a long time, recalled Zachary, because we have to take care of the production and export of wines. For now, the employees are complying with the agreement and the family's idea of sharing the land with them was great. I learned that, after their parents' death, the children took on the responsibility of managing both their property and ours. But there is a need for more efficient administration on our part. As Uncle Jefferson said, "the occasion makes the thief"".

"Well, I think it's time for us to divide responsibilities. Together with Orson I can take one of the ships that are going to France and see how things are going on at the farm, commented Samira. In the meantime, you will be busy with the girls here who have certainly gotten used to your presence. Soon we will continue with our plans, okay?"

When Samira and her son arrived at the winery in 1446, they saw major improvements. Everything went perfectly to her surprise. The quality of the grapes improved through new grafting and the purchase of seedlings from Bordeaux, the city where King Richard II of England was born (1367-1400). In the vault left by the parents, Samira found the money from the sales and all the wine export receipts. They inherited honesty from their parents and Samira was able to confirm that they are super-truthful.

At night, a magnificent idea occurred to Orson. The Vivone family could provide two of the brothers with a course at the Royal School with all expenses paid. They would stay at the school for two years and could subsequently participate in an institution identical to that of London to be instituted in Marseille. There would be a lottery to choose the two candidates, which was done with joy the next day. Brothers Claude and Jean Pierre Demignon were selected. Samira left them the necessary resources for the trip, gave them a letter to Jefferson, authorizing the enrollment at the beginning of next year. As for the other two brothers, she promised that they would be sent shortly after Claude and Jean Pierre's return. The celebration party was watered with Bordeaux wine produced at the farm.

Samira thought that Jean Pierre and Claude should be accompanied by Orson, because despite being the youngest, he was the most responsible and smart. In this way he could help the two French boys to get used to it and, at the same time, take a letter communicating the sale of the ship and the receipt of money for the goods sold to Tangiers' customers. In that letter she asked if her husband would like to sell the other ship, considering that he would not have so much work due to his age.

Chapter 22

The three became friends during the trip and arrived in Southampton in 1447 and, in 1448, at the Vivone estate where the school was located. The sad news they received on arrival was the death of Jefferson, Lilian, and Anderson. The three had been attacked by an unknown disease that affected the joints and all the muscles of the body. They were getting weaker and weaker and although under the care of the best doctors available at Windsor Castle, they died shortly before the three travelers arrived. Frederic had sent a letter to Samira in Portugal communicating the sad news, but she was still on her way.

Frederic decided to replace Jefferson in his work at the school. Orson was completely bewildered by the news. Having already graduated from the Royal School he decided to monitor the studies of the two Frenchmen.

Meanwhile, without knowing what had happened, the two brothers Zachary and Gordon did not want another life. They had only one problem: they did not know how to decide between staying with two or four girls a week. They never thought that they would be so lucky. But the joy ended quickly when they heard about the death of their father and uncles. Samira was also heartbroken upon receiving the news and decided that the family should return to England as soon as possible.

After the graduation of the two French brothers in 1450, Orson, Claude and Jean Pierre returned to the winery where they gave the brothers Hugo and Olivier Demignon the funds for expenses in England and the letter authorizing the enrollment in the Royal School. Gordon, Zachary, and Samira took care of the administration of the courses together with Frederic.

Hugo and Olivier left in 1451 and graduated in 1453 and then returned to France. Orson decided to form a partnership with his four friends to encourage wine exports. As for the sale of the last ship, the family authorized him to make the necessary decisions in case the Portuguese came back with another offer.

In that year, news about the war with France reached the family's ears informing that the English had been defeated in the Battle of Formigny, which marked the last phase of the War with the conquest of Normandy by the

French, when their troops made use of artillery for the first time. Despite the 3,500 men sent to Cherbourg by Sir Thomas Kyriel, the English were defeated and ended up losing the important city of Caen.

The war finally ended in 1453 with the victory of France in the Battle of Castillon and the capture of the city of Bordeaux[41]. The hundred-year war lasted 116 years (1337 to 1453). The English were only able to keep the city of Calais in the north of France in their power and there was no treaty at the end of hostilities, as they were obliged to devote their attention to internal problems when the War of the Roses unfolded[42], a dispute between two English factions: one from the House of Lancaster and one from the House of York. Both claimed the throne based on kinship with King Edward III, a dispute that began in 1453, exactly at the end of the Hundred Years war.

[41]https://www.britannica.com/event/Battle-of-Castillon.
[42]https://www.britannica.com/event/Wars-of-the-Roses.

Chapter 23

It is opportune at this point to update the family tree as of 1453.

<u>Vivone´s Family Tree in 1453</u>

Francesco Vivone (1201-1257) and Larissa Vivone (1201-1258)
Rolando (1232-1310) and Giovanna (1234-1311)
  Alfredo (1273- 1338)
  Salvatore (1273- 1338)
Sinibaldo (1232-1303) and Anabela (1236-1316)
  Alina (1274-1338)
  Bianca (1274-1338)
Godofredo (1232-1312) and Matilda (1235-1313)
  Michele (1274-1338) and Robert Valois (1273-1338)
  Luigi (1295-1367 and Sigrid Andersen (1305-1369)
    Houston (1338- and Grace Baltimore (1346-
      Anderson (1374-1448) and Samira Amal (1390-
        Zachary (1416-
        Gordon (1416-
        Orson (1418-
      Jefferson (1375-1448)
    Harold (1338-1404) and Audrey Baltimore (1346-1404)
      Lilian (1376-1448) and Frederic Swinston (1390-
      Emily (1377-1377)

All teachers were trained at the Royal School and faithfully interpreted the fundamentals created by Francesco Vivone. There was no need to hire outside professors, as most students were eager to continue contributing to the institution's success after they graduated. Frederic accepted alumni as administrators of the college, seeking to replace him as soon as his health prevented him from fulfilling his duties. This way, there would be no interruption in the event of his death.

In 1454 the family had to make decisions about the future. Everything revolved around their age and desires. Frederic already sixty-four-years old, was having serious problems to move due to his arthritis and was unable to manage his work at the school. Although Samira was sixty-four, she still longed to see her homeland again. Zachary and Gordon, planning to continue with their life in Lisbon, yearned to see the beautiful girls they met there. The two, aged thirty-eight, were at the height of their virility and lacked the patience for administrative services needed by the school. Orson, at the age of thirty-six must have inherited Anderson's restless nature and had a passion for foreign trade and doing big business. The best example of the exceptional quality of his father was the transaction he closed with the Portuguese for the sale of the twenty ships. However, the last one still needed to be sold.

Following the recent shipment of wines to England, the Portuguese again showed interest in buying the last ship that was anchored in the port of Marseille. Orson calculated that the cargo of wines was worth much less than the ship. However, even if the Portuguese paid twice the amount of the cargo, the Vivone family would incur a loss.

"Orson, please explain your reasoning to me. Why would we have a loss if they pay twice the value?" asked Samira.

"I'm going to simplify with an easy example. Let us say that the cargo of wines is worth one hundred and the value of the ship is 150. Therefore, if they pay in double, we would be receiving a total of two hundred. These two hundred would be divided into two parts. One would represent the wines to be delivered in England (that we would receive anyway). The other one hundred would correspond to the sale of the ship, but it is worth 150 which means that we would be losing 50. Did you understand?"

"So, I already know what to do, commented Samira. We will ask for twice the value of the wine and demand a cash difference. They will be able to receive the value of the cargo in England, we would keep the money in advance and the ship would be paid. Let us see if they accept this offer.

The reaction of the Portuguese was different from other times. They were willing to deliver the cargo in England but did not agree with the cash return. They thought that the work of taking the ship from Marseille to Southampton would have a prohibitive cost and, therefore, paying twice the value of the cargo would already be a very reasonable deal for both parties.

Orson finally gave in and accepted the terms proposed by them. He recognized that the Portuguese would have an additional cost for the delivery in England and it was worth not to lose the deal.

Samira, happy with the outcome of the transaction and money in her pocket, returned to Tangiers the following year where she was received enthusiastically by her relatives. Before leaving in 1455, she learned of Frederic's death, weakened by his arthritis and unable to move. Frederic died at the age of sixty-five having made a major contribution to the success of the school.

This year, Orson received information about an unusual invention made in Germany by a German named Johann Gensfleisch zur Laden zum Gutenberg or simply Johannes Gutenberg (1398-1468)[43], born in the city of Mainz, Germany. He was a genius. Gutenberg simply revolutionized the world's printing industry with his invention.

It was a printing method based on movable types, made with the aid of a mold, with matrices in which the types of letters could be manufactured in massive quantities. He based his idea on the presses used to make wine, oil, or paper. It was a technology that neither the Chinese nor the Koreans knew about. His extraordinary idea was to invent a practical system that allowed for the mass production of printed books and was economically profitable for printers and readers.

Around 1450, Gutenberg met an investor named Johann Fust who lent him eight hundred guilders because he found that the invention had achieved a superior sophistication. Two years later, Fust lent him another eight hundred guilders on the condition of becoming his partner. Unfortunately, the two had a disagreement that affected Gutenberg's life in financial terms.

The greatest work produced by Gutenberg was the Bible written in Latin with forty-two lines per page. He printed two hundred Bibles and this work lasted five years until 1455. At the time, only a few priests understood Latin which caused a delay to reach the hands of the believers. However, the revolution caused by Gutenberg's invention was responsible for the immense progress in the graphic arts of the Middle Ages.

---

[43] https://www.britannica.com/biography/Johannes-Gutenberg.

Orson immediately realized the scope of this fabulous invention and thought of the advantages that the printing of "Morality and Ethics" would have for the Royal School. He correctly imagined that each student could have a copy of the book instead of everyone consulting only one (the original, existing at the time). He then decided to undertake a trip to Mainz, Germany, to meet Gutenberg and show him the copy of Francesco´s book.

The distance from Marseille to Mainz is about 625 miles. Despite the precariousness of the roads, travelers on horseback were able to get around faster than carriages and other transport vehicles. Orson decided to face the distance between the two cities on one of the winery's best horses.

After twenty-five days, stopping at inns along the way, Orson managed to reach the inventor's hometown. It was not difficult to find his shop, because every citizen of Mainz knew him. When he heard of Orson's intention, Gutenberg was appalled by the courage of the young Englishman who was prepared to face terrible roads and storms along the way just to ask if it would be possible to obtain a certain number of copies of his ancestor´s book.

"My boy, what does this book contain that is so important?" asked Gutenberg.

"Great Master, our distant relative was named Francesco Vivone, a man with strict moral principles, of absolute honesty, without sin and without falsehood. He was law-abiding, had a real aversion to lying, a total purity of purpose and decency, an unblemished reputation and was incorruptible. He authored a book showing how people should behave in life by adopting these principles. The book was his masterpiece, and he became famous. At that time, there was no invention as wonderful as yours, so he wrote the work by hand. He managed to produce five copies, but due to a series of circumstances, four were lost and only one copy remained in Italian. Well, Francesco's family founded a school that now exists in England called The Royal School of Moral Integrity, where his moral concepts are taught, and it was at the school where the students translated the original into English."

"When I learned of your brilliant printing press, I came to Mainz to ask if you would be willing to print fifty copies. The translation into English is in separate sheets that are clearly legible and would not cause any problem of understanding. I would make the payment in advance and wait to take the books to England."

Gutenberg was impressed and asked to borrow the book brought by Orson. Gutenberg understood Italian perfectly and would have no difficulty in reading the original. Orson immediately put the book at the German's disposal and told him that he would wait until the following week to see if he liked the subject.

"I read with immense pleasure the wonderful work of your ancestor and he really was a genius, said Gutenberg. For this reason, I am going to instruct my staff to print fifty-one copies of the book. I added one more, because I would like to have the privilege of keeping a copy if this is allowed by you."

After two weeks of intense work, Gutenberg handed the books to Orson who was amazed at its perfection. However, the weight of the fifty copies was excessive to be carried by his horse, which forced him to purchase another animal for the trip back to France.

"Dear Orson, my new English friend, I would like to congratulate you once again on your enthusiasm and I wanted to take the liberty of giving you a copy of the Holy Bible that I produced this year. It was the first printed bible in the world, and you deserve to have one. Have a good trip and I hope to see you in the future."

It is possible to imagine the sacrifice of taking two horses on a journey of almost 650 miles. But Orson's determination was unshakable. He managed to arrive at the winery a month later with the fifty copies, the Holy Bible and the original "Morality and Ethics." The fifty books would be sent to England along with a cargo of wines. Each of the forty students would have a copy that should be returned at the end of the course and the remaining ten copies would be carefully kept in the school´s safe.

Chapter 24

"I think it's time to go back to Portugal, suggested Gordon. We are already in 1458, at the age of forty-two and getting old without having the opportunity to see our Portuguese friends. We must leave the school with the new administrators while we verify the existence of beautiful creatures in Lisbon and its surroundings. Orson is at the farm and must be invited. The only thing he knows is work and it is time to change this inopportune behavior. The school is already in possession of the books printed by that genius Gutenberg and the new managers are fully qualified to solve any kind of problems. In addition, the separate sheets in English used by Gutenberg to print the fifty copies are safe, kept with the original in Italian at the Baltimore Estate in a vault located in the attic of our house."

Despite Orson´s resistance, the three brothers went to Lisbon in 1460. In less than three or four days they returned to the wonderful life they were used to. Orson, due to his inexperience with the female sex, was the first to fall in love with a beautiful girl aged twenty-six by the name of Manuela Dias, born in Lisbon. Gordon found his old passion Margarida de Souza, twenty-two years old, born in the city of Porto on the banks of the Douro River. Zachary was more demanding and took a little longer to get involved, but he was unable to resist the charms of the twenty-eight-year-old Joaquina Querubim, originally from Braga, a city located thirty miles from Porto and 230 from Lisbon.

At one of the dinners with the three girls, Gordon asked about an important Portuguese who died in the present year (1460). His name was Henry the Navigator (1394-1460)[44].He had the titles of Prince Henry, Duke of Viseu and Lord of Covilhã and was born in the city of Porto, Portugal. Margarida lived there during her teenage years, she knew the full story and was willing to tell it.

"Prince Henry was the fifth son of King John I (1357-1433) and his wife Philippa of Lancaster, sister of King Henry IV of England. Born in Porto in 1394 and died in 1460, recently. When he was twenty-one, Dom John I made him a knight, and he participated heroically along with his brothers Dom Duarte and

---

[44]https://www.britannica.com/biography/Henry-the-Navigator.

Dom Pedro in the invasion of the island of Ceuta, located in the Strait of Gibraltar off the coast of Morocco."

"Dom Henry had in his blood a desire to explore the mysteries of the ocean. His brother, D. Pedro, knew of his love for adventure and, at the end of a trip begun in 1416 to Asia, Africa, and other countries, he presented him with the book written by Marco Polo which he obtained in Venice. Always planning his future in terms of discoveries, the prince called the famous cosmographer Jaime de Maiorga and created a school of cosmography and navigation which attracted famous personalities. They were responsible for guiding the caravels of Dom Henry in his ventures."

"If you are tired, I can stop and tell you the story later, said Margarida."

"Absolutely, we are learning major events in the history of Portugal. Please continue."

"Well, the owner of a considerable fortune, Henry sent his ships to the African coast where they discovered the island of Madeira, the Azores and the Canaries. His intention was always to colonize the discovered islands. At that time, it was considered impossible to sail in a dark sea like the Atlantic Ocean, because everyone thought that it would end at a certain point and the ships would fall over a precipice and the crew would be punished by God. However, Dom Henry, in 1434, dispatched his squire Gil Eanes who managed to pass the Cape Bojador, a place that was considered an impossible feat, due to the "existence" of sea monsters. Later, in 1443, Henry continued his discoveries and Diogo Gomes, at his service, discovered the archipelago of Cape Verde. Other destinations reached were Sierra Leone and Gambia. João Fernandes, in 1445, reached Sudan, being the first European to explore the interior of Africa".

"Henry´s name and fame reached foreign countries and many men eager for adventures came to ask him to participate in his navigations. Passionately devoted to cosmographic sciences, Henry was the greatest mathematician of his time; he applied the astrolabe and invented the flat charts. He gave an important impulse to the art of oceanic navigation and contributed to spread his knowledge around the world."

"Now you can rest, because you've heard a lot about Portuguese history."

The three brothers knew exactly what was going to happen next. In 1460 they decided to concentrate their attention on the lovely ladies and arranged a joint wedding in Portuguese style, with a party and local songs called "fados". It was the most fantastic wedding that Lisbon had ever witnessed, with the presence of the mayor of the city and the buyers of the ships. The Vivone family conquered a durable friendship in Portugal.

Unfortunately, in 1461, they learned of their mother's death in Tangiers at the age of seventy-one, victim of food poisoning. They also received news regarding an award received by the Royal School as the best school in England.

After the death of Dom Henry in 1460, during the reign of Dom Afonso V (1432-1481)[45], a bourgeois from Lisbon named Fernão Gomes obtained the monopoly of Portuguese discoveries through a leasing agreement with the king and became in charge of continuing the discoveries on the African Coast. However, due to the pressure by his nobility, Dom Afonso decided to fight Muslims in North Africa.

Consequently, the great supporter of the discoveries was King John II (1455-1495)[46], son of D. Afonso V. His plan was to explore the South Atlantic to look for a passage to India where he would receive information about the spice trade. Therefore, he sent two of his emissaries, Pero de Covilhã and Afonso de Paiva to the Mediterranean. With the purpose of guaranteeing his conquests and defending the interests of the Kingdom, King John II ordered the placement of patterns (a series of columns that were fixed on the land with the coat of arms of Portugal). He likewise ordered the construction of fortresses and maintained total secrecy about his initiatives.

---

[45]https://www.britannica.com/biography/Afonso-V.
[46]https://www.britannica.com/biography/John-II-king-of-Portugal.

Chapter 25

The visit to the winery in France and the Baltimore Estate in England was a success. Margarida confided to her sisters-in-law that she had never seen anything so beautiful. They also visited the school, and all were unanimous in saying that the education they received in childhood was exactly the one taught at the Royal School. Therefore, everything indicated that the three girls could be qualified as virtuous.

Unfortunately, three years later, in 1466, when Orson and Manuela arrived in Marseille, Claude, Jean Pierre, Hugo and Olivier, were in a panic. A plague spread throughout the property that completely wiped out the vines. There were brown spots under the leaves that caused them to fall, the branches dried up completely and the winery stopped producing. Nobody knew what caused the plague, and the experts never saw such a strange disease.

Orson, responsible for the winery, immediately decided to take Manuela to Bordeaux where the producers sold him the new seedlings. Upon arriving, they learned that the winery' was also attacked by the plague. The solution, for general sadness, was to cut all the feet of the trees two inches from the ground and wait for the shoots to grow without the disease. This measure would be a disgrace for France and would take at least five years without being able to export wines. The same would certainly happen with the Vivone winery. The couple returned to Marseille extremely concerned.

"How are we going to live in this period?" asked Claude.

"Well, before cutting the vines like the Bordeaux company, let us write to my brothers, and ask if there was a similar plague in England or Scotland. I know that all of this takes time, but it is important that we make sure to adopt a right procedure. In the meantime, we will only cut fifty trees and wait for the shoots to come out. We must not be discouraged, as we have enough space to plant other products. The land will certainly give us enough to maintain an acceptable result.

"Dear Orson, I'm glad you're with us in this hour of distress. Tomorrow we will start to prune the fifty trees and see what happens. In the meantime, let us get together to decide what to plant in the undeveloped area."

The brothers' reply came at the beginning of 1467. No one in England or Scotland knew this kind of problem. Orson, however, was not satisfied with the answer and argued with the four brothers that there should be another solution. He went back to examining the vines and discovered a real battalion of beetles on the back of the leaves. They left a brown trail that was responsible for the misfortune.

Jean Pierre produced a new idea. He said he heard about a neighboring farmer of a certain age who knew much about vineyards. On the same day, the five partners went to see him to expose the drama.

"To what do I owe the honor of receiving so many neighbors"? asked Auguste Simon, a nice and friendly old chap.

After reporting the whole adventure in Bordeaux and the finding of the beetles on the leaves Auguste laughed and said that he witnessed similar episodes repeatedly and managed to find a way to eradicate the pest.

"Just plant a special type of beans which emanate a very unpleasant smell that will keep the beetles away and save the vineyard. It is called "haricot bleu." What you must do is just cut the leaves and not the grapevine feet like the people in Bordeaux. The bean seedlings can be purchased at my friend Leon Masson's farm, where he has a field full of these beans. Leon will be happy if you pull them out and clear his field. The farm is one mile from here. Plant the beans between the vines and when the sprouts come out, the bugs will disappear as if by magic."

"How can we thank you for your wonderful suggestion?" said Hugo.

"Too easy. You will send me two bottles of wine when you pick the first grapes. But please put two or three beetles in a glass and send them to your friends in Bordeaux. Also send the name of the beans."

Happiness returned quickly and the partners hurried to find Leon's farm, who confirmed Auguste's explanation. Since they had a good supply of wine, they sent a box of twelve bottles to their dear neighbor and another one to Leon Masson.

In the year 1468, wine production was small due to the damage caused by the beetle, but the beans eventually solved the problem. The plague was totally eradicated. Orson received a letter from the Bordeaux winery thanking him for the solution sent but, unfortunately, they had already cut the grape vines and the production would be delayed.

After that scare, life went more smoothly in the following years. In 1471 the children of the three couples had already been born. The wives wanted to give their sons and daughters Portuguese names. There was no discussion about it and the names were all chosen by the ladies.

Joaquina, Zachary's wife had two girls named Clarinha and Esmeralda, born in 1467 and 1468. Then, two boys appeared to Gordon and Margarida in 1470 and 1472 under the names of Florencio and Fabiano. The two sons of Orson and Manuela were born in France in 1470 and 1472 respectively and were named Bartolomeu and Cristiano.

Unfortunately, age does not forgive. With a life expectancy of around forty-five years in most European countries, the three brothers had already passed this range thanks to their healthy way of life with better eating and hygiene habits than the continent's population, especially in France, Portugal, and England. It was no surprise therefore, that, in 1472, they reached the ages of fifty-six for Zachary and Gordon and fifty-four for Orson. The physical resistance of the three brothers was extraordinary. On the other hand, the wives were much younger. Manuela was thirty-eight, Margarida thirty-four and Joaquina forty. Clarinha, age five, was the oldest of the children. Esmeralda four, Florencio, Fabiano, and Bartolomeu two and Cristiano a few months old.

Another family tree is important at this stage.

Vivone´s Family Tree in 1472

Francesco Vivone (1201-1257) and Larissa Vivone (1201-1258)

 Rolando (1232-1310) and Giovanna (1234-1311)

  Alfredo (1273- 1338)

  Salvatore (1273- 1338)

 Sinibaldo (1232-1303) and Anabela (1236-1316)

  Alina (1274-1338)

  Bianca (1274-1338)

 Godofredo (1232-1312) and Matilda (1240-1313)

  Michele (1274-1338) and Robert Valois (1273-1338)

  Luigi (1295-1367) and Sigrid Andersen (1305-1369)

   Houston (1338- 1404) and Grace Baltimore (1346-1404)

    Anderson (1374-1448) and Samira Amal (1390-1461)

     Zachary (1416- and Joaquina Querubim (1432-

      Clarinha (1467-

      Esmeralda (1468-

     Gordon (1416- and Margarida de Souza (1438-

      Florêncio (1470-

      Fabiano (1472-

     Orson (1418- and Manuela Dias (1434-

      Bartolomeu (1470-

      Cristiano (1472-

    Jefferson (1375-1448)

   Harold (1338-1404) and Audrey Baltimore (1346-1404)

   Lilian (1376-1448) and Frederic Swinston (1390-1455)

   Emily (1377-1377)

In 1473 Orson and Manuela returned to England for the sole purpose of meeting with the brothers and their wives to evaluate the situation prevailing in the country. The War of the Roses between York and Lancaster started worrying the family. There was no indication of a truce[47].

"As you know, things are really complicated," said Orson. If this war lasts longer than expected, I think we should leave for Portugal. It seems to me that the war is useless. Eventually, there will be a reconciliation between the opponents, leaving everything as it was before. Anyway, even though we have

---

[47]https://www.britannica.com/event/Wars-of-the-Roses.

nothing to do with it that could affect us. Our luck so far is that nobody has bothered to close our school."

"What a beautiful idea to return to our homeland. We were really missing our relatives and the children will be able to improve our language and meet their grandparents, concluded Manuela."

Chapter 26

In 1475 they returned to Lisbon and the wives proposed a visit to each family. It would be a beautiful adventure to get to know Lisbon better and finally travel to Braga and the city of Porto. At the same time, the husbands could oversee wine exports to England, using the services of their Portuguese friends.

Ten years passed and, in 1485, the family remained in Portugal. At that time, the children had already been enrolled in the best educational institutions in Lisbon. As religiosity was something of great importance at the time, the girls Clarinha and Esmeralda were sent to a school of nuns called "Escola Fraterna de Lisboa" (Brotherhood School of Lisbon) and the boys, while attending a Jesuit school, also received instructions from two preceptors who taught them the art of shipbuilding, mathematics, and astronomy. They soon fell in love with the adventures of Portuguese navigators, because at that time, Portugal represented the dominant nation of the seas since the discoveries initiated by Prince Dom Henry.

"Did you know that the War of the Roses ended in 1483? asked Zachary to his brothers. Luckily, our property was not overrun, and exports are growing steadily with better quality due to the lessons received from our friends in Bordeaux. We even managed to conquer the English market because of the advantage we had with the discovery of the bad smelling beans. Our competitors had a delay of almost five years in relation to our production."

Meanwhile, the Royal School has grown to such an extent that the facilities could no longer cope with so much demand. The moral principles taught at the institution spread throughout England and the students, after graduating, began to influence the behavior of the population, especially the poorest. The number of virtuous citizens increased each year, causing a real uproar among the nobles.

In 1487 Gordon and Orson decided to help the directors of the Royal School and study a way to increase the number of classes to allow a greater number of enrollments. When they arrived in Southampton, they were prohibited to enter the country by soldiers who called them "personae non gratae" (undesirable persons).

"What is the meaning of this? asked Gordon. We are English citizens and we always lived in this country. We were absent because we had to place our children in Portuguese schools. At the same time, we are owners of a property that belonged to our ancestor Lord Baltimore."

"Your argument is useless. We have orders to arrest you if you refuse to return to Portugal. We have been informed that you own an illegal school near Windsor Castle where you teach moral principles that are unacceptable to the English population. It has just been considered illegal by King Henry VII, and all those linked to the so-called Royal School will be sent to prison."

"But I think there must be a terrible mistake, said Orson. Our school is not illegal and everyone at the school is honest which means that they are people of the best character, they are all taught to be good to others, do no evil, they are educated people and unable to offend anyone. They are taught to respect kings, popes and accept any religion or belief. The school has been in existence for over 40 years and has never caused any harm to English society, quite the opposite, it has improved the culture of the population. What we do not understand is how a king who was responsible for ending the War of the Roses between the Houses of York and Lancaster and who is currently dedicated to rebuilding the kingdom after all the devastation that occurred during the war decided to close the best English school? He is presently stimulating trade with other nations, developing the country's merchant fleet, he is a king who wants to do good, and I am surprised that these orders came from him."

"The orders did not come directly from King Henry. They were given by Lord Ashbury, the owner of a large school in West Sussex. He intends to influence the English nobility to close the Royal School."

"Now we understand that the king had nothing to do with it. It is time for us to have a private conversation with this Lord Ashbury. Would you agree to let us travel as far as West Sussex? We promise to return to Southampton after talking to him, otherwise we will have to communicate this to our friends at Windsor Castle."

The threat worked, the soldiers accepted the proposal and took Orson and Gordon's word that they would return immediately. As the distance was fifty miles, they could be in Sussex in two days and decided to leave at once.

They initially went to Sussex Secondary School located on a huge estate in the countryside. When asked if Lord Ashbury would be available, the school principal received them. They learned that Lord Ashbury would have a meeting in an hour.

When he heard that Gordon and Orson owned the Royal School, the principal was frightened, already wondering why the two brothers were present.

"Who knows, you may be welcomed by him before the meeting, I will try to schedule this right now, pondered the director. In fact, there he is."

He was a grouchy individual who did not look very friendly. But the two brothers were willing to stand up to anyone and showed no fear of the Lord's temperament.

"What can I do for you?" asked Lord Ashbury.

"We are here to pay you a courtesy visit and we would like to have your permission to visit your school, as we have heard that this is the best school in England. We came here to learn how to manage such a famous school as we are having problems that concern us immensely. From what we have been informed, your system is the most efficient in terms of didactics, with teachers personally chosen by you. We also know that our school does not compare with yours and we wanted to take this opportunity to congratulate you, said Gordon."

"Well, I did manage to train teachers who are the elite of England and maybe that's why we are considered the best. King Henry VII was here recently and praised our organization during his visit. But I will be happy to show you my work. I welcome you and I will personally take you to know the facilities and our best teachers."

"Before returning to Southampton, we would like to point out that there was a slight problem when we arrived from Portugal, as some soldiers prevented us from reaching our school located at the Baltimore Estate and we would like to ask Your Excellency to provide us with a document requesting the soldiers to release us."

"There must have been a mistake on their part, as I would never give such an order, much less to offend such distinguished gentlemen and professional colleagues!"

"Then we will take the liberty of inviting you to visit the Royal School at your convenience, said Orson."

"I will be delighted and will schedule my trip for the next month. I wish you a safe return and sincerely thank you for your visit."

On the way home, Orson and Gordon were happy with the outcome. In addition to escaping the soldiers, they also became friends with their main competitor. Nothing like diplomacy to deal with a person's pride, thought Orson.

On their way to school, the two brothers stopped at an inn in Winchester, tired from the trip and from Lord Ashbury's episode. The next day the plan was to arrive at the Baltimore Estate before dinner and surprise the principals of the Royal School. Unfortunately, the inn was inhabited by criminals who had destroyed the facilities and were waiting for unprepared travelers.

Immediately upon entering, the brothers were surprised by the bandits who stole all their money. Orson and Gordon, in 1488, were already seventy and seventy-two years old respectively and were not used to great physical efforts, much less to face six thieves with the appearance of violence.

"Don't be afraid of us," said the chief of the gang. The worst that can happen to you is what I call "involuntary disappearance." It is a term I produced when I made the king's soldiers disappear. We managed to convince them to hand over their weapons to us, and then they just disappeared. They are still being sought today."

"And what do you intend to do with us?" asked Gordon.

"We are thinking of having a little fun and we will give you a chance to get out of here without any problem. You will fight against two of our strongest men and if you manage to defeat them, you will be free."

The proposal was not the most attractive for the two brothers, not only because of their age, but mainly because the two young adversaries looked extremely strong.

In less than two minutes, Orson and Gordon were dead. They had no chance to defend themselves against the outlaws. According to the system they called "involuntary disappearance," they dug a pit outside the inn, simply dumped the corpses and covered them with soil.

Chapter 27

The two brothers left Portugal in 1487 to assist the Royal School board to increase their attendance capacity. This task could at the most last for a year, including the round trip. Therefore, at the end of 1488, they should have returned to Lisbon.

Without any news from the two brothers, the family began to seriously worry about what could have happened to Orson and Gordon. The age of the four sons was already between sixteen and twenty and the two girls were twenty-one and twenty, respectively. Everyone was old enough to act promptly to look for their parents. The best way to proceed would be to travel to the school and ask the principal about their whereabouts. Thereafter they could plan a more detailed investigation. Margarida and Manuela, like most women, felt that something serious could have happened to their husbands.

It was decided that Florencio and Bartolomeu, the older children of Gordon and Orson, should travel to England and try to solve the mystery. Zachary did not feel strong enough for the trip, as he was deeply depressed by the absence of his brothers. Furthermore, there was the need to continue with the farm's wine exports.

The search started in 1488 with the arrival in Southampton, the first stop for the investigation in England. They tried to contact the port authorities and consult the list of passengers landed at the port. When they mentioned that the parents owned the Royal School, one of the guards remembered the two brothers who were initially prevented from entering the country and mentioned that the order had come from a noble person named Lord Ashbury, who owns a school in West Sussex.

Immediately the two cousins decided to find Lord Ashbury. When they mentioned that they were children of Orson and Gordon, he immediately welcomed them warmly and remembered the great satisfaction he had to make their acquaintance. He found it strange, however, that they had not given any more news to the family for so long.

"Do you know if they decided to return to Southampton?" asked Bartolomeu.

"For sure, and then they would go directly to the Royal School. They even kindly invited me to visit the school, which I would do with immense pleasure."

Back in Southampton, they decided to take the shortest road that would take them to the Baltimore Estate. As they passed Winchester, they looked for an inn to rest, but found only one that was destroyed by fire, so they continued their journey and stopped at another one in Farnborough where they asked if two old Englishmen had stayed there about six months or less ago. No results.

"Did they make it to school? Let us hurry up to find out where they've been," said Florencio.

The directors of the Royal School did not know who the two brothers were, as they had never been to the school. When they presented themselves, they caused a great surprise, since the board was eager to receive the owners to report the problems that currently occur, relative to the huge demand for vacancies.

"We came here as quickly as we could in search of our parents, Orson and Gordon, who came to England to talk to you, said Bartolomeu. From what we understand, they did not arrive here, which is very strange. What could have happened to them? They left Portugal a year ago and were initially prevented from remaining in England by soldiers in Southampton, by order given by a Royal School competitor, Lord Ashbury, the owner of the Sussex Secondary School in West Sussex. However, they managed to contact him and had his full cooperation."

"When we were with Ashbury, he informed that our parents would follow immediately to the Baltimore Estate. They couldn't have just disappeared!"

"No doubt they must have taken the shortest and fastest route from Southampton through Winchester and Farnborough and would finally reach Windsor, argued director Mark Preston."

"We followed exactly that route and passed Winchester where they could not have rested, since there was only one inn destroyed by fire, pondered Florencio. We inquired in the neighborhood about what happened and learned that it had been invaded by bandits who set the place on fire. They said it happened recently, so we had to sleep in Farnborough, but the owner of that inn does not remember seeing them. They stayed somewhere between Winchester and Farnborough."

"I'm trying to remember other trips I took on the route you described, said Mark. I always stayed at the inn in Winchester and do not understand how anyone could destroy such a lovely place."

"As we will have to return through that road to Southampton to embark for Portugal, we will try once again to ask the authorities of Winchester if there was any news regarding our parents. As for problems with the school, I will suggest to our uncle that he send enough resources to expand the facilities. We will give you news as soon as we arrive in Lisbon."

"Have a safe trip and wish you luck in Winchester," said Mark.

Upon arriving in Winchester, they went to the local police to inquire about the criminal fire. According to the information, the bandits had been arrested and would be hanged shortly.

"Would it be possible to speak to them before the execution? asked Bartolomeu. We want to know if they saw our parents when they arrived at the inn."

Authorized by the police, the brothers asked for protection to speak to the wrongdoers, as they could try to attack them. The conversation was extremely unpleasant due to the hatred of being arrested and convicted, but they said they saw two old men who came from Portugal and were going to Windsor.

"Except that they must not have reached their destination" said the head of the group, laughing. I have the impression that they were victims of a game I call "involuntary disappearance." But before that, I invented another game. I selected two of our strongest men and challenged the old men to fight them. If they won, they would be free to continue their journey. But they were no match for Mac and Leo."

"But what did you do with our parents"? asked Florencio.

"Didn't you hear what I said? They disappeared."

"What do you mean, disappeared? Nobody disappears!"

"Let me repeat once more: they disappeared from the face of the earth. I guarantee. I buried them in front of the inn. Now do you understand? said the outlaw. Then we set the inn on fire and went to the forest where the police arrested us."

"You are barbarians, shouted Bartolomeu. How can there be so much evil? Didn't you see that they were old and couldn't defend themselves?"

The police officers who watched the conversation were also amazed by the courage of these criminals. They were hanged the next day, while the brothers returned to Southampton.

The reunion with the family could not have been sadder. Bartolomeu did not tell all the details of the drama, but he had to mention the murder by the bandits. For a virtuous family, an episode of this nature was a real test of resistance.

Chapter 28

At that time, Portuguese navigators already had the necessary experience to explore unknown regions of the African coast. Admired by the achievements of the Portuguese, Zachary's, Orson´s, and Gordon´s children were ecstatic with the discoveries and longed to participate in the trips across the ocean. It seemed incredible that daughters Clarinha and Esmeralda were also interested in something that would normally be just the burning desire of men. Zachary and Joaquina admired their daughters' passion and predicted that the family's fate was about to turn around.

It would even be an opportunity for the Vivone family to judge if the quality of these discoveries were truly valuable. Before any further decision, however, it would be necessary to attend the Royal School and undertake this research after graduation.

The family unanimously decided that the six should attend the two years necessary to acquire all the notions taught at the school in England. They left for the Baltimore Estate in 1490. Zachary would take care of wine exports with his wife and two sisters-in-law while their children would stay at school.

In 1494, after graduating, they returned to Portugal with another view about life, especially regarding the moral principles that would guide their future. Unfortunately, news arrived informing the death of Zachary, father of Esmeralda and Clarinha, 77 years old, due to kidney complications that had been bothering him for more than five years.

The two-year period in England was of immense value to the six students who became increasingly united. The plan regarding ocean voyages was still on everyone's mind and their meetings were about the discoveries of the Portuguese in that century. They made a list of the main achievements since the conquest of Ceuta in 1415 until 1494. The discoveries and conquests of the navigators were placed in chronological order and described by the brothers:

1415-Conquest of Ceuta in Africa, representing a key point for navigations to the south of the continent.

1418 -Discovery of the Madeira Archipelago. Gonçalo Zarco and Tristão Vaz Teixeira landed on the island of Porto Santo.

1427-Landing in the Azores Archipelago by Diogo de Silves, by order of Prince Dom Pedro.

1434 -Gil Eanes passed Cape Bojador, also known as the Cape of Fear.

1437 -The Portuguese attacked the city of Tangiers where they were defeated. The Muslims demanded the surrender of Ceuta and as a guarantee of the agreement they held Infante Dom Fernando as hostage[48].

1444 -Discovery and conquest of Guinea after the defeat at Tangiers. The plan was to try to reach the sources of raw materials.

1456 -Discovery of Cape Verde, achieved as a service for Prince Dom Henry.

1471 -Conquest of Arzila and Tangiers. With four hundred ships, the Portuguese assaulted the Plaza de Arzila. Then, Dom Afonso V conquered the fortress abandoned by its defenders.

1488 -Bartolomeu Dias passes the Cape of Storms, later renamed Cape of Good Hope. With this feat, the Portuguese opened a new route to the East.

1492 -Christopher Columbus[49] discovers America, thinking he arrived in India. He also discovered the islands of Haiti, Cuba, and the Dominican Republic, then returned to Spain.

1494 -Signature of the Treaty of Tordesillas. The treaty was signed in the Spanish city of the same name and divided the world "discovered and undiscovered" in two parts, with the exploitation rights granted to Portugal and Spain.

"Do you know who Christopher Columbus was? asked Florencio. I was talking to sailors in the port who told me about his life. I'll tell you what they said to me."

---

[48] Infante is a person of the Portuguese nobility with a position below the title of prince. It can also mean an infantry soldier.
[49] https://www.britannica.com/biography/Christopher-Columbus.

"Christopher Columbus was born in Genoa, Italy in 1451. Since he was a boy, he had a passion for the sea and lived among ships and sailors. Columbus believed that it would be possible to sail anywhere, be it east or west and then return to the place of departure. He was one of the few who believed that the earth is round."

Everyone at that time wanted to trade with Asia for commodities that everyone in Europe needed, such as silk and spices, and other products. This trade was done by the Venetian merchants who followed the route discovered by Marco Polo.

Columbus began his career as a navigator in the Portuguese merchant navy, having survived a shipwreck in Cape San Vincent on the southern tip of Portugal. His life was very rough between 1476 and 1488, because in addition to being a widower of his first wife Felipa Perestrello and Moniz, he joined another woman named Beatriz Enríquez de Harana, from Cordoba. With his first wife he had a son named Diego and with the second a boy named Fernando.

Columbus tried to raise funds for his desired westward journey to reach India. For this purpose, he appealed to King John II of Portugal, but his request was denied. He continued to fight for his goal by contacting the Spanish Catholic monarch Ferdinand II, king of Aragon, married to Queen Isabela I of Castile. In January 1492, the king agreed to supply the funds for the expedition and gave Columbus three ships, named Santa Maria, Pinta and Nina.

The trip would fulfill several objectives. First, it was essential to increase the power of Castile and Aragon, whose kings were afraid of Portuguese competition. Second, the Christian missionary fervor and the hatred of Islam that prevailed at the time was another important reason. In addition to his own passion for adventure, coupled with the hope of finding gold, silver, pearls and spices (which Europe so desperately needed to cook, preserve and for medicine), all this caused a burst of energy that resulted in his first trip.

Finally, in August 1492, Columbus left the port of Palos in Spain, aiming to reach Asia (the Indies) heading west. The first stop was at the Canary Islands where he had to wait for stronger winds which only arrived in September, allowing him to continue his journey.

However, the trip went on beyond what he planned, to the point of almost causing a riot by the crew. To contain the uprising of the sailors, Columbus prepared two different travel diaries, one showing the actual distance traveled daily and the other indicating a shorter distance and kept the first as a secret. This artifice calmed the crew, as it reduced the actual extent sailed so far.

The device lasted until October when the riot threat returned. As a last resort, he promised the sailors that they would return to Spain if they did not find land within two days. The next day, however, the land was sighted.

On October 12, 1492, the "Admiral" (Columbus attributed the title to himself), landed initially on an island called Lucayos or Guanahani in the Indigenous language, one of the islands of the Bahamas. Upon disembarking, he was surprised that the natives walked without clothes. There was fruit, an abundance of water and very green trees. At that time, he ordered his auxiliaries to confirm possession of the land in writing for the king and queen of Castile and Aragon.

Therefore, Columbus opened the world of the Americas to Europeans. But, despite bringing European culture to America he caused great suffering to the natives, as he enslaved them, forcing them to work hard in gold and silver mines. In addition, the Native Americans contracted diseases brought by Europeans. We can affirm, with certainty, that Columbus did not qualify as a virtuous person. He should have attended the Royal School to learn the necessary moral principles indispensable for a navigator of his kind.

His ships reached Cuba on October 29 and on December 6 stopped at the island of Hispaniola (today divided between Haiti and the Dominican Republic). He built a fort there and in January 1493 returned to Spain. He loaded his ship with parrots, plants, gold, clothes, and Indigenous people and was considered a hero by the monarchs.

The most important detail of his trip was his illusion of having reached the East Indies, which is why he called the natives "Indians."

109

Chapter 29

In 1494, the Vivone family was composed of nine members. The three mothers were already around sixty to sixty-two years old, and the age of the children ranged between twenty-two and twenty-seven years. At a time of great maritime adventures by the Spanish and Portuguese, other feats were expected from navigators, and it would be difficult to predict the extent to which discoveries and explorations would affect life, especially in Portugal where the family lived.

Although the children thought it would be wonderful if they could participate in the explorers' trips, common sense indicated that the dangers would be much greater than their compensations and/or rewards. One of the beautiful qualities of all family members was their logical way of thinking, so the idea of facing storms and being subject to shipwrecks was not exactly what everyone wanted. Therefore, this project has been pushed aside completely. They decided by consensus that it would be smarter and less risky to take advantage of the discoveries of new markets by Portuguese adventurers and use their parents' expertise in international trade. It would be fair to imagine that the countries discovered and exploited would be good consumers of the family's products, especially their French wines.

"Think about it, Esmeralda argued, we must not neglect the experience acquired by my father and my uncles with wine exports to England and Portugal. We have the advantage that we no longer need the fleet of ships that was only deteriorating. In addition, we have a good relationship with the Portuguese who have always served us magnificently. Therefore, it is a unique opportunity at a time when the world is witnessing great transformations and enormous growth. I would even propose that we organize a small company based here in Lisbon for this purpose. What do you think of the idea?"

Everyone was enthusiastic and, in 1497, the export company was in full operation. They named it FRANCESCO VIVONE WORLD EXPORTS, in honor of the oldest ancestor of the family.

"I think that our age does not allow an active participation in the company, argued Margarida. Gordon and I decided to live in Braga where I was born. My parents left me a large farm where we will be very well accommodated. You young people, will have more freedom to deal with export issues and we would be just an extra burden in your activities. As soon as you can, visit us so that we don't miss you too much."

In 1508, the export company completed eleven years of existence, eight years after the beginning of the 16th. century. During this period, they were able to travel to England and France to see the development of the Royal School and the wine business. In fact, the family now owned properties in three countries, and everything indicated that the future would be splendid, mainly because the six had the necessary moral principles to manage the family businesses in the best way. Clarinha, who was responsible for the company's administration, had a history degree and reaffirmed to everyone that the chances of success in the future would be immense, especially due to the possibilities provided by the new countries discovered by Portugal as part of the recent Treaty of Tordesillas.

"Could you give us more details about this treaty, and about Pedro Alvares Cabral's recent trip? How can we take advantage of what they discovered and the countries they will find in the future?" asked Margarida.

"Let's see if I can sum up all this, because it is a very long story", replied Clarinha.

"The Tordesillas Treaty[50]constituted an agreement between Spain and Portugal aimed at resolving conflicts over lands recently discovered by Christopher Columbus and other explorers, in the late 15th. century. In 1493, after reports of the discoveries arrived in Spain, Kings Ferdinand II and Isabela I asked Pope Alexander VI (Rodrigo Borgia, of Spanish nationality), to support their demands regarding the World, to inhibit the Portuguese and other rival claimants. To accommodate the wishes of Spanish kings, the Pope established a 100-leagues (about thirty-five miles) pole-to-pole demarcation line west of the Republic of Cabo Verde Islands, giving them exclusive rights to all areas already discovered and those to be discovered west of the line, while the Portuguese would be the owners of the eastern part. However, neither Spain nor Portugal could occupy any territory in the hands of a Christian sovereign."

---

[50]https://www.britannica.com/event/Treaty-of-Tordesillas.

"King John II of Portugal was unhappy because his country's rights were insufficiently recognized. Meeting in the city of Tordesillas, the Spanish and Portuguese ambassadors accepted the Pope's division, but agreed to increase the Portuguese share by a line situated 1,185-miles west of the Cape Verde Islands, which was finally approved by Pope Julius II in 1506. With the new demarcation, Portugal won the right to explore and occupy a much larger area, as the dividing line was fixed farther west than before[51]. With this increase, the Portuguese occupation reached the eastern part of Brazil.

"You asked for details about Pedro Alvares Cabral's life. Before that, however, you must let me to talk about another great Portuguese navigator called Vasco da Gama[52](1460-1524) who preceded Cabral."

"Vasco da Gama was born in Sines in Portugal in 1460. He opened the route that goes from western Europe to the east, through the Cape of Good Hope, located in the extreme south of Africa. Vasco da Gama, however, was not the first one who reached it. Bartolomeu Dias, another Portuguese discovered it in 1488 and named it Cape of Storms due to the violent see that the navigator and his crew suffered in the region. King John II, however, considering that the passage through the cape would provide a new path for the Indies, decided to change the name to the current Cape of Good Hope."

"In 1495, King Manuel I, the Fortunate, ascended the throne and chose Vasco to open the route to Asia and to ward off the Muslims who had a monopoly of trade with India and the Eastern countries".

"Vasco da Gama took three interpreters with him, two of whom knew the Arabic language and one who was proficient in some Bantu dialects, spoken in Nigeria and the Congo. With a fleet of four ships, he left Lisbon in 1497, crossing the Cape of Good Hope at the end of the year. After anchoring in Maputo, capital of the Island of Mozambique, in Mombasa and Malindi, Vasco da Gama set the so-called patterns, columns that proved the property of the Portuguese. In May 1498 they arrived in Calcutta in India. His sailors died of scurvy and Vasco returned to Portugal in September 1498 with only fifty-five survivors, from an original crew of 170 men. The arrival was triumphant, and

---

[51]https://www.nationalgeographic.org/thisday/jun7/treaty-tordesillas/.
[52]https://www.britannica.com/biography/Vasco-da-Gama.

King Manuel, I awarded him the title of Dom and an annual pension of 1,000 cruzados in addition to real estate".

"I will now tell the story of the Portuguese Pedro Álvares Cabral[53], said Clarinha."

"Cabral was born in Belmonte, Portugal (1467-1520), son of Ferdinand and Isabel Cabral Gouveia, a Portuguese noble family. Among his achievements, two important ones stood out. The first was the discovery of a new country which he named Terra de Vera Cruz. Second, he reached the Indies from Europe via the route around the Cape of Good Hope that had been bypassed by Vasco da Gama in 1498. It is also said that a Spanish explorer named Vicente Yánez Pinzón (who accompanied Columbus on his first trip to America), was there three months before Cabral's arrival. Another one who apparently has been in Terra de Vera Cruz was Duarte Pacheco Pereira in 1498."

"But how was he chosen to undertake these trips and what happened during his voyages?" asked Esmeralda.

"Cabral was esteemed by King Manuel I and received several privileges in 1497, such as a personal allowance, a title of consultant to His Majesty and the Habit of the Order of Christ. Three years after Vasco da Gama's pioneering trip, the king granted him the command of a second expedition to India. Declaring his immense confidence in Cabral, he named him Supreme Admiral of a fleet of thirteen ships that left Lisbon in March 1500 and should follow the route adopted by Vasco da Gama to strengthen the commercial ties and the achievements of his predecessor."

"In the middle of the trip in the Atlantic Ocean, however, his ships deviated to the southwest and, on April 22 of the same year, the fleet arrived at the Brazilian coast on an Easter Sunday in front of a hill he named Mount Pascoal."

"On April 24, the ships took shelter in a natural port, baptized as Porto Seguro (Safe Port). They remained in the country until May 2 and, in contact with the natives, obtained information about the recently discovered territory. To inform King Manuel I of his accomplishment, Cabral dispatched a

---

[53] https://www.britannica.com/biography/Pedro-Alvares-Cabral.

ship to warn his sovereign and instructed Pero Vaz de Caminha, the registrar of the fleet, to write the letter that was later considered Brazil's birth certificate."

"The name Land of Vera Cruz ("Terra de Vera Cruz") was used until 1501. From 1501 to 1503 the country was called Land of Saint Cross ("Terra de Santa Cruz") of Christian reference and from 1503 onwards it was called Brazil due to the abundance of a tree called brazilwood which had a reddish color sap".

"Cabral made a significant effort to treat the inhabitants cordially and even invited them to board his caravel. After staying ten days in Brazil, he left for India on a trip plagued with problems. He lost four of his ships around the Cape of Good Hope and arrived in Calcutta only in September 1500 where he built a fortified trading post. However, the post was attacked by Muslims who killed all of their defenders before reinforcements could arrive from the fleet anchored in the bay."

"Cabral bombarded the city, captured ten Muslim ships and executed their crews. On the return trip to Portugal, he stopped at Cochim in India and loaded his six remaining ships with spices. He completed his cargo at Carangolos and Cananor on the same coast and, in January 1501, started his voyage back, in which he had two more shipwrecks. He arrived in Portugal in June 1501 and was praised by King Manuel I".

"Later when he requested support from the king for a new trip, he was passed over by Vasco da Gama. Cabral never again held a prominent position at the court and ended up retiring to his home in Beira Baixa."

"Cabral was a true hero. He had an extraordinary courage to undertake all these dangerous journeys," commented Esmeralda.

"What if we were able to travel to Brazil and discover the mysteries, talk to the inhabitants and explore the wealth of the new country?" asked Cristiano.

"It is an excellent idea, but we have to think about our properties, said Bartolomeu. In France, we own the winery that is being run by our partners Claude, Jean Pierre, Hugo, and Olivier (deceased) and currently by Paul, son of Claude, and Eric, son of Jean Pierre. In England it is the Baltimore Estate and the Royal School. Here in Lisbon, we must take care of our residence and should not forget our company Francesco Vivone World Exports."

"Bartolomeu, what do you suggest then?" asked Clarinha.

"Look, there are six of us. I think you and Esmeralda should take care of the winery, because it is well organized, and you would be at ease with our French partners, suggested Bartolomeu. As for Florencio, I think he should manage the Royal School. He showed a special love for it and has an incredible ability to learn and teach languages."

"Talking about Cristiano, his greatest asset is foreign trade, inherited from our father. I do not have his ability to do big business the way he does, therefore I feel he should be responsible for the export company. At the same time, he can continue living here in Lisbon and take care of our residence."

"We have to see what Fabiano would like to do and, of course, what would be my goal, informed Bartolomeu".

"I would like to see other newly discovered countries," said Fabiano. There must be a way to get to Brazil. On one of the trips authorized by the Portuguese king, I could work as a sailor and spend time with the natives and research the riches of the new land. I am sure that these treasures must be incalculable. But I know that, momentarily, Portugal is not interested in Brazil despite the great abundance of brazilwood. For this reason, I believe that invasions from other countries in search of this wood will alert the Portuguese court to defend its property and its wealth. Therefore, I could embark on one of these defense expeditions. You, Bartolomeu, what do you intend to do from now on?"

"Today we are in 1508, said Bartolomeu. I think we should both focus on the family's assets until the Portuguese court start to protect their possession in Brazil. In the meantime, we will help the family to fulfill their obligations and visit the city of Braga to see how our mothers are doing. I also suggest that we visit all properties, regardless of who is taking care of them. For example, the cousins will be at the winery and that does not prevent us from staying. Then we will go to Baltimore Estate and try to increase the export company's sales."

The strategy gave excellent results and protected the properties of the Vivone family. A happy episode occurred at the winery with sisters Clarinha and

Esmeralda shortly after their arrival. They found themselves surrounded by Paul, son of Claude Demignon and Eric, son of Jean Pierre Demignon and ended up falling in love with them. The consequence was Paul's marriage to Clarinha and Eric to Esmeralda.

Unfortunately, in 1510, when Bartolomeu and Fabiano arrived in Braga, they learned that due to the flu epidemic that hit the city in 1509, the three died. The communication about the sad episode was not made due to the generalization of the disease that did not spare the inhabitants of the region. The two cousins brought the news to Lisbon and sent correspondence to Clarinha and Esmeralda in Marseille.

Chapter 30

In 1516, the Portuguese navigator Cristovão Jacques (1480-1530), of the nobility of the Portuguese Royal House was sent by King Dom Manuel I to Brazil to protect the coast and expel the French from the territory. His voyage was also meant to start trade with the Indigenous people and buy local products, especially brazilwood, a wood that was in great demand in Europe. Cristovão Jacques had previously travelled with Gonçalo Coelho in his fleet in 1503. Coelho was also a Portuguese navigator who led the first two exploratory expeditions to the land discovered by Cabral and was accompanied by Americo Vespuccio (1454-1512)[54].

The two cousins were enthusiastic about sailing and decided to contact Cristovão Jacques to ask if they could board one of his ships. They soon discovered his whereabouts.

"Why do you want to go to Brazil? asked Jacques. What do you intend to do when you arrive? If you really decide to embark with us, you will have to work like other sailors and will not receive any payment."

"We are fully in agreement with the conditions, as we fervently wish to know the new country and we want to have a better knowledge of its inhabitants. Just let us know the date of departure."

"Exactly fifteen days from now. Be at the port at five in the morning on time and be aware that we are going to fight French pirates who are stealing brazilwood, which represents a considerable risk of life."

"We are aware that a trip to Brazil is in itself dangerous; therefore, we will face whatever comes along," confirmed Bartolomeu.

Fifteen days later, the two cousins embarked on the greatest adventure of their lives. They worked incessantly as sailors under the rigor imposed by Cristovão Jacques. But it was all a programmed sacrifice, and nothing could affect their goals, even though they did not know what awaited them. The fleet was made up of two caravels that were supposed to patrol the Brazilian coast and fight the French privateers.

[54]https://www.britannica.com/biography/Amerigo-Vespucci.

The trip went as planned and the arrival, in the opinion of Fabiano and Bartolomeu, was simply wonderful considering the natural beauty. The landing took place in November in a huge bay that Jacques called Bay of All Saints ("Baía de Todos os Santos") where a celebration took place with local people who received gifts from the crew and looked at the foreigners with great curiosity.

Cristovão established a fortified trading post on the island of Itamaracá, in Pernambuco which constituted the first defense structure for the coast of Terra de Santa Cruz. The main reason for the establishment of the fortress was due to the enormous quantity and excellent quality of brazilwood existing in the region. Cristovão then went south to the Silver River ("Rio da Prata") where he imprisoned French pirates, destroyed their fortresses and vessels, and confiscated their cargo.

Fabiano and Bartolomeu followed all these adventures, increasingly amazed by the new world they were getting to know. They regretted, however, the brutality with which Christopher treated French prisoners, as he sent them to Portugal or executed them. It can be said about him with certainty that he was not a virtuous character.

Finally, the two cousins decided to stay on the island of Itamaracá, not only for its beauty, with an abundance of fruits, lush foliage, and rare birds, but also for the loving treatment they received from the Indigenous people. They fell in love with the wild animals that lived there, especially monkeys, macaws and parrots, something never seen in all the countries of Europe where they have been. The natives, in addition to their normal occupations, cut wood in exchange for axes, scythes and iron rakes, performing the so-called barter with the navigators. This contact supplied greater intimacy between them, which brought them closer to the Portuguese or to others who reached the Brazilian coast.

"Where are we going to find a place to sleep? asked Fabiano. We can´t sleep in the forest. I will ask Cristovão to see if he can accommodate us among the Portuguese who will remain in the trading post or even with the Indians if that is possible."

Before leaving for coastal patrols in search of more French privateers, the noble person granted them the privilege of settling in the trading post together with the sailors they met during the trip.

The caravel companions said that the Indigenous people belonged to the Caeté tribe. They inhabited the region between Itamaracá Island and the São Francisco River, they speak the Tupi language and were known for their ferocity and the practice of cannibalism rituals.

Despite all this, Bartolomeu and Fabiano managed to set up a cordial relationship with them. It is strange that this happened, as it was not the custom of the tribe. They made friends with the French and hated the Portuguese.

Every morning the cousins went into the forest to get close to the Indigenous village They were immediately surrounded by the natives who touched them and sometimes wanted to tear off their clothes to see what was underneath. Fabiano, who had excelled at the Royal School in languages, began to hear the words spoken by the members of the tribe, trying to guess their meaning. He wanted to learn the language at any cost.

On one of his trips to the village, luck was a friend of Fabiano's. He met a beautiful girl who penetrated him with her eyes. There was an incredible symbiosis, a connection between a person born in Europe and an Indian with a precious face and sculptural body. She touched him like the other members of the tribe, wanting to know what this man was made of.

Fabiano knew that she spoke the Tupi language[55], used by all the Indigenous people of the coast. It would, therefore, be necessary to conquer the good will and the trust of the native girl and start a dialogue based on touching objects and hearing their names pronounced by her. He also knew that the Portuguese who stayed in Brazil learned the language of the natives, which they called "the Brazilian language." In this way they started to communicate with the natives more easily.

Fabiano decided to point to an object and through gestures he would ask her for the name in Tupi. As soon as she said it, he spoke the word in

---

[55] https://www.britannica.com/topic/Tupi-Guarani-languages.

Portuguese. That way, two goals would be achieved, that is, he would learn Tupi, and she would learn Portuguese. The first one he pointed out was a huge tree that was in the village. Soon the young woman realized what he wanted and pronounced the word "Ybyrassú" and Fabiano immediately said Árvore Grande.("big tree") She laughed a lot due to her different way of speaking and said Paraná, pointing to the river that ran beside the village and Fabiano completed with Rio ("river") The two ended up laughing at each other looking like two children playing the guess game.

Fabiano quickly learned the words. On the same day, she remembered words that he translated for her as soon as they found an object or a person. That day they exchanged the following words:

Ybyrassú	Big tree
Ybyrá	Tree
Itú	Waterfall
Pirá	Fish
Oka	House
Xe-py	My foot
Îakaré	Alligator
Pereba	Wound
Ixé	Me
Ita	Stone
Ygara	Canoe
T-obá	Face
Kunhã	Woman
Tab	Man
Paraná	River

They repeated the joke the following days until a group of curious Indigenous people joined them, laughing each time Fabiano said the words in Portuguese.

Meanwhile, Bartolomeu stayed longer in the trading post where he met a Portuguese lady named Angelica de Albuquerque, sister of Aloisio de Albuquerque, a noble person sent by Dom Manuel I to inspect the second caravel of Cristovão Jacques. She was twenty-three years old and had recently divorced her husband.

Unfortunately, the trading post did not exactly meet the expectations of Angelica and Aloisio, who had to adapt to the precarious conditions of the accommodation and the lack of hygiene of the place. The trading post was simultaneously used as a fortress, a market warehouse, support for navigators, customs, and tax collection office in the king´s name. They were easily supplied and defended by sea and had the monopoly of the trade of the Atlantic. They were also in charge of extracting brazilwood.

From the start, a friendship between the two cousins and the Portuguese brothers appeared, due to their similar ideas. Aloisio reported that he had a small school in Lisbon where foreign languages were taught, French, English, and Italian. He was keenly interested when he heard about the book written by the ancestor Francesco Vivone, called "Morality and Ethics." Fabiano soon supplied further details regarding the Royal School curriculum.

"Do you think it's possible to come together around this idea and show our people what it means to be virtuous?" asked Aloisio.

"We will return to Portugal soon, so we can seriously think about it, and it would be an honor to have your support in Lisbon" replied Fabiano.

During the period they stayed at the trading post, between 1516 and 1519, Bartolomeu and Fabiano had different experiences from those in the other countries in which they were. He managed to learn the Tupi language and teach Portuguese to the natives. Yjara was the name of the young girl which meant "mermaid, mother of water." Fabiano devoted his full time to her. The daily contact pleased Chief Tuxaua, father of the young Native American. He ended up spending hours listening to Fabiano's classes and learned enough to communicate in Portuguese.

Yjara, twenty-one years old, was already able to write letters and words in both Portuguese and Tupi. She also learned to count and write numbers. It was a success. This period of constant contact aroused a mutual dependence and an increasing attraction between them. Fabiano could not resist Yjara's charms, and she felt something in her heart that she had never imagined. It took a while for him to make a courageous decision twenty days before his departure for Lisbon.

Interrupting his class, he stared into Yjara's eyes and confessed his love to the beautiful creature, stressing that he would not be able to live without her, wherever he was.

"But you are going back to Portugal, what will my life be like without you? asked Yjara."

"I want you to be my wife and I would like to take you with me. I know it is a sudden and surprising proposal, but I cannot leave Brazil without you. These years we spent together were enough to confirm my deep love for you."

"I wouldn't know what to do anymore if I had to live without you by my side," said Yjara. I have not had the courage in all these years to confess that you have fulfilled my dreams since you arrived in the village. My love grows every day, and your proposal was what I most expected. I am delighted, I accept with the greatest affection. I also know that my father would have no objection, as he has a deep admiration for you."

"I know the adaptation problems you will have when you live in a totally unknown place where they will look at you with the same curiosity that your tribe looked at me when I arrived in the village. Of course, you will have to adapt to the kind of clothes that Europeans wear, but I know that this may even be a pleasant surprise for you."

"This problem of adapting to the new life will not affect me, as I already felt that things were changing with the arrival of foreigners in our land and that there would be a turnaround in customs on both sides."

"I am eager to communicate our decision to my cousin Bartolomeu, who you already know. At the same time, I will ask Angelica to provide you with the clothes you can wear on the trip. She will certainly choose pretty ones. But we still have about twenty days to prepare for the move, and I must also communicate the fact to Commander Cristovão Jacques and talk to your father."

After a series of rituals and indigenous festivals, they all embarked in the caravel towards Portugal. Yjara was stunning in the dress chosen by Angelica. Only when boarding was it clear that there was something different between Bartolomeu and Angelica, as they walked hand in hand. Fabiano was warned of this fact by Cristovão who, in these three years became fond of all passengers.

"Bartolomeu, what is going on between you and Angelica? Can I assume that she is your girlfriend?" asked Fabiano.

"We had agreed to leave our romance as a mystery until we arrive in Lisbon, but our secret was discovered too early. But there is no reason not to show that we are engaged, and we are going to get married as soon as we arrive in Portugal. We also know that your intentions regarding Yjara are the same as ours, am I right?"

"I think that this trip to Portugal will remain in the history of our families, and it can even be said that it is a pre-nuptial expedition that requires a celebration with a good wine," said Aloisio.

The two caravels arrived in Lisbon at the same time due to the favorable winds and calm sea, sailing side by side in the entire route.

Chapter 31

Cristiano almost fell on his back with the sudden arrival of Bartolomeu, Fabiano and Yjara. Angelica decided to stop by the residence and store the souvenirs brought from Brazil, while Aloisio left on a trip to the palace of King Manuel I (1469-1521) in Évora, approximately eighty-five miles away. He would be absent for at least two weeks.

Fabiano's first step was to introduce his bride and tell them how they fell in love and how he managed to teach her to speak and read Portuguese, something unthinkable for someone who had never attended school in childhood and youth. She soon relaxed and reported her satisfaction for learning so much. Fabiano informed that they intended to visit the vineyard in France and the school in England as soon as it was practical.

"My dear Fabiano, I want to congratulate you for your courage to undertake such an unusual trip to a recently discovered land and I have to say that I am excited about the arrival of my sister-in-law and your future wife Yjara, said Cristiano. I want her to feel like a member of our family right now. Florencio is in England and Clarinha and Esmeralda in France, see how we are all spread across Europe. And you, Bartolomeu, I heard that you also brought your bride. We would love to meet her."

While Aloisio remained in Évora, the atmosphere at the residence was of immense joy at the arrival of Yjara. She reported incredible things from her past, recalled the courage of her father, Chief Tuxaua in the fight against enemy tribes and against Portuguese who tortured and enslaved his tribe.

Angelica brought luggage with a set of clothes for Yjara that were at once approved by everyone. At the same time, she described how her brother Aloisio met King Dom Manuel I, the Fortunate[56]. We lived near Alcochete where Dom Manuel was born. The city was chosen due to the outbreak of the black plague that occurred in Lisbon. It is located on the banks of the Tagus River, opposite of Lisbon. Our parents kept a farm where they planted grapes and supplied wines to neighboring villages and our brand became famous and known in the aristocratic circles of that region of Portugal. Dom Manuel was

---

[56]https://www.britannica.com/biography/Manuel-I.

the adopted son of Dom John II and continued to encourage Portuguese navigations, notably to India and Brazil."

"With Vasco da Gama's trips to the East and Cabral´s to Brazil, Dom Manuel accumulated an enormous fortune, proceeded Angelica. His conquests were confirmed by the Pope and recognized by Spain where he had an excellent relationship. Thanks to Dom Afonso de Albuquerque (1453-1515)[57] sent to India in 1506, key ports such as Goa, Malaga and Ormuz were conquered, which formed the foundations for the State of India and allowed the Portuguese to control an important part of the eastern maritime trade. Dom Manuel was married three times. The first in 1497 with Isabel, daughter of King Ferdinand II of Aragon and Queen Isabel I of Castile, who oversaw the unification of the Iberian kingdoms in the country that later became Spain. She died a year later. The second took place in 1500 with Princess Maria of Castile and the third in 1518 with Leonor, sister of Charles V, Holy Roman Emperor. Dom Manuel lived in Lisbon. A regular customer of our wines, he visited our winery and became our friend. It was on that occasion that he met my brother Aloisio who seemed ideal for him to play a relevant role in the king's court. He appointed him inspector of shipbuilding and Portuguese navigation. For this reason, you met him as inspector during Cristovão Jacques' trip. Aloisio returned to Lisbon at the beginning of 1520 shortly after the visit to the king."

"I brought important news for the family, said Aloisio. King Dom Manuel received news about the arrival of Fabiano's bride, the first Caeté Indian present in Portugal. He insisted on meeting her on his return to Lisbon, which would be soon. Secondly, he asked to be godfather of Aloisio's sister's wedding to Bartolomeu and, finally, he wanted to attend Fabiano's wedding with Yjara."

"Fabiano, you managed to teach me Portuguese with a lot of effort, said Yjara. I also did my best to please you not only for the privilege of learning, but for my love for you. I knew I could own you faster if I spoke your language. Now that I can have a good relationship with the Portuguese language, I ask if you would be willing to teach me English and French. Maybe I could even attend

---

[57] https://www.britannica.com/biography/Afonso-de-Albuquerque.

classes at the Royal School when we arrive in England and so I could learn other important subjects."

"My love, I will be delighted to teach you these two languages, said Fabiano. With reference to the moral principles, one of the main topics of the curriculum, I would like to give you an example that will clarify its meaning. I am going to tell you the story of a family that lived in the last century until recently, the Borgia family[58]."

"The Borgias were of noble origin in Spain. They took root in Italy where they became important in the field of politics and of the Catholic religion between 1400 and 1500. Two of its members became popes and others were political and religious leaders."

"In 1455, Alfonso Borgia (1378-1458) was elected pope and assumed the name of Calixto III. Another member of the family was Rodrigo Borgia who managed to be elected Pope through the purchase of votes from the cardinals responsible for the appointment of the pontiffs. He adopted the name Alexander VI (1431-1503) and had four children with his lover Vanozza dei Catanei, with the names of Cesar, Lucrecia, Gioffre and Juan".

"In addition to banning the marriage of members of the Catholic church and having sex with women, Alexander VI simply ignored this determination and continued to attract other women to his bed."

"Alexander VI's papacy was known for bribes, murders, poisonings, corruption, embezzlement and other crimes, such as torture and persecution. It was customary at the time, to burn heretics in the public square, something barbaric. These crimes were committed by the pope and his children. An example of the type of evil that existed in the family was the murder of son Juan, by his own brother Caesar. Anyway, if you think about it, none of these characters had what is called Moral Standards. For a person to adopt these principles, he must live without sin and falsehood, have good habits and honesty. In addition, he must have an aversion to lying and must act with purity of purpose and be incorruptible. From this story, you will see that none of the members of the Borgia family had any of these qualities."

---

[58]https://www.britannica.com/topic/Borgia-family.

"Now I understand the subject of your ancestor´s book," said Yjara.

"Exactly."

"But then my relatives do not embrace these moral standards, because some of them kill Indians from other tribes and eat them! Here in Portugal such a thing would be horrible. Imagine if a Portuguese man kills his friend, cuts him in pieces and eats him? Is there a difference between the Borgias and the Caeté Indians?"

"I think it's a question of culture, answered Fabiano. The Indigenous people were accustomed by their ancestors that anthropophagy is not a crime and did not understand what is right or wrong. The Borgia, however, committed crimes knowingly out of sheer malice and thirst for power and knew exactly what they were doing. They had the necessary culture to understand that this or that was wrong. Even so, they preferred to choose crimes and not decency."

Upon arriving, Angelica proposed that the wedding of the two couples be held on board the ship commanded by Cristovão Jacques in which the four returned from Brazil. It would be a nice memory and King Dom Manuel could attend the ceremony because he ordered this trip to the new continent.

Jacques was excited about the idea of celebrating a wedding on board his ship, currently anchored in the port of Lisbon. Dom Manuel, invited by Aloisio, agreed with the 25th. of July 1520, in fifteen days. The Portuguese friends from the French-Portuguese Company of International Trade would also be invited. Sisters Clarinha, Esmeralda and their respective husbands would be absent because they were currently in Marseille and Florencio was at the Royal School.

Bartolomeu proposed that the respective honeymoons be spent, partly at the winery and partly in England at the Baltimore Estate residence. The program could not be nicer and was enthusiastically received by everyone.

With the curiosity of a child, Dom Manuel was anxious to get to know the Indian Yjara and was already devising a plan for the future of his navigations. He kept this project a secret that would be exposed shortly after the wedding.

During the ceremony, the brides shone for their beauty, for the exuberance of their wedding garments and for the joy on their faces. As captain of the ship, Cristovão Jacques celebrated the wedding alongside King Dom Manuel, godfather of Angelica and Bartolomeu.

During the ceremony, it was possible to notice an increase in the king's intimacy with those present, especially with Fabiano and his wife Yjara. Extremely anxious, he was unable to keep his secret and asked the two couples to listen to his proposition.

"It was with intense pleasure that I find myself in this wedding ceremony and I want to congratulate the newlyweds who have just arrived from our new country bringing with them this beautiful maiden from Brazil. I thought long before I decided to make my proposition to Fabiano and Yjara about a project that I have been working on. I want to officially invite you to be my advisors for the purpose of teaching the Tupi language to members of my court and to the navigators who will soon leave for Brazil. I think that knowing the language of the people who live there will be of wonderful use so that there can be greater harmony and greater understanding between so diverse cultures in terms of habits and customs. The classes could be taught at my palace where I receive the nobles and the navigators."

"Your Majesty honors us greatly for the trust you now place in us," said Fabiano. I have been talking to Aloisio, who as Your Majesty knows, owns a school that teaches foreign languages. He was willing to include the Tupi language among his courses and, if Your Majesty agrees, we would be happy to teach the language at your palace."

"If Your Majesty allows me, I would like to say that I feel immensely honored by the invitation and I can assure you, with the indispensable help of my beloved husband, that I will do everything in my power to teach my language. I must mention that I am happy to receive, just after my wedding, a proposition as wonderful as the one that Your Majesty made to us."

"Then enjoy your honeymoon and come back refreshed to start this new stage of your life."

Upon arriving at the winery, another surprise. Clarinha, Paul, Esmeralda and Eric were static with the arrival of the two couples. They could never imagine that Fabiano was going to get married, mainly because he was the shyest of the family. It did not take long for them to bond with Yjara and the newlywed Portuguese couple, but Paul and Eric Demignon did not speak Portuguese, and had communication problems with the new guests.

The forest that surrounded the property at once attracted Yjara to awaken memories of her life in Brazil. She took off her shoes, went into the woods singing and dancing as if it were an indigenous party. Everyone ran to go with her and enjoy the show, but soon lost sight of her. After a long search, they heard her voice calling everyone. She was on top of one of the highest trees in the forest, laughing at the awe of her pursuers.

After everyone returned home, Paul informed that the exports brought great profits to the winery due to the seedlings received from Bordeaux that improved quality of the wine. Orders from England and Portugal increased year after year. They recently received an offer from the Bordeaux producers to buy the entire winery at a price well above its true value. This matter would be discussed with all those present at the dinner to celebrate the coming weddings.

The couples received the best accommodation of the property and decided to disappear for a while. The next day, during lunch time, Yjara wanted Fabiano to talk about the pope and his attributions.

"This is an interesting question. In fact, the subject will take time because it is difficult to describe, started Fabiano. The Pope is the head of the Roman Catholic Church. He lives in a palace called the Apostolic Palace in the Vatican City in Rome, Italy and in in charge of disseminating all the teachings of God contained in a sacred book called "The Bible". Those who believe in the existence of God also accept the man who lived about 1500 years ago called Jesus Christ, considered the son of God by all Christians. He was born to spread his father's word on earth."

"The population of most countries in western Europe adopted a religion called Christianity. As you will remember, Catholics believe that there is only one God who created the universe in seven days. Those who adhere to the

Catholic religion also believe the teachings of Jesus Christ. Due to his name, the word Christianity appeared and is adopted by all those who consider Jesus the "Son of God and Savior of Humanity."

"Jesus was born in a tiny village called Bethlehem and grew up in a town by the name of Nazareth. His mother was called Mary and his father Joseph. But what they say is that Jesus was placed inside Mary's womb by the Holy Spirit, that is, there was a divine intervention without Joseph having had any contact with her. An interesting detail about his birth was that his mother was a virgin and remained a virgin for the rest of her life, something that people at the time called a miracle."

"I can't believe this story argued Yjara. It would be the same if we both had a child without your participation in the matter. Another thing that I do not quite understand is the difference between the Catholic religion and Christianity," asked Yjara.

"I also had those same doubts. As for the pregnancy, I can only agree with you. Regarding Christianity, it has three different churches: The first is the Roman Catholic Church, which is that of the Pope. The second is the Eastern Orthodox Church[59] that does not recognize the Pope's authority and does not believe in the virginity of Mary, the mother of Jesus. Furthermore, they accept the marriage of priests who were already married before conversion to the Orthodox Church and only bishops cannot marry. The third is the Protestant Church that I will explain shortly."

"It is said that Jesus Christ was endowed with divine gifts and that during his life he preached kindness, respect for others and was dedicated to save people from their sins. He would have performed miracles by healing sick people. You could say that Jesus was what Francesco Vivone would call a virtuous person. Unfortunately, his ideas did not please Jewish leaders because the morality he taught was against their principles and interests. Consequently, Jesus was crucified, suffering terrible pain for hours and died shortly afterwards. But it is said that he resurrected and returned from death. After appearing to people for forty days, they say he went up to heaven."

---

[59]https://www.britannica.com/topic/Eastern-Orthodoxy.

"Therefore, the Pope is the person responsible for the administration of the Vatican and, through his subordinates (cardinals, archbishops, priests, and other lower-rank prelates), he works to disseminate the teachings of Jesus Christ among followers of the Catholic religion."

"My love, this is all very interesting," Yjara said. My father taught me who are the gods of our people, and it is very much like the God of the Catholics. He told me that the God of the Indians is called Thunder God and that he created the entire world. He was also known as Tupã. He had the help of the goddess Araci when he came down to Earth and created everything that exists, including the ocean, forests, animals, and stars. My father explained to me that Tupã created humanity with statues of people made of clay, mixing things he took from nature. Then he blew life on them and left. As my father is the chief and teaches all this, we could say that he is the Pope of the Indians."

"Yjara, you are absolutely right. Your father is the Pope of the Caetés. You know that today is the year 1521 and the Pope who is in Rome is called Leo X, appointed in 1513, well before our trip to Brazil. He became pope number 217, imagine the number of popes that existed since the year 30 after Christ. The first was St. Peter, who remained as Pope for 37 years and is said to have had the keys to heaven".

"Aside from Catholicism, there are other religions. For example, in 1483 a man named Martin Luther (1493-1546)[60], born in Eisleben, Saxony, Germany, dedicated his life to study religions. Although he believed in God as Catholics do, he reformulated ideas of Christianity with a movement that resulted in the so-called Protestant Reformation, creating Protestantism, causing a division between Roman Catholicism and the new Protestant traditions, the Lutheranism. He was one of the most influential figures in the history of Christendom."

"Luther presented ninety-five theses (ideas), among which it is worth mentioning two that are different from the traditions of the Catholic religion. First, Protestant priests are allowed to marry. Second, unlike the contact with God that was made through Catholic priests in absolving the sins admitted by the believers, Luther thought that salvation should be done

---

[60]https://www.britannica.com/biography/Martin-Luther.

through faith and not through a messenger as it happens in confessions. He created the first Lutheran churches for his followers. Luther translated the Bible from Latin into German, which allowed a greater number of readers, who did not know Latin, to have access to the book."

"Based on Luther's ideas, a Frenchman named John Calvin (1509-1564)[61] was the creator of new religious ideas. He considered the regular clergy of the church unnecessary, criticized the cult of images and only admitted the sacraments of the Eucharist and Baptism, and considered the Bible the basis of religion. He extolled the individual characteristics necessary for commercial practice, which pleased the bourgeois class. His ideas were soon accepted throughout Europe and reached Scotland, Holland, and Denmark especially. His followers were called Presbyterians."

"I would like to mention two more important religions. One is the Jewish religion (practitioners of that religion are called Jews) and the other is Islamic (those who practice it are called Muslims). There are differences between these two and Catholicism and Protestantism. Jews base their beliefs on the laws of a book entitled Torah that is equivalent to the Christian Bible. It is interesting to hear the history of Judaism to understand its fundamental principles."

"The Jews lived in a country called Egypt and were slaves of the Pharaoh, king of the country. Considering the immense population of Jews, the Pharaoh thought they could start an uprising and gave an order that no Jewish child should remain alive. But among the Jews there was a boy named Moses[62], who was born in the year 1500 BCE[63]. To protect him, his mother made a basket and placed it in the Nile River where he floated until he was found by an Egyptian princess, daughter of the Pharaoh. Moses ended up being educated at the royal palace and the Pharaoh wanted to prepare the boy for a high office or even for the throne of Egypt. He stayed in the country until he was forty."

"At that age, on one occasion, Moses saw an Egyptian beating a Jew and was so angry that he killed the Egyptian and buried him in the sand. When they heard about the murder, Moses fled to the Midian Desert where he met a man

---

[6161]https://www.britannica.com/biography/John-Calvin.
[62]https://www.britannica.com/biography/Moses-Hebrew-prophet.
[63] BCE | meaning in the Cambridge English Dictionary.

named Jethro who hired him to take care of his flocks and ended up marrying one of his daughters."

"Yjara, are you tired of hearing this story?" asked Fabiano.

"You can't imagine how curious I am to hear the whole story. Please continue," said Yjara.

"Well, on that occasion, God contacted Moses and sent him back to Egypt to free the Jewish people. Accompanied by his brother Aaron, his spokesperson before God, Moses convinced the people to flee, but they were stopped by the Pharaoh´s troops. In retaliation God sent ten plagues to Egypt and caused a real calamity to the country. Finally, the Pharaoh allowed them to leave, but he soon repented and sent the army after the Jews who were camped close to the Red Sea. To escape from the Egyptian troops, they would have to cross the river which would be difficult for so many people. Moses, however, performed his famous miracle, opening the waters of the Red Sea for the Jews to pass through. When the army arrived at the see, Moses made the waters return, drowning the Pharaoh's troops."

"After crossing, the Jews concentrated at the foot of a mountain called Mount Sinai. Moses, who was the only one who could communicate with God, went up to Mount Sinai and stayed there for forty days without eating or drinking. It was during this period that God taught him the ten commandments of the Torah and asked him to carve them on two tablets of stone so that the people could get to know them. As he descended the hill, he found that the Jews were revering a golden calf as their God. He found out that the people were concerned about his delay in returning and asked Aaron to mold a new God they could worship, an idol who would lead them back to Egypt where they had been slaves. Aaron then asked the Jews to remove the gold earrings that women and children wore, poured the gold into a mold and made a golden calf saying that it was this idol that brought them out of Egypt."

"When God heard of the incident, he hated the Jews because they replaced him by the image of an animal. Moses, in anger, broke the two plates with the commandments written by God and destroyed the calf by melting it in a fire. Then God called Moses again to the top of the hill and promised that he would write the same commandments for him to carve on the stone. Moses stayed there for forty more days without eating and drinking and returned with the stones to inform the people that God would not destroy them as He had promised. It is said that Moses lived to be a hundred and twenty years."

"The Jews believe that at a future date the Messiah, a descendant of King David will come to bring perfection to the world. Christians, however, think that Jesus Christ is the Messiah since Mary and Joseph were descendants of David. You might ask, but who was this King David? He was the greatest king of the Jews, born in the year 1040 BCE and died in 970 BCE".

"There are two major differences between the Catholic religion and Judaism. First, the Jews do not accept that Jesus' mother was a virgin. Second, there is a controversy about the coming of the Messiah. As Jesus was already among us, if he came back as Messiah he would have come twice. The Jews, on the contrary, say that the Messiah will only come once, so he will be the true Messiah. Anyway, these differences are not important, because only the future will tell who is right."

"And how different is Islam? asked Yjara."

"Just to summarize and show the dates on which each of these religions was founded, it can be said that Judaism was founded by a leader named Abram, in the year 2,000 BCE and the Torah was written around the year 1,250 BCE. Jesus Christ founded Christianity in the year 30 after his birth (CE)[64] and the book that holds the word of Jesus is the Bible. Islam was founded by Muhammad who was born in the year 570 CE in the city of Mecca, Saudi Arabia and the book that decides the obligations and rules of Muslims is the Koran. According to Muslim tradition, God revealed the Koran to the prophet Muhammad in visions and messages over a period of twenty years. The Koran is considered the true word of Allah, or God. The Koran has the final word on Islamic social, religious, and legal issues."

"Islam[65] has some similarities to Christianity. For example, on the issue of life after death: According to Christianity, the believers will meet with God in heaven and non-Christians will be cast into hell forever. Those who are faithful

---

[64] Controversy over the use of CE and BCE to identify dates in history (religioustolerance.org).
[65] https://www.britannica.com/topic/Islam.

Muslims, will be sent to Paradise and infidels will be cast into a lake of fire. This seems to be almost the same."

"Christians claim that the Bible was inspired by God and made without errors, while for Islamists the Bible has been corrupted and is only correct when it agrees with the Koran. Muslims do not believe that Jesus died on the cross. Both religions are monotheistic (believe in only one God). Each one believes that their God is the only one. In Christianity it is God and in Islam it is Allah."

"Christians think that God lives in heaven, and it is where they will enjoy his friendship, while for Muslims Paradise is a place with unimaginable joys, a garden with trees and food, with beautiful virgins just for men and nothing for women."

"Anyway, I tried to summarize what I could in order not to overextend and not tire you, said Fabiano. What I conclude from all this is that all religions have a good side and a bad side. There are things that can be accepted by logic and others are doubtful. But it is worthwhile for someone to adopt a religion and have faith in its commandments because everyone has the right to believe what they want."

"Honey, I agree that everyone has the right to have faith in whatever they want, said Yjara. You also said that there are dubious things in the various religions, but I think you should have said that they are absurd, and I cannot accept them. Based on what you told me, for example, this business of Moses opening a passage in the Red Sea for Jews to flee from the Pharaoh, the birth of Jesus of a virgin mother, God speaking to Moses on Mount Sinai when no one has yet seen God, Jesus' own resurrection and his ascent to heaven are things I refuse to believe. This is also true of the history of the Muslims' paradise with beautiful virgins and Christians going to hell for those who do not believe in God. Another absurdity is to force poor Catholic priests into meaningless chastity. In my tribe there are also some nonsenses such as believing in the Thunder God or Indians having to eat their enemies at lunch."

"Yjara, you really understood the most incredible aspects of the different religions, and I have to admit that all of these gods seem kind of strange to me. Everything is a matter of faith. If someone decides to believe in something, it is difficult for others to convince them to change their mind. He or she believes and that's it."

"Imagine if I tell my father that I do not believe in the Thunder God. I am sure he will send me away from the tribe and will never speak to me again."

It is time to assess the changes in the Vivone and Demignon families as of 1521.

Vivone´s Family Tree in 1521

Francesco Vivone (1201-1257) and Larissa Vivone (1201-1258)
    Rolando (1232-1310) and Giovanna (1234-1311)
     Alfredo (1273- 1338)
     Salvatore (1273- 1338)
    Sinibaldo (1232-1303) and Anabela (1236-1316)
     Alina (1274-1338)
     Bianca (1274-1338)
    Godofredo (1232- 1312) and Matilda (1240-1313)
     Michele (1274-1338) and Robert Valois (1273-1338)
     Luigi (1295-1367) and Sigrid Andersen (1305-1369)
      Houston (1338- 1404) and Grace Baltimore (1346-1404)
       Anderson (1374-1448) and Samira Amal (1390-1461)
        Zachary (1416-1493) and Joaquina Querubim (1432-1510)
         Clarinha (1467-   and Paul Demignon (1461-
         Esmeralda (1468-   and Eric Demignon (1463-
        Gordon (1416-1488) and Margarida de Souza (1438-1510)
         Florêncio (1470-
         Fabiano (1472-   and Yjara (1495-
        Orson (1418-1488) and Manuela Dias (1434-1510)
         Bartolomeu (1470-   and Angélica de Albuquerque (1495-
         Cristiano (1472-
       Jefferson (1375-1448)
      Harold (1338-1404) and Audrey (1346-1404)
      Lilian (1376-1448) and Frederic (1390-1455)
      Emily (1377-1377)

Demignon´s Family Tree in 1521

Claude (1430-1503) and Gabrielle (1434-1504)
  Paul (1461-   and Clarinha Vivone (1467-
Jean Pierre (1433-1505) and Jeanette (1436-1497)
  Eric (1463-   and Esmeralda Vivone (1468-
Hugo (1435-1505)
Olivier (1436- 1500)

Chapter 32

"I think we should return to Portugal to fulfill our commitment to His Majesty to teach the Tupi language to the navigators. We are already at the beginning of the year 1521 and he must be surprised at our long absence, said Fabiano".

Upon returning to Lisbon, Fabiano asked Aloisio to take them to King Manuel I to speed up the invitation to the candidates. The nobles present in the palace had already been informed about the "savage" who would teach the "mysterious" language. They were totally dazzled by Yjara's beauty and soon surrounded her for a more detailed examination. It was unusual in Manuel I's palace to receive a creature from another "planet."

Six were interested in the new language course. They were all strong, rustic, and authoritarian. But they obeyed the wishes of Dom Manuel I to serve him in the best conceivable way in Brazil. They also bowed to the charms of the teacher, respecting her effort and honesty. The course lasted three months, with the collaboration of Fabiano, who sometimes came to Yjara's aid when she did not know a term in Portuguese. It was an extraordinary success, as everyone, without exception, was able to understand the Tupi language and speak well enough to be able to communicate with the natives. King D. Manuel, immensely grateful for Yjara's effort, as a reward asked the painter Vasco Fernandes de Viseu (1475-1542), one of the most famous of the time, to portray her. The painting was shown in the palace as D. Manuel was in love with art.

Only one more course was given by Yjara and Fabiano, because she was anxious to travel to England. Fifteen more Portuguese, eight of the nobility of Manuel I and seven future navigators took part in the last class. During one of the breaks between classes, Fabiano told those present that Yjara used to hunt with her father in the Brazilian jungle and therefore it was necessary to run long distances to hunt the animals that would feed the tribe. The subject interested the students because most had been trained for war. They wanted Yjara to show them her skills anyway.

"I ran inside the forest, on very narrow trails, which made it difficult to move. Here I have more space, which should increase my speed a little. We will see the result," said Yjara, anticipating the failure of her competitors.

They decided to run around the King's palace. She decided to run barefoot as she did with her father. As soon as the dispute started, the men obtained a considerable distance easily in front of here and Yjara accompanied them calmly, feeling that they would not have the breath to continue at this pace until the end of the race. Suddenly Yjara decided to show her skill and exploded on the dirt road and quickly left everyone behind. Any effort to reach her would be impossible given her amazing speed. The noble gentlemen had never seen somebody running that way.

Dom Manuel I, known as the Fortunate ("O Venturoso") conducted great performances in the fields of Portuguese navigation. Vasco da Gama in 1497 unveiled the sea route to the Indies. Furthermore, the discovery of Brazil by Pedro Álvares Cabral in 1500; the appointment of Francisco de Almeida as the first viceroy of India; the conquest of important places like Málaca, Goa and Ormuz; ensured control of the Indian Ocean and Gulf trade routes. It is easy to imagine that all these achievements were the basis of the so-called Portuguese Empire at the time one of the richest and most powerful countries in Europe and proved his dynamism as king of Portugal. Despite all these achievements, however, Dom Manuel's kindness reached a limit by pleading with the Pope the establishment of the inquisition in Portugal. Such a request fully proves his disrespect for human beings by allowing the punishments inflicted on those who refused to accept the Catholic religion.

With the death of Dom Manuel on December 13, 1521, his son Dom John III succeeded him as King of Portugal[66](1502-1557), known as the Pious due to his religious belief. He was the fifteenth king of Portugal. At the age of twenty, shortly after taking office, he married Catherine of Austria. Concerned about the dissemination of culture, he oversaw the evolution of the University of Coimbra and the Royal College of Arts, having been called Protector of the University and considered the patron of culture.

---

[66]https://www.britannica.com/biography/John-III-king-of-Portugal.

Portugal, through the Treaty of Tordesillas, became the owner of half the world, but the administration of such a large territory caused an increase in the country's problems. The Portuguese properties suffered attacks especially from Turks and Arabs who did not accept Portugal's monopoly, which needed the permanent deployment of troops and weapons to the east. With all these difficulties, Dom John III changed his priorities and started to dedicate his attention preferentially to Brazil in its colonization and growth of the country's population.

Fabiano and Yjara remained in Lisbon until 1523 when, finally, he decided to fulfill Yjara's desire to visit England. They closed the house in Lisbon, entrusting the property to the employees to take care of cleaning and necessary payments. During the time they stayed in Portugal, Fabiano managed to teach his wife the main terms and phrases of the English language and was amazed by her interest and dedication. Obviously, she would arrive with sufficient knowledge to communicate with the directors of the Royal School.

The pleasant surprise was that Bartolomeu, and Angelica accepted the invitation to join them on the trip, as Angelica had never been to England. Aloisio had to continue his duties as inspector general of Portuguese navigation.

Luckily, the loyal friends of the French-Portuguese International Trade Company had a delivery in Southampton and kindly made two cabins available to the couples. During the voyage, Yjara complained of severe seasickness that could have resulted from the waves which rocked the ship violently. As the sickness continued even after the bonanza, Fabiano thought that she was pregnant. Unfortunately, upon arriving in England, his assumption was not confirmed. It was a consequence of food on board.

Fabiano was optimistic to see his brother Florencio, who spent all this time running the Royal School. Despite being the most versed in languages, Florencio would certainly recognize Fabiano's merits when he managed to teach Portuguese and English, moreover, learn the Tupi language. The arrival at Baltimore Estate was a surprise, as Florencio had just returned from the school and was elated by the arrival of his brother with friends. Immediately a dinner was arranged in honor of the visitors, and it was only then that he learned of

Fabiano's marriage to this exuberant girl and of Bartolomeu to Angelica. The beauty of the Vivone residence impressed the two girls while Bartolomeu remembered the good times he spent at the Royal School.

The conversation over dinner consisted of an account of the family's adventures. It lasted until 5:00 o´clock in the morning, as it was necessary to describe the main events, such as weddings, the trip to Brazil, staying in the trading post, contact with the Indians and with the chief of the Caetés, Yjara's father, the plans of Portuguese navigators for the next voyages, the victory of Yjara in the race against the Portuguese nobles, the death of Dom Manuel I and the change in strategy of his successor John III in relation to the east, giving priority to the colonization of Brazil.

The next morning, they visited the Royal School where the graduation party for more than forty graduates from the year 1524 was being prepared. After the meeting with the school board, Yjara wasted no time in applying for registration for the school year 1525, which encouraged Angelica to also take part in the course. Florencio, at once obtained two copies of "Morality and Ethics," translated into English, and presented them to both candidates.

"I think we should take the opportunity to discuss a little bit about our future," said Fabiano. Clarinha and Esmeralda are fifty-eight and fifty-seven years old, respectively. They are married to Paul and Eric who are sixty-four and sixty-two. Since they had no children because they were married late, they will have no heirs. What will happen to the winery?"

"Florencio is fifty-five years old and has not married, which is a shame. He is a wonderful person and has an enviable physical stamina. I think that his dedication of body and soul to the Royal School prevented him from having a more intense social life and we are curious about his plans. On the other hand, I am fifty-three and Yjara is thirty. As we decided to remain without children for a while, Yjara will be busy with the course, and I intend to collaborate with Florencio in teaching foreign languages."

"As for Cristiano, he dedicated himself entirely to foreign trade and managed, through his efficient commercial strategy, to generate extraordinary profits for Francesco Vivone World Exports, of which we are all partners. Now we must study a way to provide a bigger share for him, as long as everyone agrees."

"What about Bartolomeu and his wife Angelica? asked Fabiano. He is fifty-five and she is thirty. We know that Angelica will attend the Royal School in the year 1525, which will occupy her time for two years. As for Bartolomeu, I know that he is a man of multiple abilities, and I would like to know which one he will choose for his future. Anyway, do you have any idea?"

"What I really want is to see our wives finish the course. We will also avoid having children right away, said Bartolomeu. Thus, I will be able to remain here in England and become a representative of our export company in partnership with Cristiano. We can even organize a branch here at Baltimore Estate. If I need any help, I may hire one of the students to help me."

"I wanted to talk about the winery, said Cristiano. As our cousins and their husbands are a little older, they need help in managing the property. So, I suggest that we help the four in whatever necessary and, in addition, I can start exporting from there. If you agree, I will leave for France as soon as I receive King Henry VIII's invitation to dinner at Windsor Castle, said Cristiano. I think I'm a lucky person, because I got this relationship that I will describe to all of you later."

"I have a little secret that I would like to reveal, said Florencio. I was very jealous of Fabiano when he went to Brazil. I would really like to see this wonderful country and, who knows, find a beautiful wife like Yjara. In that case, I would have to leave the school in the hands of Fabiano, who is more than capable of replacing me."

"Now I just need to locate a ship to take me to Brazil," said Florencio. I will write to Uncle Aloisio and ask him to contact King John III to see who is scheduled for the next trip to Brazil, perhaps even Cristovão Jacques."

"Well, in relation to Florencio's trip to Portugal, as I said, I managed to contact King Henry VIII (1491-1547), informed Cristiano. Our family has always been lucky in their relationship with sovereigns. In fact, the main reason was our wine. The production of Marseille is being exported to England and the nobility fell in love with our wines. With the new Bordeaux seedlings, we practically dominated the English market. Shortly before the arrival of Fabiano and Yjara from Brazil, I was able to make friends with the nobles of Windsor Castle, presenting them with boxes of our special red wine. On one of my trips to the castle, I happened to meet the king, whom I reported to be the producer in France and at the same time one of the owners of the Baltimore Estate and the Royal School. All this impressed him, and he ended up visiting the school with his entire court. It was a real glory for me and the students to receive the King of England! It was a consecration and a privilege for everyone."

"What do you teach in this school?" asked the king.

"Here we teach moral principles, foreign languages, such as French, Italian, German, Portuguese and music," replied Florencio. I do not know if Your Majesty has heard that there was an extraordinary improvement in the customs and the education of the English students in general due to these teachings. The institution has been running for years with participants from many countries. Now I would like to ask Your Majesty most respectfully about your writings and compositions. We heard that Your Majesty is an expert in these two modalities. Could we have access to them?"

"Certainly, my dear Florencio, but we must do it in my castle after a dinner to which I invite you with great satisfaction. We should schedule this event in about 30 days, because I will be busy with other programs until then. You will receive the invitation within that time."

"Therefore, I have to stay here until I receive the invitation," concluded Cristiano.

In fact, the king's invitation to the whole family came after twenty days and the dinner was scheduled for December 18th, 1524. Everyone was excited about the occasion, especially Yjara and Angelica, as it would be an event to be remembered forever. Cristiano, more accustomed to the palace protocol, instructed everyone on how to behave at a royal table and see the right moments to taste the food served by the king's personnel. Upon arriving at Windsor Castle, they were ecstatic with the pomp and the presence of the nobility who would attend the dinner. As Cristiano suggested, the king had agreed to show his gifts in the fields of music and his literary works, which was the main reason for the invitation.

The elegance and beauty of the two women impressed the king and the nobility and aroused curiosity about Yjara, already perfectly integrated into English life and customs. The nobles were curious about her origin and the main differences between the two societies. Yjara spoke at length about the customs of the indigenous people, about their economy based on hunting and fishing, she also explained that her father was the chief of the Caeté tribe, mentioned the ability of Indians with bows and arrows, described the type of food of the Indians in general and gave special emphasis to the type of contact with the white men from Europe. After her speech, the participants suggested that this occasion should be repeated and that they intended to visit Brazil and learn more about its riches. They also asked Yjara to prove her skills in hunting and fishing with the bow and arrow, an idea that excited the king who was an expert partridge hunter.

Yjara mentioned that at the beginning of the year she would be attending the course of the Royal School of Moral Integrity with Angelica. At that moment, Cristiano reminded King Henry VIII of his promise to show his musical compositions and poetry which was a success.

Chapter 33

At the beginning of the 1525 school year, the two girls began to study at the Royal School. It was not easy to understand Italian and French, although certain words sound like Portuguese. Students of various nationalities attended the course as well as Scots, Irish and nobles from Windsor Castle. Yjara and Angelica were admired for their effort and for their beauty and friendliness.

The moral principles advocated by Francesco Vivone were assimilated by the class, causing the mentality previously in force to be modified. One of the subjects that drew attention during the classes was certainly the analysis of the behavior of King Dom John III of Portugal due to his wish to implant the inquisition in the country. All students felt that such a plan was against moral standards. The graduation of Angelica and Yjara took place in December 1527.

The grand prize, given to Angelica two years after graduation, came in the form of an unscheduled pregnancy. There was an "accident on the way," as they did not want to have children so soon. Finally, the joy was twice as great when, on January 1, 1531, the son Teodoro was born, named after a close relative of Angelica, living in Portugal.

Aloisio's reply arrived in January 1529 with news about Cristovão Jacques. He had been in Brazil since 1526, due to his appointment as Governor of Brazil. In 1527 he returned to command six ships to fight French pirates in Bahia in a struggle that was the first major naval battle of the country where he imprisoned three French galleons.

Aloisio also discovered that a childhood friend of King Dom John III, Martim Afonso de Souza (1500-1571)[67] would be sent to Brazil in 1530. Martim was a military man, from a noble family, born in Viçosa, Portugal. He was considered a man of unbreakable character, austere, brave, and tenacious. Well before the trip, Dom John asked Martim Afonso to accompany the widow of Dom Manuel I who was returning to Castile, his native land. Castile was the kingdom of Charles V (1500-1558) from Spain who asked Martim Afonso to help him in his struggles against France. Charles had an infinite number of titles: he was

---

[67] https://www.britannica.com/biography/Martim-Afonso-de-Sousa.

Emperor of the Holy Roman-German Empire, heir to the kingdoms of Castile, Aragon, and Navarre. He was chosen emperor of Germany and heir to the House of Austria, the Netherlands, the kingdoms of Naples and Sicily, Lombardy, the Franco County, the Duchy of Milan, Artois, and the lands conquered by Spain.

Martim got married on that occasion and returned to Portugal in 1525, accompanying the Spanish princess Catherine (Carlos V´s sister), who would marry Dom John III, and thus become Queen of Portugal.

Aloisio obtained authorization from King John III for Florencio to board one of Martim Afonso's ships in 1530. In the meantime, Yjara would have enough time to teach him the Tupi language and the customs of her tribe. She also asked him to take gifts to her father, Chief Tuxaua and to his brothers.

Florencio arrived in Lisbon at the end of November, as the expedition was scheduled to sail on December 3, 1530. Martim Afonso's main purpose was to colonize Brazil. Before leaving, Dom John appointed him Counselor to the Crown. The fleet, with a crew of 400 men, was composed of four vessels, the flagship commanded by Martim Afonso and his brother Pero Lopes de Souza, plus a galleon called San Vicente, commanded by Pero Lopes Pinheiro and the caravel Rosa, with Diogo Leite who had had experience in Brazil following the bodyguard expedition of Cristovão Jacques and finally the Princess caravel, led by Baltazar Fernandes, experienced in fighting the French.

Florencio embarked on the Princess caravel. Despite his sixties, he was still strong enough to withstand the storms that often plague ships in the Atlantic. Upon arriving at Itamaracá Island, Florencio was present when Martim Afonso fought French smugglers who stole brazilwood. After taking their ships, he incorporated them into the Portuguese fleet.

Unfortunately, Florencio could not be housed in the trading post built by Cristovão Jacques, since it had been looted, but he was received by Diogo Alvares Correia (named Caramurú by the natives) He had been in Brazil for twenty-two years and was married to an Indigenous woman called Paraguassú. With Diogo's help, he reached the village of the Caeté Indians where he was taken to the presence of Yjara's father, Tuxaua. Gifts brought from Portugal were a success that eased his life among the Indigenous people.

Martim Afonso went south, where he installed the first real landmark of the colonization of Brazil in the Captaincy of São Vicente. There Martim Afonso built a fortress and set up the first permanent settlement. King Dom John III decided to divide Brazil into hereditary captaincies and appointed Martim Afonso as donor of the captaincy of São Vicente and granted that of Pernambuco to Duarte Coelho. Martim Afonso was the first Governor General of Brazil.

In the absence of suitable accommodation, Florencio managed to stay with the Native Americans of the tribe at the invitation of Tuxaua whose Portuguese was already fluent. In a conversation with the chief, Florencio reported in Tupi all the adventures of his daughter Yjara, her course at the Royal School and her tenacity. He also told him that she spoke English and Italian perfectly in addition to Portuguese.

He spent his days teaching greater notions of Portuguese to the tribe, telling stories about Portugal, France and England, a success among the adults and young natives. Tuxaua introduced him to his youngest daughter, Yjara's sister, who is also stunningly beautiful. Her name was Mayara which means "wise." The outcome could not have been different. In 1531 Florencio proposed to marry her which was happily authorized by Tuxaua. The return of Martim Afonso and his fleet was scheduled for mid-1533. Thus, there would be time to take care of Mayara's clothes and instruct her about Portuguese customs and the various countries through which they intended to pass. In December 1531, a son was born who received the name of Pyatã, meaning "strong, tough, vigorous". Undoubtedly it would be one more unusual event for the Vivone family.

Florencio learned that Martim Afonso, in 1532, went to S. Vicente where he met an adventurous Portuguese explorer named João Ramalho (1493-1571). Ramalho arrived in Brazil in 1512, looking for his "Paradise Island", but his ship sank in front of the Captaincy of San Vicente, but he survived and went deep into the forest where he met Guaianases Indians. Ramalho became a friend of the tribe and married the Indian Bartira, daughter of Chief Tibiriçá and his wife Potira. Ramalho named his wife Isabel with whom he had nine children, in addition to children with other women of the tribe, since there was total sexual freedom in the tribe. As Ramalho was very smart, he set up trading posts on the Brazilian coast with his sons to establish trade with Europeans, but he was also responsible for selling Native Americans as slaves. He was an extremely cruel individual to the enslaved natives, but he played a key role in helping Martim Afonso de Souza by leading him along the trails to the top of the mountain where the land was more fertile. When he arrived at the plateau, Martim Afonso founded a city which he named Santo André da Borda do Campo.

Finally, in mid-1533, Florencio, Mayara and their son left for Portugal, from where they would proceed as quickly as possible to England. They stayed temporarily at the Vivone residence in Lisbon and took the opportunity to familiarize Mayara with a completely different civilization. Mayara was a much reserved and shy person, different from her sister Yjara and had difficulty communicating in Portuguese. Slowly, however, she got used to the new life.

Early in 1534 they boarded one of the ships of the Portuguese friends of the French-Portuguese International Trade Company and arrived in Southampton. in a week and in four more days at Baltimore Estate. Fabiano and Yjara thought that Florencio had died, as he was absent for almost four years without sending any news. Yjara's joy was indescribable when she learned of her sister's wedding with Florencio. He was sure that they would form an invincible pair together with the two brothers. The good news that Florencio and Mayara received was the birth in 1531 of two twin boys from Yjara, whose names were respectively Ybyajara, meaning "Knight of the Plateau" and Cauã, meaning "Hawk". Mayara's shyness was quickly forgotten and turned into a dance that attracted Yjara, Angelica and the two brothers. They were also happy when they learned that Angelica had a boy named Teodoro, born in 1531. By coincidence, Piatã, son of Mayara was also born in 1531.

Yjara told her sister about the wonderful time she had at the Royal School, highlighting what she learned, especially in terms of moral principles and foreign languages, such as Italian, French, and English. To Florencio's happiness, Mayara took a keen interest and asked to enroll her in the next school year, which was at once provided.

Mayara's graduation coincided with a sad fact that occurred in 1536. Pope Paul III authorized Dom John III to institute the Court of the Holy Office in

Portugal[68], an institution created by the Iberian countries to discover and punish crimes against the catholic church. It was the so-called "Inquisition." In May 1536, the Pope appointed the bishops of Ceuta, Coimbra and Lamego as his commissioners and inquisitors to go ahead against the new Christians (Jews converted to Christianity) and against all those guilty of crimes of heresy. The Court was controlled by the king and the inquisitors reported and dispatched directly with the monarch. The Holy Office Court extended its action to the whole country and the Portuguese territories. The church considered itself the only valid one in the world and accused all those who refused it as infidels or heretics.

"Well, it's time to head to Marseille and help our cousins and their husbands to manage the winery, said Cristiano. It would be wonderful if Florencio, Mayara and Piatã went with me to get to know the farm and taste our wine. As Fabiano is indispensable as director of the Royal School, I think it would be better for him to stay here, but Angelica should accept our invitation to accompany us with Teodoro, while Bartolomeu would stay with Fabiano."

"We also want to go, shouted the two brothers, Yjara's children. We want to play in the woods with Piatã and Teodoro and you could make a bow and arrow for us. Then we can look for ants and birds. Please, mother."

"We cannot leave your father alone because he will be very sad without you."

"You will have a lot of fun at the farm, and I will be alone until you return, but you can be sure I will be very busy while you are there," said Fabiano. You can go without any problem. If I need help, Bartolomeu can give me a hand when he is not busy with wine exports."

---

[68]http://self.gutenberg.org/articles/eng/Holy_Office_of_the_Inquisition.

Chapter 34

The trip took place at the end of 1537, but sad news surprised them on arrival. Paul, already seventy-six years old, and Eric, seventy-four, could only move around with effort. Clarinha with seventy and Esmeralda with sixty-nine, was dedicated exclusively to taking care of their husbands. They also lacked the strength to manage the essential daily tasks. That is why they got the help of faithful employees who took care of grapes and wine production. The arrival of relatives was a real relief for them. It also awakened a new life expectancy for them. The joy of the boys and the beauty of the two Indians and Angelica was a balm for Paul and Eric, who always resented the lack of children. The next day, they managed to straighten up and walk with the family. They even played with the children, showing them everything that would serve as a toy. They seemed to be resurrected.

It is unnecessary to mention that the children's play area was in the forest of the farm. Yjara and Mayara built huts for the boys, prepared small bows and arrows, and made wooden hatchets. The stay in the grove lasted for hours until Angelica called them for lunch. The language used by everyone, including Florencio and Angelica, was Tupi. She learned the language during the three years she stayed in Brazil and already spoke it with fluency. Teodoro, aged nine, had no difficulty in learning Tupi. The only ones who did not understand anything were the two couples who lived at the vineyard.

Piatã, son of Mayara was the calmest of all and managed to perform a completely unusual feat. He sneaked up to a bird's nest and watched the mother feeding the chicks. He started talking to her and saw that the bird was in no way frightened. Then, Piatã extended his hand to the nest and to his surprise the mother jumped on his hand, hooting. Everyone was appalled by the episode and even more when the boy took the bird home with him on his shoulder. It must be a special gift to identify with the animals.

Paul and Eric, as good Frenchmen, followed in detail the news of French domestic politics and from Rome about the activities of the Catholic Church.

"I am going to tell you an interesting story that occurred between Pope Clement VII (1468-1534) and King Henry VIII of England, said Eric. Henry was married to Catherine of Aragon[69], Princess of Spain, daughter of the Spanish king Ferdinand of Aragon. She was the first wife of Henry VIII and ruled England from 1512 to 1514. As she did not give him a son, Henry asked Pope Clement VII for permission to divorce his wife, which was denied, as the Catholic religion prohibited separation. However, with the help of Thomas Cromwell (1485-1540)[70] and the Bishop of Canterbury, the divorce was permitted".

"As a result, the Pope excommunicated Henry, who proclaimed himself Supreme Head of the Church of England and founded the Anglican Church. Aided by his new chief minister, Thomas Cromwell, he dissolved the monasteries, increased the land of the Crown, definitively consolidating the absolutism of the monarchy by separating it from the Catholic Church. In 1533 he married Ana Boleyn, Catherine's bridesmaid, with whom he had only one daughter, Elizabeth I. The marriage lasted three years and, in 1536, Ana was accused of adultery and beheaded".

"Henry VIII married four more times, reaching a total of six. One of his wives, Anne Howard behaved in a manner considered inappropriate and the king ordered her decapitation. Based on these episodes of unparalleled barbarity, it can be said that Henry VIII, despite being considered "one of the most charismatic rulers to occupy the English throne," failed in terms of moral principles."

"The successor to Clement VII was Pope Paul III (1468-1549)[71] whose name before being named pope was Alessandro Farnese. When he was still a cardinal, he had four children with Silvia Ruffini, something strange and at odds with the celibacy law of the Catholic Church. In 1534, the year of his appointment as Pope, he was the first to establish the so-called counter-reform that consisted of his efforts against the advance of Protestantism".

"One of his most important acts for the population and certainly for Yjara and Mayara was a bull Paul III launched in favor of the freedom of the Indians of the Americas. In terms of art, during his pontificate, Michelangelo painted the "Judgment Day" on the altar of the Sistine Chapel, a work that began in 1535 and had been commissioned by his predecessor, Clement VII".

69[69]https://www.britannica.com/biography/Catherine-of-Aragon.
[70]https://www.britannica.com/biography/Thomas-Cromwell-earl-of-Essex-Baron-Cromwell-of-Okeham.
[71] Paul III | pope | Britannica.

"In 1537, Ignatius of Loyola, a man in love with the doctrines of the Catholic religion, founded the Society of Jesus, a religious order formed by members known as Jesuits who took vows of poverty and chastity and dedicated themselves entirely to the dissemination of the Catholic religion. Approved by Pope Paul III, the Order of the Jesuits had a significant role in the propagation of the Catholic Church in Brazil and other countries."

"But how did you manage to know so much? asked Mayara. It is incredible that someone has such a memory."

"Well, I'm seventy-four years old and you're thirty-nine. It is twice your age, which shows that I have accumulated much more experience than you, my dear. That's why I kept so much in my memory."

The boys stayed in France until mid-1538 when it became clear that they should return to England with their mothers to relieve the loneliness of those who stayed. Before embarking in Marseille, Piatã returned the bird to its young so that they would not run out of food, but the farewell was difficult for the boy. The sadness of the couples who stayed was even greater, as they ended up falling in love with the visitors.

The trip this time was dramatic. The ship was surprised by high waves in the Strait of Gibraltar. Panic took hold of travelers who experienced moments of terror. The waves of the Mediterranean rose more than four meters and washed the deck continuously. It was a terrible experience for everyone except for the boys who thought it was great. During the rest of the trip, Ybyajara decided to talk about the story told by Eric.

"Daddy, you told us that the Indians in our tribe were anthrophologists. I wanted to know what King Henry VIII did to Queen Anne Boleyn. Did he eat the queen after he cut off her head? Did he also eat another wife, that girl named Ana Howard? Is he not a Caeté Indian like us?" asked Ybyajara.

"Well, your idea is interesting, but first I want to say that the word is not anthrophologist, but anthropophagous. The other thing is that the king is not an Indigenous person, but he is certainly a bad man. Imagine if he comes here and cuts off my head. Don't you think that would be terrible?" asked Fabiano

"Do you think we have to eat people too? Are we born bad? I do not think we are, because Piatã did not eat the bird and became friends with him, so he is not bad, is he? And will my grandfather Tuxaua and mommy ever eat people?" pondered Ybyajara.

"My father never ate anyone although it was the custom of the Indians to eat their enemies after defeating them in the war. And I never ate anyone either because it is horrible. It turns out that the Indians learned this custom from their ancestors who were educated like that in the past," argued Yjara.

"I even think that, in a way, we can compare kings and popes to the Caeté Indians," intervened Florencio. Do you want to know why? Popes are the heads of the Catholic religion which teaches that God lives in heaven and that he created the world. King Henry VIII also believes it. However, there are people who do not accept any of this and for this reason are considered criminals and called heretics. They are arrested and, if they do not repent, they are tortured, hanged, burned alive or beheaded, because Catholic kings and popes hate those who do not accept their religion. But what do the Caetés worship?" asked Cauã.

"Caetés believe in a God called Thunder God and say that he created the world, just like the God of the Catholics. Whoever does not believe this is killed by the tribe. If you think about it, it is similar as Popes and kings punish those who do not believe in their God and Caetés punish those who do not believe in the Thunder God."

Back at Baltimore Estate, they decided to enroll the children in a British school before they could attend the Royal School. The idea was to find a college where there was not an excess of discrimination of foreign students or differences from most students, as was the case with the three little boys, mainly because they are not fluent in English.

They opted for a college that accepted candidates from other countries. Among them were Germans, Italians, French and Spanish, an excellent mix that would be ideal for children, as they would have contact with different languages. The three were looking forward to the start the classes scheduled for September 1540 and were still two months away. The school was called British Elementary School.

Already fully acclimatized in the new residence, Yjara and Mayara went back into the forest, this time accompanied closely by the four boys and by Angelica. In 1540, the four boys were nine years old. Yjara and Angelica were forty-five and Mayara forty-two. Everyone, without exception, had the energy needed for adventures in the woods. Fabiano and Florencio continued to dedicate to the Royal School and to import wines from France.

Fearing to venture too deep into the forest without knowing its dangers, the seven explorers decided to ask which animals normally inhabit that territory. Bartolomeu thought it convenient to go to Windsor Castle where there would certainly be someone who could provide this information. The guard at the entrance showed the way to the library, where they managed to find a book about the animals that inhabited the forests of England. They had to be studied as to their customs and their ferocity. The main ones were:

Animal	Features
Red Squirrel	Tame
Badger	Tame
Red Fox	Dangerous
Brown Frog -	Tame
Red Deer	Tame and scared
Mole	Tame and scared
Crow or Rook	Scared bird
Heron	Tame and scared
Otter	Tame and fearful
Boar	Dangerous
Poisonous Snake	Dangerous
Salmon	Fish

Bartolomeu examined the list of animals and concluded that only the boar, the fox, and the snake could be dangerous in the forest, but that the rest would not be of concern. To avoid stepping accidentally on a snake, he decided to buy tall boots for everyone. The two mothers, used to wild animals, made bows and arrows for any emergency, and took two hatchets to cut wood.

Bartolomeu, who was the most skilled, offered to build a tree house and a very tall and secure observation post against the most dangerous animals. Florencio and Fabiano were unable to collaborate due to their occupations at the Royal School.

It was necessary to find the proper woods to assemble the structure of the house as well as the necessary tools for the project. In less than a week the house was perfect, and both the children and the adults could fit in it. It was a success. After the work was finished, the boys asked to stay at the house the first night, which was denied, as it would be dangerous for the four to be alone without lighting.

The next day after breakfast, they ran into the forest, quickly climbed the house at the top of the tree and soon saw the first animals. It was a pair of foxes with cubs spotted from above the observation post. Cauã, Teodoro and Ybyajara did not want to go down because they were afraid of wild animals, but Piatã went down the rope and watched the animals. Realizing that they had no intention of moving away, Piatã approached the foxes and then sat down on the floor in front of the cubs. He held out his hands in their direction while the adult foxes carefully watched what was going on.

The puppies were beautiful. They came close and started to lick his hands as if they wanted to play. A fight broke out between the cubs, but Piatã grabbed them lightly and began to caress them. It was what they wanted, and they lay on their backs like dogs that want affection. Teodoro, Cauã, and Ybyajara were appalled by their cousin's courage to face four wild foxes. Slowly and still in fear, they decided to come down to see what could happen, when the fox couple approached the new participants of the adventure. The three imitated Piatã, extending their hands towards the animals and realized that they were tame.

At that moment, the boys' mothers appeared, which caused a certain commotion among the foxes who quickly went into the bush and disappeared. It was a general disappointment.

"Mother, said Piatã, you cannot imagine what happened. I managed to talk to the foxes, and they came to play with us. Now I do not know if they will be back, but we should wait a little. Maybe they will get used to you."

No sooner said than done. In just under ten minutes, they appeared and stood on the edge of the bush without moving. Yjara was delighted and sat on the floor, accompanied by Mayara and Angelica. As they realized that there would be no attack by humans, they started approaching the women with their characteristic sound. It was not a bark, but a cry, it seemed to be a friendly one. After this episode, the women took the initiative and started to pet the animals, which was accepted with pleasure.

"Mother, can we take the foxes to our home?" asked Cauã.

"If they want to, they can, but how are we going to feed them? We do not know what they eat, and they are hunting animals and at home we do not have anything like that, answered Mayara. But I think we could stay with them during the day and then they would go back to sleep in the forest, what do you think?"

The idea was unanimously approved by all, but the foxes needed to be convinced to accept the invitation to play at the Baltimore Estate. Piatã knew somehow that it would be easy. He turned his back to the foxes, pretended to walk away from the forest and started to leave. The foxes at once followed him closely.

"This boy really understands animals and will certainly be a master at it" added Angelica, laughing. Do you remember when he talked to the bird that ended up riding on his shoulder?"

Upon arriving for lunch, they received sad news sent by Cristiano from the winery, informing the death of Paul and Eric Demignon due to a strong flu outbreak that came from Spain in 1540. Paul died at the age of seventy-nine and Eric seventy-seven. Esmeralda and Clarinha also contracted the flu but managed to recover reasonably. Cristiano, aged sixty-eight, was not infected.

In September 1540, the boys were enrolled at the British Elementary School, eager to meet other students and learn the English language more quickly. They did not suspect, however, that their colleagues would certainly be surprised about the three boys coming from an unknown country, something never seen in England.

The four nine-year-old boys were enrolled in the same class. With about thirty students per class, they would certainly find a reasonable number of friends to mingle with. As for Teodoro, no one was surprised. However, right at the beginning, the students looked at the boys in a strange way, others showed their tongue and still others examined them from top to bottom as if they were animals. But as their mothers had warned, they did not mind and even found it funny. It was difficult to understand the English spoken by the teachers. They had to pay attention twice as much as the English classmates. At night, at home, they were able to express their opinions about what they learned during the day.

With the afternoon free, they returned to the forest to see if the foxes would appear. The search was useless until they heard a grunt that looked like someone was suffering. They ran to see what it was and saw the fox trapped with iron teeth squeezing his left leg. The poor animal looked at the three as if asking for help. They had to try to open the trap and free the unfortunate thing. Immediately the fox jumped on Piatã and licked him effusively as if he were thanking them for their favor. The final friendship with the foxes was finally celebrated.

"Who put this trap in the forest? asked Cauã. This is terrible and we must find the author. They ran home and found Mr. Jack, one of the employees who lived near the residence. He confessed that he himself had put the trap to catch wild boar, as it was his favorite meat."

"But Mr. Jack, said Ybyajara, the trap almost killed our fox, and we had a tough time setting it free. He is our friend, and he wants to live with us here in our garden. He has a fox wife and two small cubs."

"I will take care of them while you are at school, okay?"

"Tomorrow we will bring our friends for you to meet" replied Piatã.

The boys went to sleep in the tree house and sometimes Fabiano and Yjara, or Angelica and Bartolomeu spent the night with them. Happiness was general and any problems that could occur with the school students did not affect the three boys at all. Jack took care of the foxes during the day and took them back to the forest at night so they would not lose the habit of living on their own. They received names that they soon assimilated. The father was called Joe, the mother Daisy, the puppies Chris, and Mike.

At the beginning of 1541, Cristiano communicated by letter that unfortunately the two cousins died, partly due to the sorrow about the death of their husbands and partly due to lung problems and infection. Although they drank wine daily as a remedy for a better life, the drink did not prevent their death. Cristiano, already sixty-eight years old, was still strong and healthy, but he had to hire more people to manage the vineyard and to continue exporting.

It is important to update the family tree as of 1541. The tree of the Demignon family can be found in Chapters 31.

Vivone's Family Tree in 1541

Francesco Vivone (1201-1257) and Larissa Vivone (1201-1258)

    Rolando (1232-1310) and Giovanna (1234-1311)

      Alfredo (1273- 1338)

      Salvatore (1273- 1338)

    Sinibaldo (1232-1303) and Anabela (1236-1316)

      Alina (1274-1338)

      Bianca (1274-1338)

    Godofredo (1232-1312) and Matilda (1240-1313)

      Michele (1274-1338) and Robert Valois (1273-1338)

      Luigi (1295-1367) and Sigrid Andersen (1305-1369)

        Houston (1338- 1404) and Grace Baltimore (1346-1404)

          Anderson (1374-1448) and Samira Amal (1390-1461)

            Zachary (1416-1493) and Joaquina Querubim (1432-1510)

              Clarinha (1467-1541) and Paul Demignon (1461-1540)

              Esmeralda (1468-1541) and Eric Demignon (1463-1540)

            Gordon (1416-1488) and Margarida de Souza (1438-1510)

              Florêncio (1470   and Mayara (1498-

                Piatã (1531-

              Fabiano (1472   and Yjara (1495-

                Ybyajara (1531-

                Cauã (1531-

            Orson (1418-1488) and Manuela Dias (1434-1510)

              Bartolomeu (1470- e Angélica de Albuquerque (1495-

              Teodoro (1531-

            Cristiano (1472-

          Jefferson (1375-1448)

        Harold (1338-1404) and Audrey (1346-1404)

        Lilian (1376-1448) and Frederic (1390-1455)

          Emily (1377-1377)

Chapter 35

The family was happy in England and had no intention of traveling to Brazil. The boys' classmates were eager to meet the foxes and asked Teodoro to schedule a visit to the Baltimore Estate, which pleased the four immensely. Bartolomeu decided to organize a party for the whole class, to present the animals that had already been completely domesticated. The colleagues' first reaction was of fear. However, despite the crowd of children, the foxes played with everyone without any incident.

The subject was discussed by the students with their parents and teachers and Piatã became a hero among his colleagues. No one could understand how a child could tame animals that, in general, are ferocious.

In the following years, the school emphasized studies of arts such as painting, sculpture, architecture, and science. Piatã, who was one of the students most curious about learning, told the professor that he had heard of rebirth.

"Professor, I heard someone saying that we are now in the renaissance. Is it possible for someone to die and be born again? Who died and who was born again?"

"Your idea is interesting. In fact, rebirth means to be born again, but the word renaissance, in this case, does not refer to dying and being born. It means that Europe is going through a new phase, changing things that were in the past. I will explain it a little better. You know that we are in the year 1545. Before we were born, people were already in this world. To give you an idea of those who lived before us, I will start in the year 5000"

"I think you will be interested to learn which cities existed from the year 5000 BC onward[72]. Look at the table below where you can examine the years of settlement of each city:

---

[72]https://www.worldatlas.com/articles/the-oldest-cities-in-the-world.html.

Rank	City	Date of Settlement (BC, Approx.)	Country
1	Byblos	5000	Lebanon
2	Argos	5000	Greece
3	Aleppo	4300	Syria
4	Susa	4300	Iran
5	Sidon	4000	Lebanon
6	Athens	4000	Greece
7	Jerusalem	3900	Israel
8	Gaziantep	3650	Turkey
9	Plovdiv	3500	Bulgaria
10	Luxor	3200	Egypt
11	Jericho	3000	Palestine
12	Ray	3000	Iran
13	Beirut	3000	Lebanon
14	Tyre	2750	Lebanon
15	Kirkuk	2600	Iraq
16	Damascus	2500	Syria
17	Jenin	2450	Palestine
18	Homs	2300	Syria
19	Erbil	2300	Iraq
20	Jaffa	2000	Israel

After looking at the table, Piatã asked the professor about Rome and China and why they are not in the list.

"You are asking nice questions, my dear fellow. Rome and China are not listed because they were founded later. China came into existence about 1600 BC, and Rome was founded in 753 BC.

"Could you please explain what BC means?" asked Piatã

"That is a good question. BC means Before Christ. In other words, it shows the years before Jesus Christ was born, which is considered Year 1 of the Common Era[73]. All dates after year 1 were defined with the suffix A.D., meaning Anno Domini (Date of the Lord).

---

[73] Presently the dates are defined either as BCE meaning <u>Before the Common Era or Before Christian Era.</u> Example: Year 500 BCE meaning 500 years before Year 1. Alternatively, the dates after year 1 of the

Today, there are more countries, such as France, Portugal, Italy, Germany, England where we are now and Brazil, the place where our colleague Piatã and his two cousins came from."

"Let us get back to the Renaissance, said Professor Stephenson. In each of these countries were individuals who produced new things that did not exist before. Long ago they invented the bow and arrow that the ancients used in war and hunting, as the Indians in Brazil do. In the year 1440 or so, a German named Gutenberg invented a machine for making books. It is what they call a printer. Before him, people had to write everything by hand. For example, Ybyajara's mother told me that her ancestor named Francesco Vivone, an Italian who was born in Rome in 1200 A.D. authored a book called "Morality and Ethics". Do you know how long it took him to make five identical copies of the book? It took almost two years. Imagine if at that time he could have used Gutenberg's invention. One of Francesco Vivone's descendants managed to speak to him and asked him to print fifty copies of the book. Gutenberg printed the fifty books in one week. It was he who produced the first printed bible in the world. You can see how many inventions appeared in the past."

"But you haven't said what Renaissance is, Professor Stephenson," argued James, one of the students in the class who was increasingly interested in the subject."

"I will get there. As you have seen, all these peoples produced something new. However, before the Renaissance, in a period called the Middle Ages, painters, sculptors, architects, and scientists did wonderful things but some did not like their work referred as the "Age of Darkness." The Renaissance did not start overnight. It came from the 14th century (from the year 1301 to 1399) and the 15th (from 1401 to 1499) and today we are in the 16th century (which goes from 1501 to 1599). The current era is being called the Modern Age."

"In the Middle Ages, most arts were controlled by the Catholic Church[74] and all paintings, sculptures and literature were to deal mainly with religious matters. Over time, customs and arts changed and academics returned to studying the ancient civilizations of Greece and Rome. This modification of

---

Common Era are defined as CE. Example: Year 200 CE, meaning year 200 after year 1.

[74] https://www.britannica.com/topic/Roman-Catholicism/Roman-Catholicism-on-the-eve-of-the-Reformation.

thought was what was called the Renaissance[75], because "older" cultures were "reborn," and people became interested in the literature and art of past centuries. At the beginning of the 14th century, men began to increase their studies of the Latin language, which was understood only by the priests of the Catholic Church. Thus, the church lost control over the arts and literature. Everybody started looking for old forgotten manuscripts, made corrections, elaborated dictionaries, made translations, and studied Greek and Latin manuscripts. This all made them see the world through the eyes of the Greeks and Romans and no longer through the eyes of medieval monks. They became no longer afraid of the world like the priests and started to accept the beauties of what exists and recognized that having pleasures would not be considered a sin as established by the Catholic religion. As they considered the human being good in himself, the new intellectuals were called humanists and their studies were called humanism"[76].

"The Renaissance started in Italy and has continued until now. As you know, Italy is in the center of the Mediterranean Sea and has become a place of active trade between Europe and the countries to the east and this has had influence on the cultural spread between these nations. An interesting thing is that in Italy, wealthy families sponsored the arts, paying and teaching artists to produce works for them. One of those who financed artists were the Medici family."

"At the time of the Renaissance, renowned artists such as Michelangelo, Leonardo Da Vinci, Rafael, and Titian emerged, all famous Italians. The techniques also changed, as they started to make oil-based paintings, mixing powdered pigments with flax seeds. As this mixture took time to dry, they had more time to touch up their paintings. There was also progress in sculpture and architecture, with a form of drawing called perspective that showed buildings in three dimensions."

"We are in the middle of the Renaissance. It turns out that not all changes were peaceful. A few years ago, in 1527 Rome was attacked and practically destroyed in an attack called "The Sack of Rome"[77]. Before explaining the Sack

---

[75]https://www.britannica.com/event/Renaissance.
[76]https://www.britannica.com/topic/humanism.

[77]https://www.britannica.com/event/Sack-of-Rome-1527.

of Rome, it is important that you know the story of a German named Martin Luther born in 1483. Luther is a religious person who does not agree with a series of Catholic Church principles. Although he also believed in God like Catholics, he reformulated ideas of Christianity and ended up developing a new Christian religion called Protestantism that resulted in what is known as the Protestant Reform. He was against Catholic church traditions like banning priests from getting married. He also fought what was called Indulgences. An indulgence is a kind of forgiveness for the sins that people commit. So, to enrich the church, the Pope sold indulgences, which is a shame. Luther is totally against this custom of the Catholic Church."

"Pope Leo X (1475-1521)[78], accustomed to charging large sums of money for the indulgences condemned by Luther, issued a bull ordering Luther to retract himself. Otherwise, he would be excommunicated. Luther, indignant, tore the bull in front of the crowd and ended up being excommunicated in 1521. Leo X died shortly afterwards, in mysterious circumstances. His family name was Giovanni di Lorenzo di Medici, second son of Lorenzo de Médici, the Magnificent. His cousin, Giulio di Giuliano di Medici, would succeed him as Pope Clement VII (1523-34)".

"This new religion caused a division between Roman Catholicism and the new Protestant traditions called Lutheranism. Luther is one of the most influential figures in the history of Christianity, having even translated the Bible from Latin into German so that a greater number of believers could read the Bible and not just the few who knew Latin. Luther thinks that education should not be regulated by the church, but by the state. In addition, he believes that education should be mandatory for everyone with access to universities as well. His ideas had countless followers."

"Professor, my mother told me that there was a Frenchman named Calvin who also created a religion like Luther. Could you explain who he was?" asked Cauã.

"Very well remembered. He was called John Calvin (1509-1564)[79] and he had different ideas and was an innovator. He thought priests were unnecessary and

---

[78] https://www.britannica.com/biography/Leo-X.

[79] https://www.britannica.com/biography/John-Calvin.

criticized the cult of images and only admitted the sacraments of the Eucharist and Baptism and considered the Bible the basis of religion. He extolled the individual characteristics necessary for commercial practice and for this reason he pleased the bourgeois class. His ideas were soon accepted throughout Europe and reached Scotland, Holland, and Denmark. His followers were called Presbyterians. He created a doctrine called the Doctrine of Predestination which consisted of considering individuals as predestined, that is, those who would be saved by God. To find out who would be chosen as predestined, he said that only the successful people in life would have that right and everyone else would be excluded, an idea that favored the bourgeois class."

"Before we continue, I have to tell you one more thing about King Henry VIII. He had a wife named Catherine of Aragon who was unable to give him a son, which was important for the son to inherit the throne of England. Henry then asked the Pope to allow him to divorce Catherine, but the Pope did not grant his wish. Henry was furious about the Pope´s decision, so he proclaimed himself head of the English church and created the Anglican church of Protestant doctrine. Henry did not recognize the pope's authority and was therefore excommunicated by him. In revenge, the king confiscated all the assets of the church existing in England."

"What about the Sack of Rome, Professor? What happened in 1527? Two students asked at the same time."

"Take it easy, I'll get there, but it is important to know how and why there was the Sack of Rome."

"Before talking about the Sack of Rome[80], I must tell you a little bit about King Charles V (1500-1558), Holy Roman Emperor and King of Spain where he was called Charles I. Since half of the world belongs to Spain, he is a powerful king, owner of half the world[81]."

Charles is a fervent supporter of the Catholic Religion and he had enemies, including Martin Luther. He had to face four wars against France as well as countless revolts by the German princes who took advantage of the Lutheran

---

[80]https://www.britannica.com/event/Sack-of-Rome-1527.

[81]https://www.britannica.com/biography/Charles-V-Holy-Roman-emperor.

furor against the indulgences of the Pope. With all these wars he ran out of money to pay his army."

"Charles V's soldiers revolted for not receiving their wages and decided to plunder the city of Rome where defenses were weak and where they could obtain their money. The troops were mostly Lutherans, and on May 6, 1527, members of the Lutheran legions of Charles V's imperial army started an uprising and took the city by storm. The Sack of Rome was one of the bloodiest episodes of the Renaissance. Their fanaticism reached such a point that Lutheran soldiers named Luther "Pope of Rome.""

"Just to give you some examples of the carnage: they massacred all the sick people at the Holy Spirit Hospital. Rome's population was about 55,000 and the soldiers killed 36,000 with only 19,000 left. The palaces were destroyed by cannon fire, the soldiers played sport games with the heads of the apostles Saint John and Saint Andre. The Tiber River which passes through Rome was filled with dead bodies of children and nuns."

The students were horrified by the story told by Professor Stephenson. He took the opportunity to mention that there is a school at Baltimore Estate where students learn a completely different kind of behavior. This school, he said, is called "The Royal School of Moral Integrity" and is nearby. He also informed that at the end of the year, after graduation, interested students may enroll in the Royal School and learn the principles recommended by Francesco Vivone, an ancestor of Piatã, Cauã, Teodoro and Ybyajara.

Chapter 36

In November 1545 was the graduation at the British Elementary School. After this occasion, the four boys were enrolled in the Royal School, which they all gladly accepted. During the course, everyone was able to learn the various languages, especially Italian, French, and English. One of the subjects of the course of Moral Principles was the analysis of the behavior of Pope Leo X, relative to his habit to charge money to forgive sins committed by loyal believers, called indulgencies. The entire class concluded that never a man in his position who used indulgences to take money from the faithful could be considered virtuous. They also found that Luther's criticism of this practice was perfectly justified.

Following the graduation in 1547, it can be said that all members of the Vivone family attended the Royal School and were able to develop and apply the notions about the moral principles which they learned.

"Considering that a large part of our family is made up of descendants of Indians, less Teodoro and Angelica, I think we could try to disseminate the principles of the Royal School in Brazil, proposed Yjara. We were privileged to learn new languages and new customs and to live with people of other nationalities. We are a lucky family and due to the efficiency of our ancestors, we have enough resources to live a wonderful life. Our children are educated, and I am proud to belong to the Vivone family, but despite this feeling, I miss my past and my relatives who stayed in Brazil."

"I also miss the time we spent there. Let us look at our ages, which is extremely important. Bartolomeu is seventy-five years old, and I am fifty. Cristiano is in France and is seventy-three. Florencio is seventy-five years old, and Mayara is forty-seven. The four young ones are sixteen, a wonderful age. They were the youngest to pass the Royal School and can be considered almost adults with everything they learned."

"Wait a minute. I have doubts, said Mayara. First, I consider the ages of our husbands and Cristiano to be quite high, although they do not currently have any health problems. Secondly, how would the work of Cristiano in France and Bartolomeu, Florencio and Fabiano be here in England? Would it be impossible to leave everything in the hands of employees? Third, who would run the Royal School and Baltimore Estate? Fourth, the effort that such a trip would require from older people, due to the distance and the lack of comfort. It is dangerous to face these risks. And you are forgetting our residence in Portugal. In what conditions will we find it? Anyway, I would like to have your opinion and hear from our husbands about all this."

"Your doubts are extremely valid, said Angelica. How are we going to get out of this impasse?"

"I think it's time to call our dear husbands, as they may have different ideas than ours or even better," said Mayara.

"What are you talking about? asked Florencio during the dinner at which everyone but Cristiano was present."

"We are at a crossroad, explained Mayara. We would like to spend time in Brazil, but we have doubts about the three men in the family. I know that nobody is too sick or too old to travel, but an expedition like this would have some disadvantages that I tried to point out."

After clarifying the husbands on the matter, Florencio took the floor and gave his opinion.

"Although we have enough resources to live a comfortable life, the men in the family have obligations that cannot be ignored, and everyone knows what they are. I do not think we could be absent for as long as the trip will certainly last. However, since we have not been in Lisbon for a long time, one of us should see how our house is doing. But it would be a short trip. Furthermore, despite our perfect health, we must recognize that we are no longer as young as you and our age only tends to increase. Anyway, I would propose that you undertake this trip without our company because I am sure that we will be here on your return. In fact, I noticed that Fabiano nodded with his approval, and I know that Cristiano would also agree. So, I would leave it to our excellent wives and our "adult" children.

Ybyajara was most interested in history and stood out among the students at the Royal School being praised by teachers. He asked to offer his considerations.

"I think we should, initially, find out what is happening here in England. Today we are at the beginning of 1548, and you know that our king Henry VIII died last year, and his son Edward VI (1537-1553) took the throne at the age of nine[82]. He is being tutored by Edward Seymour, 1st Duke of Somerset and is the first English king raised as a Protestant. Because he is still a child, it is not known what he will do when he comes of age. Regarding the intended trip, due to the information we received from Uncle Aloisio, a trip to Brazil was scheduled for 1549 by a Portuguese called Tomé de Souza. Do you know who he is?"

"As far as I could learn, Tomé de Souza (1503-1579) was born in Portugal in a county called Rates, said Ybyajara. Souza is a nobleman and soldier who was appointed the first Governor-general of the Portuguese colony of Brazil. The king ordered him to fight the indigenous rebels and defend the Brazilian coast. He will take with him about a thousand men[83]. I heard that King Dom John III wants him to build a fortress in a village destroyed by Indians and plundered by the French and transform the territory covered by all captaincies into an organized and profitable structure at the service of Portugal."

"I think we should go to Lisbon to ask our uncle to contact King Dom John III and ask him to allow us to board one of the ships of Tomé de Souza. We do not know if he will stop at Itamaracá, but it does not hurt to try. What do you think?"

"I think is wrong, Cauã argued. We are sixteen years old and, although we took the course at the Royal School, we are not trained in anything. Such a trip to Brazil would be a kind of vacation and we are not able to waste time. For example, I would like to be a lawyer as all citizens need the services of those who know the laws. I would be happy if I could take a law course at Oxford University, Cambridge, or Paris. Oxford was founded in 1096, Paris in 1170 and Cambridge in 1209. I know they would all be excellent."

"I would also like to have a profession, said Ybyajara. I know that two of our ancestors contributed to build a chapel at Windsor Castle and their names are

[82]https://www.britannica.com/biography/Edward-VI.
[83]https://www.britannica.com/biography/Tome-de-Sousa

on a sign in the castle. Imagine if I could be an engineer like them, I could build houses, bridges, and other works."

"And I, said Teodoro, could be like my uncle Aloisio who travels all over the world. I could study foreign trade and work with Uncle Cristiano who is in Marseille, selling our wines. My father does the same thing, and I would like to follow his profession."

Mayara overheard the whole conversation and was excited about the boys' maturity. She asked Piatã what he would like to do.

"Mom, I always liked animals and I know that they like me. But I think I should be a doctor, so I can help people to stay healthy and treat sick animals. But then I would have to take two courses, medicine and veterinary. I think that would be possible despite the effort contained in this decision."

Angelica, Mayara and Yjara looked at each other and realized how the boys were right. They decided to stay in England and give their husbands full support while the four teenagers were at university. If the heads of the family agreed, the next step would be a visit to Oxford to see the conditions and possibilities for enrollment.

Fabiano, Florencio and Bartolomeu were amazed at the prospect of seeing their children at a university the size of Oxford and prepared to accompany the boys to the university. The whole family was immediately opposed in view of the ages of the three. It was Yjara's turn to give her opinion.

"I think that the four should travel to Oxford without our interference. They are just as responsible as most boys of that age and would be welcomed to the university like any other candidate. The Course Certificate at the Royal School will certainly be a positive factor for them to be accepted. We women must stay with our husbands and help them in whatever way possible. At the age of sixteen, their personality is forming and the less influence we exert on them the better. As classes start in September, they will have time before the trip, as they should arrive in Oxford at least two months before the start."

In order not to have any problems with the enrollment deadlines, they left for Oxford in June 1548. They went directly to the university and found out what are the necessary requirements to be able to attend the various courses. Upon arriving at the admissions office, they were informed that only students over the age of seventeen could be accepted. It was a general disappointment, and they had no choice but to return to Baltimore Estate.

"And now, what are we going to do? asked Cauã. Our birthdays are in June and enrollment ends in August, so we would have to spend that next year at home and study at the Windsor Castle Library, if allowed. Let us talk to the family and decide together, or we could spend the eleven months in Brazil and get back in time. We are now in June 1548, so we would have to be back by May 1549 at the latest".

"Great idea, Cauã, Teodoro rejoiced. We have to talk to our parents and, if they agree, we will put our previous plan into action."

Everything is easy for the boys. Plans get out of your brain in minutes and decisions are made even faster. The main "problems" would be the following:

1-Arrive in Portugal as fast as possible.

2-Find Uncle Aloisio.

3-Get a license from Tomé de Souza to join his expedition.

4-Schedule the return for May 1549.

At dinner, the parents noticed the excitement of the boys and Bartolomeu asked what it was about. They soon explained the plan and asked for permission to travel to Portugal to find their uncle and try to get a place in one of Tomé de Souza's caravels.

"I would love to accompany you, said Bartolomeu. However, as much as I love a program like this, I could not keep up with you, because I have a severe joint pain and I can barely walk. Florencio and Fabiano are taking care of the school and our wives are helping us with everything. I feel that travelling alone is dangerous, because you are not counting on unforeseen events, especially on a long trip like this. The only way to make this dream come true would be to convince Uncle Aloisio to join you."

"Dad, I agree with everything you said, argued Cauã. I know it would be painful for you. To locate Uncle Aloisio, it is faster to travel directly to Lisbon instead of writing to him because a letter would take twice as long and being there, we would have more chances to organize things don't you think?"

"Your idea has its logic but are you really willing to face whatever happens?" pondered Bartolomeu.

"There are four of us and we will always be together, defending each other. And we know how to speak English, Portuguese, Italian, French and Tupi. We know a little German, but not enough. Anyway, we can have a good relationship with anyone. In addition, at the Royal School we had wrestling lessons and we are strong enough to face any danger," said Ybyajara.

"If I were you, I would already be packing, said Fabiano. If our dear wives agree, we will find a way for you to embark in Southampton on the first ship to Lisbon."

Chapter 37

The Vivone family is really a lucky family. Anchored in the port, was the freighter of the Portuguese friends of the French-Portuguese International Trade Company, preparing to raise anchor for Portugal. It was with immense joy that their commander received the boys, but he informed them that they would have to work on deck with the members of the crew. It was beautiful news, as it was what the four teenagers wanted to spend time with.

The work during the trip to Portugal was strenuous for the boys with the great advantage that they became strong and capable of facing any challenge. In Lisbon they returned to the family's residence, which was in good condition, thanks to the care exercised by Aloisio.

In July 1548, Aloisio, a high official during the reign of Dom John III, had been summoned again to oversee the expedition, as he did on the trip where Florencio participated. By chance, Aloisio was a friend of Tomé de Souza (Governor general of Brazil), and it was not difficult to convince him to take the boys. Aloisio pointed out that the four speak five languages and could be useful in contacts with French pirates. At the same time, they would have the advantage of speaking to the natives without any problem.

While preparing for the great adventure, Aloisio got a place for the boys as language teachers in the palace of Dom John III. At the Royal School, they participated in various teaching classes and acquired the necessary experience. They were so successful to the point that Dom John III asked them to teach him words in Tupi. Of course, the women were curious about the three young descendants of Brazilian Indians and wondered how they were proficient in foreign languages. The children of the nobles wanted to participate in their classes. As for Teodoro, the girls were totally amazed by his physical beauty. The number of students was unexpected. The only problem they had was "resisting" the girls' harassment. The commotion was so great that they considered themselves fortunate to be able to enjoy so much success. The four were invited to all the palace's social events and aroused the envy of the Portuguese teenagers.

It did not take long for each of the four to find a girlfriend. However, they agreed with each other that even a more serious commitment to girls could not pass through their minds. They understood that it would be essential to strictly follow the plan of the trip to Brazil without any emotional interference. They also decided to inform each of the candidates that they should not expect any permanent engagement. Such an attitude was in accordance with the moral principles that they all espoused during the course at the Royal School.

While waiting for the departure date, scheduled by Tomé de Souza for February 1, 1549, they had time to study the duties that the Governor-general of Brazil would have when disembarking in Brazil[84]. It was important to know the conditions to become governor general. He must belong to the nobility and will have under his responsibility all matters related to the administration, with the obligation to render accounts to Portugal. Tomé de Souza received the instruction to promote the Portuguese settlement of all Brazilian lands and to disseminate the Catholic religion. He will have to notify the captains and governors of his arrival, asking for help with the installation of a government office in Salvador, Bahia and to find a suitable place for the construction of a fortress.

As for colonization he will distribute properties (called "sesmarias" in Portuguese) to anyone who requests them, with the payment of a tithing to the Order of Christ. The governor will be responsible for developing profitable economic production, especially the cultivation of sugar cane. He had the authority of providing land for the construction of sugar mills for those who have the resources to build them. Another obligation contained in the 1548 by-laws is the relationship with the local population. The Governor-general must preserve peace and punish people who cause conflict and promote wars. All Christian relation with natives in their villages would have to be authorized by the Governor-general. He would also determine a specific day for holding fairs for the trade with the natives, except for the supply of weapons.

To facilitate the conversion to Catholicism, the by-laws specify that Indigenous people must live close to towns and villages. As for military and defense administration, the Governor-general can authorize the construction

---

[84] https://www.britannica.com/biography/Tome-de-Sousa.

of ships and is vested with the power to provide arms to captains and governors also making them responsible to report the proximity of corsairs around the captaincies.

The great moment of departure came on February 1, 1549. The girlfriends insisted until exhaustion to accompany the four to Brazil. According to the agreement, all the cries were solemnly ignored. Tomé de Souza placed them on the deck with the crew members who forced them to do double shifts, as they saw their presence as an intrusion of daddy's little children.

During the crossing, however, the sailors found that this was not the case, as they worked happily, without any complaints, and noticed them speaking an incomprehensible language. The question that had no answer was "where did these guys come from?" The chief of the crew, one of Tomé de Souza's favorites, called them aside.

"Oh, boys, you are speaking a language that is not understood here. Only one of you looks like a normal man like us, but the other three are completely different. What country were you born in?" asked Captain Henriques.

"Captain, respectfully, I have to inform you that we are the children of Brazilian mothers, both descendants of Caeté Indians, a tribe that lives on the Island of Itamaracá where our fathers met and got married, replied Cauã. The language we speak is called Tupi, spoken by the entire country. Our relatives live in England and France, and we studied at a school called Royal School of Moral Integrity where we learned English, Portuguese, Italian and French. We are going to Brazil thanks to the generosity of Commander Tomé de Souza to whom we are immensely grateful for providing us with this opportunity. My name is Cauã, and my brother is called Ybyajara. Our cousins are called Piatã and Teodoro. The latter is the nephew of Aloisio de Albuquerque, who is also present on this trip."

"What a beautiful surprise, young man. Aloisio was my contemporary at Junqueira Braga Gymnasium where we studied together, subjects related to navigation, such as astronomy, cartography, and mathematics. I wonder if you know that Aloisio was one of the most brilliant mathematicians of our time. I was happy to know that he did not make any pressure to give you privileges on this trip, which underscores once again the very correct character of your uncle."

After an hour, the captain met the boys again.

"Dear Cauã, if I understood your name, I am curious to learn a little of the Tupi language, given that soon we will have more frequent contact with your people. As we still have almost two months of travel left, we could use your presence to practice that language and French, as we will certainly have problems with the invaders of the Brazilian lands. Would this be possible?"

"It would be an honor for us. I can even add that we can teach both languages simultaneously, that is, instead of teaching only Tupi, we would do the translation into French and give the meaning in Portuguese. Would that be satisfactory?" asked Ybyajara.

"Magnificent. As I am sure you are hungry, I invite you to accompany me to the cafeteria."

With a roguish smile, all four of them jumped off the deck and were happy to be able to put into practice the teachings received at the Royal School and transmit the languages to the Portuguese adventurers.

Captain Henriques programmed the instruction very intelligently. He invited twenty of his most trusted men, defined five for each "teacher." It was almost three hours a day and the classes became a real fun and a form of relaxation for the navigators. The subjects and words of the new language were accompanied by loud laughter, due to the difficulty of pronunciation, for both Tupi and French. Tomé de Souza sometimes participated in the recreation. The result was such that the "pupils" became confident that the Indians and the French would understand them.

Chapter 38

The ship "Salvador" of Tomé de Souza docked at Bay of All Saints ("Baía de Todos os Santos") on March 29, 1549, after two months of a peaceful voyage. Upon arriving, he found that the natives had destroyed the village where a fortress would be built. At the same time, the place had been ransacked by the French who stole large shipments of brazilwood. Therefore, the scenario was bleak with scattered settlers, mutinous Indigenous people, French smugglers, and inept administrators.

In the captaincy of Bahia, court officials estimated that there were five to six thousand Tupinambá warriors, versus only one hundred colonists. The difficulties were such that it was time to take effective possession of Brazil and make it yield to Portugal. Fortunately, Tomé de Souza brought with him a thousand men. To fulfill its mission, the armada brought together three ships, two caravels, a brigantine and two other commercial ships, which should return full of brazilwood. It was a total of approximately five hundred to a thousand people, formed by 130 soldiers, ninety sailors, seventy professionals (carpenters, blacksmiths, woodworkers, and other professionals), civil servants, Jesuits commanded by Manuel da Nóbrega, five hundred exiles and other workers for heavy tasks.

Aware of these problems, the four boys were willing to assist the officers of Tomé de Souza, in their contact with the natives. Tomé de Souza started by founding the city of Salvador on March 29, 1549, which would be the first capital of Brazil.

The lack of Portuguese control over the Brazilian colony was so great that, in 1548, Luiz de Gois, brother of Pero de Gois, donor of the captaincy of San Tomé, asked King Dom João III for help: "If, with time and brevity, Your Highness does not help these captaincies and the coast of Brazil, even if we lose lives and farms, Your Highness will lose the land", he wrote.

"I am finding it strange that Commander Souza was received with such sympathy if it is known that the Indians were angry, Piatã asked Captain Henriques."

"What I learned was that a Portuguese man named Diogo Alvares Correia, a teenager was shipwrecked on the coast of Bahia around 1510. He became a friend of the Tupinambá Indians and ended up marrying an Indian woman called Paraguaçú, daughter of chief Taparica. I know he was called Caramurú by the tribe and, imagine, he celebrated the wedding with Paraguaçú in France where she was baptized Catarina Alvares Paraguaçú, before returning to Brazil. They say that Caramurú was a noble person of the Royal House of Portugal. His companions were killed by the Tupinambá Indians but he managed to survive and started to live among them. The Caramurú name means "moray eel," a dangerous electric fish living among the rocks, and this nickname was given because he was found in the sea between the rocks. Others consider him a smuggler who could have come with the French in search of brazilwood. However, he was helpful in mediating between the Indians and the Portuguese and that is why Tomé was received so well when he arrived. I also learned that Paraguaçú, in 1530, organized the construction of a church, the first in the city. In that church Manuel da Nóbrega said the first mass of Salvador, in 1549. In fact, it is worth noting that Salvador was declared the capital of Brazil."

"Right after the arrival, Tomé de Souza located a hill that fell vertically on the beach. It was the highest point in the region, a perfect natural defense, with water sources and a river flowing in the opposite direction of the sea. This point is seventy-five yards high and ideal for the public administration buildings and the villas, while the warehouses, the Treasury, and the gunpowder storage would remain close to the shore. Starting in April 1549 Manuel da Nóbrega dedicated himself to the catechesis of the Indigenous people. Aided by Caramurú, Tomé de Souza summoned the natives to work in the construction of buildings as there was a shortage of Portuguese labor. The Governor was the first to roll up his sleeves and carry rafters and timbers for the construction of houses."

"I think that, due to the way Tomé de Souza fulfilled his duties throughout the journey from Portugal to Brazil and then in Bahia itself, he can be considered a serious and honest lieder, Cauã argued. Logically, a Governor-general had to deal, at times, with crimes committed by exiles and with problems such as the absence of Portuguese women, which increased the miscegenation between the colonizers and the Indigenous population."

The whole situation was duly observed by the four boys who felt perfectly at ease, as they had no problem communicating with anyone. They slept in the soldiers' quarters, located next to the Jesuits. Manuel da Nóbrega noticed the intention to collaborate with the Portuguese who decided to entrust them with a very risky mission. He asked them to visit the chief of the Tupinambá Indians, named Taparica, who lives about three miles into the forest to take gifts brought by Tomé de Souza. Nóbrega knew of their proficiency with the language and was sure that they would be successful.

"Please get in touch with Catarina Paraguaçú, Caramurú's wife, so she can show you the shortest way to get to the village, advised Nóbrega."

The following day they left towards the village. In the middle of the journey, they observed a flock of blue macaws that landed on nearby trees and watched the four with curiosity. It did not take long for Piatã to rehearse a contact with them. He adopted the same tactic used with the bird that ended up on his shoulder.

"Piatã, would you be able to catch one of these beautiful birds?" asked Cauã.

"We are going to try to be quiet and sit on the floor as if we haven't seen them. They will not be afraid of us. All of our movements have to be slow and natural, explained Piatã."

In a brief time, eight more macaws appeared and started yelling and jumping around the branches. It looked like they were starting a fight. One of them went down and stood looking aside as parrots and parakeets usually do. The four observers, without any movement, began to hope for the bird to make an approach. At that moment, Piatã extended his hand towards the macaw and stared into his eyes. The macaw shook its head in both directions and went down a little more, while Piatã was fascinated by the bird's beauty.

One of Manuel da Nóbrega's gifts was a package of cookies, Piatã slowly opened the package and broke one of them and placed it in his outstretched hand. At that moment, another commotion of the macaws started, while the bravest one descended to the ground. Piatã quietly lay on his back and pretended to be asleep. The others imitated him with extreme care.

This scene took almost thirty minutes. The silence was now complete. But the macaw continued to approach Piatã and suddenly pecked at the wafer and ate quietly beside him. With his right hand and without a sudden movement, Piatã removed a larger piece of biscuit and placed it in his left hand, where the macaw simply climbed on to it and ate the snack without moving back. After repeating the procedure three more times, Piatã placed his hand lightly on the macaw's closed wings. It was a fantastic and unopposed scene. Piatã's extraordinary ability with animals was confirmed once again. After another half hour, the macaw was sitting on his shoulder eating cookies.

"We have to go. Leave the bird there, otherwise we will arrive at the village late"

"Don't worry, I'll take him with me and introduce him to Chief Taparica, joked Piatã."

With all this excitement, the four boys did not notice that for more than an hour they were being watched by Tupinambá natives. Suddenly, they started talking at the same time. Teodoro, who seemed different from the other three, explained in a fluent Tupi that they were heading to the village to take gifts to Chief Taparica. Amazed at how easily Teodoro spoke their language, they already considered him part of the tribe and pulled the four by the arms. They pointed at Piatã with the macaw on their shoulders and burst out laughing. The ice between them was broken.

Taparica was sitting on the floor surrounded by children who ran out to see the macaw "tamer." When he noticed the approach of strangers, he also started asking questions in Tupi, quickly answered by Ybyajara. He received the gifts with joy and asked his subordinates to fetch four sets of bows and arrows and four fishing harpoons and reciprocated Manuel da Nóbrega's offer. Then he invited them to stay in the village to get to know his "kingdom." Cauã thanked him for the invitation and promised that he would return, as he would have to inform the Jesuit that the delivery had been made successfully. He would accept the invitation and remain in the village for a while.

Manuel da Nóbrega smiled when he saw the four boys returning from their assignment and was amazed at the bird Piatã had on his shoulder. The soldiers tried to approach the macaw, but they only received jealous pecks. The bird only accepted affection from his four friends.

Uncle Aloisio, strategically, remained distant, but could not refrain from congratulating them on their success in the mission with chief Taparica. He warned them, however, that his contacts would be minimal, as the job required total dedication and independence.

One of the problems of a certain gravity faced by Tomé de Souza was the absence of female representatives, especially of European nationality. It was assumed that the military and all other males would have their sexual needs unmet. Thus, it was no surprise that men were chasing women who were kidnapped and kept as concubines. The situation became so chaotic that Father Manuel da Nóbrega, asked King John III to send Portuguese women to Brazil. Without understanding the seriousness of the case, he sent only six orphans and instructed the governor to arrange husbands for them. The small number of women did not prevent a considerable miscegenation between Indians and Portuguese.

For the boys, however, the initiation of their sex life was a wonderful experience due to the attraction of the women of the tribe toward the four young men. Teodoro, however, was the absolute champion. It looked like a swarm of bees around the handsome boy.

This life continued for two years. They made friends with the Jesuits and the soldiers and earned respect for their extreme dedication and obedience. During this period, Tomé de Souza, despite being eager to return to Portugal, worked incessantly. The Governor ordered the construction of fortresses at important and strategic points along the coast for protection against foreign invasions. Manuel da Nóbrega led the process of evangelization who participated in the creation of the first bishopric in 1551. He also developed agriculture and livestock to stimulate the colonization of the Brazilian territory.

It can be said, without any doubt, that Tomé de Souza, named Patron of the Colonization of Brazil after the discovery and responsible for laying the foundations of Portuguese America and the pillars of a city with incredible political and cultural personality.

Chapter 39

In 1552, Tomé de Souza asked King John III to authorize his return to Portugal. Although he was exhausted, there were still missions to be accomplished. Accompanied by Manuel da Nóbrega, he had to travel the coast to inspect the southern captaincies and provide them with the necessary artillery for defense.

Finally, the king appointed a new governor-general to replace him. It was Duarte da Costa who arrived in Brazil in July 1553. Father José de Anchieta accompanied Duarte da Costa[85]a Jesuit born in 1534 in Tenerife in the Canary Islands, Spain. In 1551, he joined the Society of Jesus in Portugal and 1553, embarked to Brazil with the delegation of the new Governor-general. He came to Brazil to catechize the Native Americans, along with Manuel da Nóbrega.

The four boys with all the extraordinary experience gained during their stay in Brazil, returned with Tomé de Souza to Portugal. With them was Uncle Aloisio. After that long absence, they were anxious to enjoy their residence in Lisbon where they found a letter sent from England. The news was sad.

It reported the death of Cristiano in Marseille in 1553. He was old and, despite his good health, he did not resist an ischemia that occurred during a walk through the winery. Upon learning of the incident, Bartolomeu and Angelica left for France hoping that they would still see him alive, but they arrived late. He was buried on the farm by employees who continued his work. Cristiano´s, business savvy was important for the family, as he managed to convince his friend and owner of the Bordeaux winery to make an offer for the Marseille farm. The amount was presented to Bartolomeu and the cousins who immediately approved the excellent offer. Prior to his death, Cristiano accepted a proposition of his friends from the French-Portuguese Company of International Trade who wished to acquire Francesco Vivone World Exports. He provided all the necessary documentation for the sale of the two companies and was able to send money to England. With this step, the family got rid of an unnecessary burden in terms of costs and labor.

---

[85]https://www.britannica.com/biography/Jose-de-Anchieta.

They also received correspondence from their mothers, concerned about the long absence of their four children and telling them that their three husbands had symptoms typical of the age and had no more resistance to face their daily obligations. Fortunately, with the sale of the winery, Bartolomeu was released from the administration of exports and Fabiano and Florencio delegated their obligations to ex-students of the Royal School.

"Uncle Aloisio, we have to go back to England to enroll at the University of Oxford and we would like to invite you to come with us. You still do not know the Baltimore Estate," asked Teodoro.

"I've been thinking about it seriously, and I would love to visit the property. I will get the tickets to Southampton right away."

The arrival of the five in England was triumphant after their long absence. The mothers were so happy that they all spoke at the same time to hear the news. The foxes were living inside the property and had more cubs that soon became friends with the four explorers. Aloisio reported all the episodes that had occurred in the last five years and praised the boys' performance.

Oxford University accepted the boys, each one in a different specialty. Piatã in Medicine, Cauã in Law, Teodoro in Engineering and Ybyajara in Mathematics and Astronomy. This would demand a total dedication to the university for a period of six years, between 1554 and 1560.

The three wives, feeling that their husbands needed constant medical care, decided to place them in a nursing home located near the Baltimore Estate, while Aloisio returned to Portugal for his position as Inspector General of Portuguese Navigation.

During his trip to Brazil, Aloisio wrote to the family telling the latest news from Brazil. The most recent were about the problems faced with French invasions.

In 1559, the northeast coast of Brazil was being violently disputed between Portugal and France. On the one hand, according to the Treaty of Tordesillas, Portugal and Spain divided the world. France never accepted this kind of sharing that had been blessed by the Pope.

It was in that year that the graduation of the four Vivone took place, each one in its specialty. On the day of the celebration, their proud mothers attended, especially since Teodoro was chosen as a speaker for the group. His speech represented one of the most important stages of the Vivone family and would have been a source of pride for Francesco, his ancestor and founder.

"I was honored by the professors to present as a speaker for the graduating class of the year 1560, my feeling of gratitude to the University of Oxford, to the professors and, especially to our colleagues, started Teodoro. Our family, composed here by my three cousins and by myself, can be considered privileged, not only because we were admitted to this wonderful university, but because of the experience we were able to acquire together in our youth. Destiny wanted us to have the benefit of knowing a new country discovered in the year 1500, Brazil, where my aunts were born. Consequently, we managed to learn their customs similarly to what we were able to assimilate in France and Portugal, the land where my mother was born. Fortunately, our permanence allowed us to learn a total of five languages, notably English, French, Portuguese, Italian and Tupi, the language of the Brazilian Indians."

"We also had the honor of attending, before Oxford University, the course taught for two years at the Royal School of Moral Integrity, a school located near Windsor Castle where we learned that only through an extremely high degree of moral integrity is it possible to cross all the paths of the future that awaits us. Today's date consolidates for any student the dream of receiving the culture to be transmitted to his loved ones."

"The contact with our colleagues who are graduating today was indescribable in terms of fraternity and exchange of experiences. I am sure that they would all be much better speakers than I am and that is why I consider myself happy to be able to represent them at this moment."

"We are fortunate to live in England where culture is zealously distributed by the best university professors who dedicate their efforts and friendship to students. We spent the best years of our life that will remain in our memory forever. I congratulate you all and offer my sincere thanks for the privilege to join you in our road to the future."

Every year, the University of Oxford fixes a list of companies on the news panel wishing to hire recent graduates. At the same time, entrepreneurs are looking for personal contacts with alumni for initial candidate interviews. The salaries offered are, in fact, the highest in England, due to the prominent level of university education of its students.

The four boys were the most requested. At the age of twenty-nine, they had a promising future. After a week of negotiations, the group was hired, each for a different entity. Among them was a London government entity dedicated to the study of Astronomy and Advanced Mathematics that signed a contract with Ybyajara, a brilliant student in these two subjects. The entity was named British Research Institute for Astronomy and Advanced Mathematics.

Piatã was disputed by the University of Southampton to assume the position of assistant of the Department of Surgery. At the University they learned of his special talent in his operations and diagnostics. Cauã went to the Ministry of Justice of Queen Elizabeth I (1533-1603), daughter of Henrique VIII and Anne Boleyn, to analyze all the processes related to tributes of the nobility and the population in general. Teodoro was hired as an engineering assistant to take care of the reforms at Windsor Castle under the reign of Elizabeth I.

As the workplaces of the four were close to the Baltimore Estate, it would be possible to assist their mothers in managing the property and take care of their parents, who were in the nursing home.

Before starting their respective jobs, they decided to communicate the good news to their parents and were preparing to do it the following Sunday when they received a terrifying news. One of the old people of the asylum, permanently depressed by the constant deterioration of his health, caused a fire in the asylum that quickly reached great proportions and spread with an uncontrollable speed. Everyone was asleep when the flames spread and had no chance of escaping the fire, mainly because they no longer moved without the help of nurses. When help arrived, the building was in ruins and there were no survivors.

It is impossible to imagine the desperation of the four boys and their mothers on hearing the news. It would be impossible to think that an accident of this nature could claim three lives of men so dedicated to work and family. Bartolomeu, Florencio and Fabiano were known as people of unmistakable moral rectitude and who showed everyone what it is to have absolute honesty as principles.

The burial of what was left of the three deceased was held at the Baltimore Estate in the presence of a crowd of Royal School alumni. Angelica, bursting into tears, managed to thank everyone for their solidarity. The children and the wives left a tribute on the headstone for posterity that said:

IN LOVING MEMORY OF BARTOLOMEU, FABIANO AND FLORENCIO VIVONE.

Yjara, Angelica, Mayara, Piatã, Ybyajara, Cauã, and Teodoro Vivone

December 1560

Chapter 40

Below is the updated family tree with the latest developments as of 1560.

<u>Vivone's Family Tree in 1560</u>

Francesco Vivone (1201-1257) and Larissa Vivone (1201-1258)

    Rolando (1232-1310) and Giovanna (1234-1311)

      Alfredo (1273- 1338)

      Salvatore (1273- 1338)

    Sinibaldo (1232-1303) and Anabela (1236-1316)

      Alina (1274-1338)

      Bianca (1274-1338)

    Godofredo (1232-1312) and Matilda (1240-1313)

      Michele (1274-1338) and Robert Valois (1273-1338)

      Luigi (1295-1367) and Sigrid Andersen (1305-1369)

        Houston (1338- 1404) and Grace Baltimore (1346-1404)

          Anderson (1374-1448) and Samira Amal (1390-1461)

            Zachary (1416-1493) and Joaquina Querubim (1432-1510)

              Clarinha (1467-1541) and Paul Demignon (1461-1540)

              Esmeralda (1468-1541) and Eric Demignon (1463-1540)

            Gordon (1416-1488) and Margarida de Souza (1438-1510)

              Florêncio (1470-1560)   and Mayara (1498-

                Piatã (1531-

              Fabiano (1472-1560)   and Yjara (1495-

                Ybyajara (1531-

                Cauã (1531-

            Orson (1418-1488) and Manuela Dias (1434-1510)

              Bartolomeu (1470-1560) and   Angélica de Albuquerque (1495-

                Teodoro (1531-

              Cristiano (1472-1553)

          Jefferson (1375-1448)

        Harold (1338-1404) and Audrey (1346-1404)

          Lilian (1376-1448) and Frederic (1390-1455)

          Emily (1377-1377)

<u>Demignon's Family Tree in 1560</u>

Claude (1430-1503) and Gabrielle (1434-1504)

  Paul (1461-1540) and Clarinha Vivone (1467-1541)

Jean Pierre (1433-1505) and Jeanette (1436-1497

  Eric (1463-1540) and Esmeralda Vivone (1468- 1541)

Hugo (1435-1505)

  Olivier (1436- 1500)

Uncle Aloisio reported key facts about the country since the discovery. Although Brazil was discovered in 1500, the real colonization only started in 1530 with the foundation of the first villages. Portugal was faced with a fundamental problem: the excessive cost of maintaining the Hereditary Captaincies which demanded new sources of profit and the supply of labor for the cultivation of sugar cane. To face this dilemma, it was decided to enslave the natives who were working at the extraction of brazilwood. In addition, the Portuguese started the African slave trade as the main source of profits. However, the brutality with which Black people from Africa were treated became an unfortunate chapter in that story. By keeping slave ships loaded with slaves in inhumane conditions, they suffered the most barbaric torture and punishment and those who died were simply thrown overboard. After arrival, slaves were displayed in stores where they would be sold as goods to the mill owners who always chose the strongest and healthiest.

The first slave ship arrived in Salvador in 1560, that would serve two objectives of the Portuguese. First, the internal requirement to obtain qualified labor for the mills built to produce sugar, a commodity of great acceptance in Europe and, secondly, the external requirement of slave traders for this highly profitable trade to be maintained.

The four Vivones were successful in their respective professions and only occasionally returned to the Baltimore Estate to visit their mothers. As age spares no one, the three felt the relentless advance, due to the effort spent in the administration of the Royal School. Fortunately, extremely resolute, and correct alumni assisted them.

Piatã had to leave the foxes with the residence staff who completely domesticated the animals discovered by the four explorers in the English forests. It was a joy to meet them during the visits.

The years between 1560 and 1568 brought successes for the four professionals. Training at Oxford and the Royal School was the key that opened countless doors for them. Piatã was called to Windsor Castle to treat sick people of the nobility, including Queen Elizabeth I (1533-1603) of England and Ireland, daughter of Henry VIII and his second wife, Anne Boleyn. He was called once to examine her after a fall in which he broke his leg and had to receive a cast, but nothing serious.

Ybyajara, in turn, was appointed Professor of Astronomy at the British Research Institute for Astronomy and Advanced Mathematics. Cauã was invited to assume the position of Attorney of Justice while Teodoro became resident Engineer of Windsor Castle.

The best news, however, was the courtship that arose between the group and the young ladies of the nobility of Windsor Castle, which the four regularly visited. Each of them had the possibility to choose between a hive of girls which could only result in marriage. As was the custom of the Vivone family, everything should be done together. The deal was to have the "group wedding" at the Baltimore Estate with the massive presence of former students from the Royal School and the nobility of Windsor Castle. Finally, an event that was reflected throughout England. Who could have imagined the appearance of Englishmen at the wedding of three descendants of Brazilian Indians and another son of Portuguese parents?

The prospect of the event cheered up the boys' mothers. They felt ten years younger due to the frantic activity to organize the wedding party. The date set was November 10, 1567. Cauã with Sherry Paulson (born 1542), Piatã with Silvia Taylor (born 1544), Teodoro with Elizabeth Evans (born 1543) and Ybyajara with Trudy Watson (born 1542). Thus, the Vivone family registered a further increase in its members. A special invitation was addressed to Uncle Alosio and the Portuguese friends of the French-Portuguese Company of International Trade. Needless to mention, along with the parents of the brides, a veritable crowd attended the event, people of the highest nobility in England, including parents and close relatives. It was one more success.

Uncle Aloisio after returning from his trip to Brazil took the opportunity to give a detailed account of the latest events. The number of listeners was enormous.

"In 1557 Queen Catherine, widow of Dom John III, appointed Judge Mem de Sá (1500-1572)[86] to the post of third Governor General of Brazil to replace

---

[86]https://www.britannica.com/place/Brazil/Royal-governors-Jesuits-and-slaves.

Duarte da Costa. The disorganized situation left by this man needed an active, knowledgeable, and honest governor. Mem de Sá possessed all these qualities, he was known for his great heart, zeal, and prudence. He was a Portuguese noble person, trained in law with a beautiful career as a straight and energetic judge."

"Mem de Sá arrived in Bahia in December 1558. From then on, he started taking measures. With the help of the Jesuits, he encouraged the catechesis under the supervision of a priest from the Society of Jesus, an institution that gave priority to the teaching of work and of discipline. The governor showed great energy in his repression of abuse. He determined the prohibition of anthropophagy by the Indigenous people whose disobedience would generate serious penalties. When he was disobeyed by a chief named Cururupeba, he had him arrested for a year, which was enough to make him docile and submissive. He also defeated the Paraguaçú tribe, who ambushed the Portuguese and, in less than two months, appeased an indigenous revolt in Espírito Santo and forbade them from eating humans."

"Mem de Sá sustained a real war against the Indians in the captaincies of Ilhéus and Porto Seguro and, above all, in the captaincy of San Vicente where he defeated the terrible "Tamoio Confederation"[87] formed by various Indian chiefs of the north Coast of São Paulo and southern Rio de Janeiro who threatened to definitely expel the Portuguese from Brazil. The confederation that started in 1554 in retaliation for the violent action of the Portuguese against the Tupinambá Indians, causing deaths and slavery. The problem between Tupinambás and the Portuguese began with the marriage of João Ramalho, a Portuguese and right arm of Brás Cubas, Governor of the Province of San Vincente, with the daughter of Tibiriçá, chief of the Guaianazes Indians. The marriage provided an alliance between whites and Guaianazes against other Indigenous nations. In response to the attack on the Tupinambás, the chief of the village of Angra dos Reis, Cunhambebe, invested against Portuguese properties. Meanwhile, Brás Cubas imprisoned a Tupinambá chief, Kairuçú, and his son Aimberê. Kairuçú died of the ill-treatment received and Aimberê managed to organize a mass escape from the properties of Brás Cubas."

---

[87]https://www.encyclopedia.com/humanities/encyclopedias-almanacs-transcripts-and-maps/tamoio.

"Free from captivity, Aimberê formed an alliance with Goitacazes and Aimoré Indians, located in Angra dos Reis and Ubatuba that constituted the aforementioned Confederation of Tamoios, headed by Cunhambebe."

"As if the problems faced by Mem de Sá were not enough, the French arrived in Rio de Janeiro, commanded by Nicolas Durand de Villegagnon, a French knight from Malta. Villegagnon, who had embraced Calvino's religious ideas, aimed to seek fortune in new lands and aided by his friend and associate, Admiral Coligny, left for Brazil, and settled on one of the islands in the bay of Rio de Janeiro, the one that received the name of Coligny. On this island, the French built a fort that was impregnable due to the nature of the land. The fortress was named Fort Villegagnon and the whole region constituted the "Antarctic France." Villegagnon formed an alliance with the Tupinambá Indians to guarantee his permanence in Rio de Janeiro and offered arms to Cunhambebe to fight against the Portuguese. On the other hand, a tribe, named Termiminó, established an alliance with the Portuguese against the Tupinambás and the French, intensifying the fighting. After the outbreak of an epidemic of smallpox, a disease that decimated hundreds of natives, including Cunhambebe, another native by the name of Aimberê was chosen as the new chief and the conflict continued. Aimberê sought support from Tibiriçá and together they agreed to fight against the Portuguese."

"Despite the problems faced by the King of France Henry II (1519-1559), involved in religious wars, he applauded the attempt of Villegagnon to colonize and sent troops to Brazil. Villegagnon abandoned his companions in 1558 and returned to Europe while Mem de Sá received an order to expel the French. Even without having received reinforcements from Portugal, the governor managed, with 120 Portuguese and 140 Indians, to expel the French from Rio de Janeiro. Mem de Sá's victory was significant because the French had 150 good French soldiers and more than a thousand Tamoio Indians. While the French fled into the forest, Mem de Sá, after destroying the fort, returned to Bahia."

"However, the French reorganized and fortified the island again. Only in 1563 did the nephew of Mem de Sá, Estácio de Sá, arrived in Bahia, who managed to definitively expel the French from the Bay of Guanabara. The collaboration that Mem de Sá received from Manuel da Nóbrega and José de

Anchieta was essential for the expulsion of the French. Estácio de Sá, on March 1, 1565, founded the city of São Sebastião of Rio de Janeiro, but died in February 1567, victim of a poisoned arrow that hit him in the face during the battle in Uruçú-mirim, a battle that ended the French occupation. Mem de Sá spent another five years in Bahia as Governor General of Brazil."

"One of the saddest chapters of the colonization of Brazil clearly shows how much evil exists in the hearts of certain people. For example, in Salvador, Bahia, in a square close to the administrative and political center, there is a stone column called Pelourinho, where slaves were punished in front of the people to serve as an example. It is difficult to imagine how anyone can perform such cruelties."

This description was received with horror by the Vivone family, and it would be unthinkable to qualify as a human being any individual who commits such barbarities.

"Uncle Aloisio, you really are an inexhaustible source of news, Cauã marveled. How can you remember all the events with such precision? Can you talk a bit about the piracy that currently threatens the Portuguese colonies and their ships? From what we saw, it was arduous work for Mem de Sá to expel the French from Rio de Janeiro."

"Your question is very timely. I can give you an idea of the danger of these buccaneers for both Portugal and Spain."

"We are listening carefully, please continue" asked Piatã.

"Well, as you know, through the Treaty of Tordesillas, approved by the Pope, Portugal and Spain became monopolists of the world trade. Consequently, the two countries put aside the rivalry that existed between them, to a point where they became allies. As you know, both Portugal and Spain are catholic countries while other European nations are Protestant. These countries were not in the least satisfied with the Iberian trading power.

"At the same time, Spain and Portugal urgently needed labor to develop the production of sugar and tobacco for their exports to Europe and other Atlantic nations. Portugal has a strong presence in West Africa which facilitated the transport of an enormous quantity of African slaves, a highly profitable operation. Spain and Portugal established a monopoly for this traffic and created strict (and unfair) trade laws over any other country that wanted to participate in this new type of trade."

"However, the other countries, disgusted with this commercial domain, started to smuggle slaves and other goods to the Americas, an activity that was soon overthrown by the Iberian countries. Such attacks had a prohibitive cost for smugglers who then started to dedicate themselves to piracy."

"French privateers, for example, attacked Spanish settlements in Cuba, Puerto Rico and the rest of their possessions in the Antilles and attacked where defenses were weakest, leaving Spaniards at the mercy of the pirates' cleverness, mainly because it was difficult to defend their ships and possessions simultaneously."

"In 1560 the English made raids with pirate ships against the Spaniards who reacted with such violence to the point of slaughtering the English in San Juan de Ulua, located in the south of Mexico. This defeat temporarily stopped the attacks for fear of provoking war against a nation as powerful as Spain at the time. Even so, investors financed pirate incursions against the Spanish, but without significant results."

Chapter 41

With the presence in 1567 of the eleven family members and Uncle Aloisio at the Baltimore Estate, Yjara decided to promote a luncheon with everyone, as she wanted to recall facts of her life and ask questions. Initially, she made an analysis of the ages of the remnants to later expose her ideas:

Angelica - seventy-two years
Me - seventy-two
Mayara - sixty-nine
Piatã, Ybyajara, Teodoro and Cauã - thirty-six
Trudy and Sherry - twenty-five
Elizabeth – twenty-four
Silvia - twenty-three.

Looking directly at Uncle Aloisio, she started to talk about the various ages. "You are seventy years old, a little younger than your sister. Fortunately, you are still in excellent shape. The three women are bravely resisting the challenges of time and we are not giving much importance to our white hair."

"Aloisio, continued Yjara, considering that you spent most of your life in Brazil, Portugal and in other countries, I am sure that you had close contact with a number of leaders of all kinds, from kings, governors, nobles, popes, navigators, adventurers and others. Thus, you must have acquired a great deal of experience regarding the moral principles they adopted during their lives. For this reason, you are the right person to tell us which among all of them could be considered VIRTUOUS. As you know, our entire family attended the Royal School of Moral Integrity located here at the Baltimore Estate, with the only exception of the dear daughters-in-law who have just completed our family."

"It is a subject that I have been examining for a long time, replied Aloisio, I really had the privilege of getting to know many of these characters up close. It is a complex topic, as each one has merits, and it is often difficult to make an impartial analysis of their actions. Let me give you a recent example of the current Governor General of Brazil, Mem de Sá. He is one of the most evolved, educated, honest, efficient, kind, fair person. Could we consider him virtuous for having all these attributes? I do not think we can. Despite having banned the slavery and the practice of anthropophagy, he encouraged the African slave trade to Brazil. Now, in my view, it is unacceptable for someone to condone a barbarism like the enslavement of human beings. He may have had all the other qualities, but that last one did a great deal of damage to his reputation."

"But let me go ahead with other examples. Take King Henry VIII. The man got married six times, which I think is a clever idea, but he had two of them beheaded. Popes of the Catholic religion may even preach love, respect, faith in God and other beautiful things, but they were not shy about torturing, burn, hang or strangle what they defined as heretics, just because the poor men or poor women had a religion that was not than Catholic."

"Now what I consider a serious crime and a real affront to morals and good manners is the behavior of the Borgia family. To begin with, Cardinal Rodrigo Borgia wanted to become Pope by all means. To this end, he corrupted cardinals of the Holy See by buying their votes until he was elected. He chose the name Alexander VI and was known for bribery, murder, poisoning, corruption, embezzlement, and other crimes, such as torture and persecution. He fully adopted the custom of the time to burn heretics in a public square. These crimes were committed by his order and his children. An example of the type of evil that existed in the family was the murder of son Juan, perpetrated by his own brother Caesar. As if that were not enough, Alexander VI had his lovers inside the Vatican, something prohibited by the church laws, solemnly ignored by him. Despite all this, he still thought he was the representative of God on earth."

"Going back a little further, Emperor Frederick II of Germania and Pope Gregory IX who lived in the middle of the 13th. century already supported the killing of heretics. Worse still was the Hundred Years War in which thousands of French and English died in an unnecessary and cruel dispute. Another regrettable episode was that of the Crusades and the Knights Templar, troops sent by the Catholic Church to free Jerusalem from Muslim domination. These religious campaigns caused thousands of deaths on both sides. If you think about it, how could we consider the leaders on both sides who promoted such violence to be VIRTUOUS? I will stop here, because if I continue, I will have a great difficulty in finding someone who has not practiced some of these acts."

The four young newlyweds listened to Aloisio's report in amazement and looked at each other without knowing what to say about such atrocities, as they were used to the environment of Windsor Castle and its court, where everything revolved around typical habits of the nobility, such as discussions about dresses, parties, music, ballet, futile conversations, and innocent flirtations.

The husbands soon noticed the girls' embarrassment and Piatã intervened quickly to liven up the environment.

"I think that today we heard our dear Uncle Aloisio exposing his international experiences and we want to thank you for this interesting lecture, said Piatã. I think that our dear wives might not have had the opportunity to see a world as different as the one shown by our uncle. But I wanted to take the opportunity to hear your impressions about this different and somewhat sad report."

"Well, Elizabeth started, Uncle Aloisio's talk was wonderful. We had the opportunity to study these episodes in our History of Civilization classes, but we never imagined that there would be so much evil in the world. Our teachers saved us from the saddest parts. As we have been friends since childhood, we have the same beliefs regarding morals. Thus, not only do we adopt honesty as a major law for our behavior, but we fully understand and support the Vivone family's way of thinking to which we now have the privilege of belonging."

"Well, I agree with you," Trudy said. Ybyajara invited me to visit the Royal School where these concepts are taught, and I wonder if there would be a possibility to attend it. I think we would all love this opportunity."

"Wonderful," said Yjara. As the school year starts in September and we are already in December 1567, we can enroll them in 1568 and, in the meantime, I think a beautiful honeymoon would be appropriate. On the way back, we can plan a visit to the Royal School and, if they are willing, we can teach them a little of the Tupi language that we all speak it currently."

After the honeymoon, the four boys returned to their respective responsibilities while the ladies decided to follow Yjara's advice to study Tupi and learn sports such as running and archery. Mayara and Yjara were specialists in the sports of Brazilian Indians. The running was exhausting for them at first, but little by little they got used to the physical effort. The tricky thing was the practice of archery, as the shots did not even come close to the targets.

Trudy, the most enthusiastic, immediately contacted friends of Windsor Castle and invited them to participate in the fun. On weekends, the husbands assisted in teaching, as they were specialists in both modalities. Trudy's idea attracted ladies who had nothing to do. They came by the dozens, a new hit for the Vivone family. After the fear of foxes was overcome, the environment became very lively.

In 1570 the four girls graduated from the Royal School. They left in awe of what they learned, especially in relation to foreign languages and moral principles, the main theme of the course. The principles are easy to accept, but unfortunately that was not the case among the rulers.

The arrangement between them was to wait for the end of the course to think about children. Only now would they devote themselves a little more to the subject. Meanwhile, the four husbands, as was the custom of the Vivones, were accumulating an amount of money that further increased the family's fortune. Life experience gave them an extraordinary advantage when compared to Englishmen of similar professions.

In August 1573 during lunch with everybody present, an envelope arrived with a letter written by an Italian named Cornelius Lazzarini from Rome. As they were fluent in Italian thanks to the Royal School course, they had no difficulty in understanding what was written. The letter read as follows:

"To the heirs of the Vivone Family"

"I am pleased to address the illustrious Vivone family to communicate that I was authorized by the Vatican to follow an investigation that has been conducted without success since 1250. It is a mystery that still arouses great curiosity in Rome. and it relates to the existence in the Holy See of the originals of a book considered heretical by the Roman Catholic Apostolic Church, entitled "Morality and Ethics," written by an ancestor of your family named Francesco Vivone."

"From the information I was able to obtain so far, one of the four originals had been presented by the author to King Frederick II, Emperor of the Holy Roman Empire in 1231. Through other sources, I learned that Mr. Francesco Vivone, at the time, had forgotten to present Pope Gregory IX with one of the copies. It is said that, in retaliation, the Pope had the author confined in the dungeons of the Vatican where he remained for a year producing another identical book, destined exclusively for His Eminence."

"Unfortunately, Pope Gregory IX died in 1241 shortly after receiving it and, consequently, did not have the opportunity to examine its contents. I heard that the cardinals of the current Pope discovered a specimen in a case located in the crypt next to the remains of Gregory IX."

"As I was able to conclude, there must still be three original copies of the heretical book whose whereabouts are still unknown, which I intend to discover. This, therefore, is the reason for the present letter."

"Consequently, I want to ask the Vivone family if there is any specific reason for these three copies to remain in an unknown location. If my question is not considered impertinent, I would be immensely grateful if the dignified Vivone family revealed to me the fate given to the other copies. I even thought about the hypothesis that the copies could have been destroyed, as books considered heretical were burned in the public square and their authors tortured, hanged or beheaded."

Cordially,

Cornelius Lazzarini

"From what I was able to understand from this letter, our ancestor Francesco Vivone finally achieved the value he always deserved for having authored this brilliant book, said Piatã. However, what I did not understand is the interest that this gentleman has in the book and especially in the originals. In addition, I would like to know how he managed to locate us after almost 350 years after the book was written. Let us think about some hypotheses":

1- The value of the originals must be high for someone to investigate to discover the location.

2- It is possible that an ecclesiastic authority in Rome hired Cornelius to locate and sue us for hiding a book considered the work of a heretic.

3- He is not aware that the book has already been translated from Italian into English and that the Royal School adopted it for years.

"Anyway, I think we should produce a short answer and wait for a more coherent explanation about his interest in the book. As Teodoro is the most qualified to write in Italian, I suggest that he elaborate this answer, how about that?"

"With pleasure, I will do that right now."

"Dear Mr. Lazzarini

"We deduce that you are interested in reading the book. For that matter, it is not necessary to search for the original, much less the missing copies. We will be delighted to provide you with a printed copy in Italian or English. If this meets with your satisfaction, please write to us again and we will answer your request immediately.

Best regards

Teodoro Vivone"

"Congratulations, Mr. Writer, Elizabeth applauded, I did not know I had such a skillful and smart husband. In fact, I think that our honesty does not prevent us from being smart. I am sure that with that message, he will have to open the game and we will know his true intention."

Chapter 42

The Vivone family has always been lucky. The adoption of the concepts elaborated by Francesco created a shield against adversity for all of them, with rare exceptions. As could be expected, two of the wives declared their pregnancy with birth scheduled for June and August 1578. The winners were Silvia and Sherry, respectively wives of Piatã and Cauã. As for Trudy and Elizabeth, they were busy at the Royal School teaching ballet to the students interested in this noble art. Therefore, they decided to temporarily abstain from a pregnancy.

Before returning to Portugal, Aloisio asked those present if they would be willing to hear a report about another episode of foremost importance that occurred in Europe in 1571.

" Evidently " declared everyone.

"Well, initially I would like to talk about the Ottoman Empire[88]. In the 11th. century, nomadic Turkish tribes settled in a region called Anatolia in Turkey. These tribes helped to spread the Islam religion in lands that were under the rule of another empire, the Byzantine. In the last century and this one (15th. and 16th.), the Ottoman Empire became one of the strongest in the world, encompassing much of the Middle East, Eastern Europe, and North Africa. By dominating these regions, the Ottomans decided to tolerate the traditions and religions of the inhabitants. This strategy, in addition to their immense military power, was able to guarantee their expansion. Therefore, the advance of the Empire constituted a serious threat to the western countries of Europe, endangering their routes and maritime traffic in the Mediterranean, with the possibility of losing their economic power to Muslims[89]."

"This situation was becoming unsustainable. Gathered in Messina in Sicily in July and August 1571, with Christian forces led by John of Austria and at the request of Pope Pius V, Spain, the Papal States, the Republic of Venice, Genoa, Savoie and Malta, under the flag called Holy League, formed a fleet consisting of 206 galleons and six larger ships armed with artillery. Heading east, on

[88]https://www.britannica.com/place/Ottoman-Empirehttps://www.britannica.com/place/Ottoman-Empire.
[89]https://www.britannica.com/topic/Islam.

October 7, 1571, the ships met the Ottoman fleet commanded by Ali Pasha in the Gulf of Patras, off the coast of Greece"[90].

"Ali Pasha, in turn, commanded 230 galleons and fifty-six smaller ships, having left his base located in Lepanto in Greece to try to intercept the Holy League. He had about sixty thousand Christian rowers who had been imprisoned and enslaved by the Ottomans. The battle initially favored the Muslims, but the ships under the command of John of Austria were able to position themselves laterally which allowed them to bomb the ships with greater efficiency. Some failed attempts to approach were made by the Holy League until one of the Christian slaves imprisoned by the Ottomans beheaded Captain Ali Pasha and displayed his head on a pole which totally undermined the combatant´s morale."

"At the end of the fight, it was found that the Ottomans lost a greater number of ships and men than the Holy League. In addition to the death of Ali Pasha, the Ottomans lost twenty-five thousand men with three thousand captured. Of the 210 Muslim galleons, 130 were captured. The impressive Christian victory in the Battle of Lepanto avoided the expansion of the Ottoman Empire in the Mediterranean and blocked their advance to the west."

"Two interesting features occurred in that battle. The first was the active participation of the writer Miguel de Cervantes as a soldier in the Battle of Lepanto where he had an injury to his left hand that caused him to lose his movements. For that reason, he was nicknamed "El Manco." The second was more of a religious character. After ten hours of fierce fighting, Muslim's commander Ali Pasha suddenly retreated. The explanation given later by Moors imprisoned by Catholics was that a beautiful and brilliant lady had appeared in the sky, threatening, and instilling them with such fear that they panicked and started to flee. It was the Holy Queen of the Rosary[91]."

"While the Battle of Lepanto continued, it is said that Pope Pius V had a supernatural vision in which he learned that the Catholic army had just achieved a spectacular victory. And immediately, exulting with joy, he turned to

---

[90]https://www.britannica.com/event/Battle-of-Lepanto.
[91]https://www.ncregister.com/blog/the-pope-the-rosary-and-the-battle-of-lepanto.

his companions, exclaiming: "Let us thank Jesus Christ for the victory he has just granted to our fleet."

The miraculous vision was confirmed only on the evening of the twenty-first of October (two weeks after the major event) when, finally, the news arrived in Rome. While the battle was being fought against the Turks in the waters of Lepanto, Christianity asked for the assistance of the Queen of the Holy Rosary. In Rome, Pope Saint Pius V asked all Catholics to redouble their prayers. The Brotherhoods of the Rosary promoted processions and prayers in the churches, pleading for the victory of the Catholic army.

"Devotee of Our Lady of the Rosary, Pope Pius V instituted the Feast of Our Lady of the Rosary to be celebrated every day on October 7th. The news of the victory of the Christians spread throughout Europe where the bells of all the churches rang. On the other hand, the Venice Senate had a picture painted representing the naval battle with the following inscription: "Non virtus, non arma, non duces, sed Maria Rosarii victores nos fecit". (Neither the troops, nor the weapons, nor the commanders, but the Virgin Mary of the Rosary gave us the victory)."

"From what you told us, the Pope in Rome had a vision of the victory of the Holy League on the day that they defeated the Ottomans in Lepanto and called on the population to intensify prayers in the churches, pleading for the victory of the Catholic army, said Ybyajara. In addition, as shown in the picture painted by order of the Senate of Venice, those responsible for the victory would have been neither the troops, the weapons, nor the commanders, but the Virgin Mary of the Rosary. I am sorry, but I can´t believe this story. If they lost the battle because they were terrified by the apparition of the Virgin Mary of the Rosary in the sky, the Virgin would only have to frighten Ali Pasha before the fight and he would already surrender in fear, avoiding the stupid and useless killing of soldiers from both sides. In fact, she only appeared when it was turning black. Do you mean that the soldiers of the Catholic Armada and their commander Dom John of Austria who used all this huge fleet had no merit? What wins a war is not prayers or a saint who suddenly appears, but a strong army that applies smarter strategies and tactics or that overcomes the enemy with a greater number of soldiers or equipment. Anyway, I hope that Pope Pius V does not hear what I have just said, because he would certainly consider me a heretic and send an executioner to torture, hang or decapitate me."

"Ybyajara, I have to agree with you, replied Aloisio. On the other hand, I think that everyone should believe what they want. In fact, we must admit that having faith is important for people, because it is a feeling of identification with something, with someone or with a higher being. He who has faith transmits the idea of loyalty and is committed to what he believes. Thus, people can choose the Christian faith, or the Islamic faith or whatever, provided they believe in the respective commandments and obey them. As for Pope Pius V, he really believed he had such a vision, just as the Venetians thought it was the Virgin Mary of the Rosary who was responsible for the victory of the Holy League. For us, these episodes are nothing more than an illusion."

Aloisio returned to Portugal in 1578 shortly after the birth of Sherry and Silvia's children, respectively a boy named Bruno and a girl named Elza.

This time, however, Aloisio resisted invitations for new trips to Brazil, as he wished to enjoy his last years in the country where he intended to author a book with his memories. It would be something exciting, because his life had episodes that needed to be recorded for posterity.

Yjara, Angelica and Mayara also decided to lead a more serene life and to stop working at the Royal School. Their vigor had diminished sharply, since at almost eighty years of age it would be difficult to maintain the rhythm of yesteryear. Piatã did everything to save them from further efforts and devoted a good deal of time to examine them closely. His diagnosis indicated that Yjara was in better health than her sister and Angelica, who already had severe hearing and vision problems. Mayara also complained of tremors in her hands and a stiffening of the joints, diseases still without any possibility of cure.

Chapter 43

"I would like to tell you that I was invited by my head of the Department of Surgery at Southampton University to give the inaugural class of the medical course that will begin in September 1578, communicated Piatã. The Head of the Department also asked me to address the subject of the development of medicine in ancient times and in the modern world. Logically, I am worried if my performance will be acceptable, and I would not like to fail in what I consider a terrific opportunity in my life."

"My love, you are considered the best surgeon at the University of Southampton, and you will present a real show of culture," said Silvia. I know how far you have progressed, and I am sure the lecture will be a success. In addition, everyone will be present, except your mother and Aunt Angelica. Your father would be more than proud."

After the presentations and the usual preamble, Piatã began his lecture.

"As the son of a Brazilian Indian mother and a father born in England, I was fortunate and honored to be appointed Professor of the Department of Surgery at this University where I met some of the most brilliant professors in England. Since my childhood, still in Brazil, my destiny was traced to a total dedication to human beings by helping them to overcome physical deficiencies whenever possible."

"It was what our predecessors have done since ancient times when looking for the best way to treat diseases. In the Indian tribe to which I belong, the procedures for curing the sick members of the tribe are performed by a figure of foremost importance called "PAJÉ." He is the most experienced and oldest tribal member, responsible for transmitting his culture, history, and traditions. He is called Healer, because he knows the rituals and the healing power of herbs and plants that exist in the forest."

"The Indians of the tribe believe that the Pagé is capable of contacting the spirits and protective gods of the tribe. They also believe that he can make rain and improve the outcome of hunting and fishing. During his work called PAJELANÇA, he contacts his dead ancestors so that they can pass on their experiences and cures to the living. These beliefs are transmitted from generation to generation, just as the customs of the tribe told by parents to children. Unfortunately, not all customs could be called human, as is the case of the chiefs of my tribe who eat their enemies defeated in the war. Fortunately, I learned that the Governor-general of Brazil, Mem de Sá, in 1558, prohibited indigenous anthropophagy".

"Although we consider the indigenous techniques of shamanism to be difficult to accept, we must admit that they are customs rooted in the culture of the Indians and should be considered as such. But we can also learn a little from the habits they had before the discoverers arrived. Their food, for example, was natural, as they lived on manioc, corn, game meat, fish, roots, wild fruits, hearts of palm, chestnuts, coconut, without any addition of spices and enjoyed excellent health. It is widely known that this type of nutrition is partly responsible for their strength and energy, allowing them to endure long runs and walks while hunting. However, when I was in Brazil, I noticed that they began to show certain symptoms when they consumed cane sugar from the Portuguese plantations. One of the effects of this consumption was the visible deterioration of their teeth, showing holes and an unpleasant smell. The other problem was with men. They started to urinate more than normally, were always hungry, and thirsty and started to lose weight. Some lost their sight and even died. As we learned in our medical course, in the past, these symptoms were common. What drew attention at that time was the sweet taste of urine which, in the case of Brazilian Indians, could be related to the sugar contained in the sugar cane."

"Another product recently added to the indigenous diet was salt. Unfortunately, due to the lack of time spent on my stay, I was unable to identify problems resulting from its excessive consumption. However, I examined English patients who love to season their food with salt and noticed that they had swollen legs, which was not the case for those who guarded against this practice. Transporting the example to Brazil, I imagine that we would find Indigenous people with these same symptoms. Undoubtedly, it is important that we dedicate ourselves to further research on these two substances, as such a study could result in great benefits for the health of humanity."

"As a surgeon, it is valid for you who are starting a new and wonderful phase of your lives, to make a brief review of the surgical techniques currently used as opposed to the procedures of the past. To tell you the truth, I cannot be proud of the methods that are still used in our century. However, I confess that I do not have all the answers at my fingertips. Each of you will have to concentrate to solve some of the problems that cause illnesses, to improve what our predecessors taught us."

"For example, one of our main concerns is with hygiene in operating rooms and hospitals in general. The clean environment is of fundamental importance for the success of an operation. This also refers to the storage of food, surgical instruments and the eradication of harmful animals such as mice, insects and the like."

"Worse than the lack of hygiene, I call attention to the system adopted by many false doctors, such as monks and even kings, who took it upon themselves to carry out surgeries and felt that they were endowed with special powers to treat the diseases. The system consisted of using an anesthetic called Dwale, composed of a mixture of garlic juice, hemlock juice, opium, vinegar, and wine. To this day unskilled people still use it. Hemlock juice alone can be fatal. It is such a strong anesthetic that the patient simply stops breathing. It is necessary that we urgently find another product that does not endanger the patient's life and that at the same time can relieve their pain during the surgical procedure."

"Another issue that will require profound reflection on your part both now and after becoming professionals is the widespread belief among Christians that prayers have a powerful healing power. While prayers and religious beliefs must be respected, it is important to note that less serious illnesses can disappear without requiring any type of medication or surgical intervention, just by keeping the patient at rest, with healthy food and trusting your physical endurance to promote the recovery. In addition, one must meditate on what happens when the patient does not improve or dies despite the prayers."

"You, as future medical professionals, should analyze the idea of the Catholic religion that the disease is a form of punishment from God. To avoid the bubonic plague, it was said that the victims should do penance and confess their sins to a priest. If they admitted their guilt, their lives would be saved. If you are curious to study the bubonic plague or black plague that, in 1347, killed almost a third of the European population, including five of my ancestors, you will see that it was not a lack of prayers or requests to God that would save the infected through faith. Whoever contracted the plague was not being punished by God. He had been infected by the transmitters of the disease which, as incredible as it may seem, were the fleas of a species of rat, the so-called black rat. After spreading, the plague is also transmitted by contact between the sick. One of the only ways to control it is to isolate its victims for longer than the average duration of the disease."

"Finally, I would like to share with you some of the concepts that I was able to learn not only during my life but at this wonderful university. First, always analyze the facts objectively, trying to listen and respect the thoughts, customs, and ideas of others, without being carried away by abstractions without logic and without proof. Secondly, your dedication must have as a priority the patient, to whom you must show your notions of ethics, prove your competence, keeping the patient up to date and inform frankly about the positive and negative possibilities of his condition. Third, always try to plan your actions with a view to better alternatives and increasingly improved techniques. Finally, I consider the feeling of love for the patient comparable to the love felt for your family and your profession as well as to your fellowmen as the most crucial factor of the profession."

"Congratulations to all and a great medical course."

Piatã had a standing ovation by the entire audience, by his family and, especially by the students who will start the course in 1578.

Chapter 44

The following years were filled with joy and sadness. Among the joys were the continued success of the husbands and the pregnancy of Trudy and Elizabeth, despite the agreement to avoid it due to the ballet classes. Trudy had a boy by the name of Charlie in 1580 and Elizabeth in 1581 also a boy by named Alex. The sad news was the death of Angelica, Mayara and Yjara in 1580, all for reasons related to old age. Even Yjara, the healthiest of the three, could not resist the passage of time. The burial was held at the Baltimore Estate with the presence of a multitude of friends made during their lives. Unfortunately, Uncle Aloisio also died for the same reasons. He still had time to appoint a family representative who would take care of the residence in Lisbon until the arrival of its owners.

Sad news also reached Baltimore Estate about an event that deeply affected the Portuguese. The drama took place in 1578 in Morocco, in the city of Alcacer Quibir[92]. In a battle that became known as the Battle of the Three Kings, because three sovereigns died in it, the Portuguese armies led by King Dom Sebastian, were defeated by the Moors of Morocco.

To try to get rid of the pressure from the Moors on their fortresses, Portugal constituted a military force composed of seventeen thousand men, among whom there were 5,000 foreign mercenaries. The fleet left Lisbon in June 1578 and, after making a stopover in Cádiz, Spain, landed in Tangiers and went to Arzila, northwest of Morocco and then to the city of Larache a little further south.

Instead of using the sea route, which would allow the troops greater rest, they were forced to make this route on foot, which reduced their physical resistance and increased the need to use more food and water. After arriving in Larache, the force moved away towards Alcacer Quibir located inland to the southeast of the sea. With this maneuver, the Portuguese lost their biggest advantage, as they were used to winning their battles in the coastal area where they used the firepower of their warships.

---

[92]https://www.britannica.com/place/Ksar-el-Kebir.

The troops began to face a scorching heat from the semi-desert region and were confronted with an army of sixty thousand men, far superior in number and fighting in their own territory. King Dom Sebastian had adamantly refused to follow the advice of his most experienced officers. The strategy adopted by the Muslims paid off, because instead of advancing on the Portuguese, they decided to wait for their attack. At the start of the battle, Muslim leaders used two tactics, the first being to fire their muskets at the Portuguese, and then send a light cavalry charge that forced the enemy lines to retreat. The Portuguese army was exhausted and withdrew in disorder. After a quick reaction, they were subdued by the Moors and half of their troops died and the other half was captured. King Dom Sebastian disappeared. The battle of Alcacer Quibir affected the Portuguese finances significantly.

The absence of Dom Sebastian caused a dynastic crisis in Portugal. To succeed him, Cardinal Dom Henry, his great uncle, took the throne, but died two years later. The crisis that subsequently developed threatened Portugal's independence, as one of the candidates for the succession of the Portuguese throne was Philip II (1521-1598) from Spain who took the throne in 1580 after a long dispute. He was renamed Philip II of Spain and Philip I of Portugal[93].

Philip II was son of Charles V, Emperor of Germany. Philip wanted in every way, to consolidate his power over Portugal. In this regard, he used the services of a renegade called Cristopher de Moura who was appointed as his agent. His nickname was "demon" and he managed to bribe five governors with Castilian gold. With this act of corruption, Philip obtained the government of the country. Although the people hesitated to recognize him as king of Portugal, he decided to conquer the kingdom by force, which was easy, considering that the governors were "creatures" of Christopher de Moura.

One of his opponents was Dom Antonio, Prior of Crato, whose army was insignificant. Philip then assembled a powerful army under the command of the Duke of Alba, entrusting the Navy to the Marquis of Santa Cruz and camped close to the border of the city of Badajoz. Subsequently the Duke sent his troops to Lisbon and defeated the Prior of Crato at the Battle of Alcantara in

[93] https://www.britannica.com/biography/Philip-II-king-of-Spain-and-Portugal.

May 1580 and proceeded to the province of Minho where he prepared the kingdom to receive the visit of their new king[94].

In 1582, Philip defeated a remaining resistance in one of the islands of the Azores archipelago called "Ilhas Terceiras" (Third Islands) where the Prior of Crato was sworn King of Portugal with the support of France. The designation Terceiras referred to the entire archipelago of the Azores (composed of nine islands) because it was the third archipelago discovered in the Atlantic (the archipelago of the Canary Islands was designated as "Ilhas Primeiras" (First Islands), and the archipelago of Madeira was called "Ilhas Segundas" (Second Islands), according to the chronological order of discovery). With the advance of the years, the island came to be known only as Third Island[95].

It is important to consider the immense power conquered by Philip II. His real empire in Europe encompassed the entire Iberian Peninsula, Naples, Sicily, Milan, Sardinia and Belgium; in Asia: the Portuguese trading posts in India, Persia, China, Indochina, and Arabia; in Africa: Angola, Mozambique, Madeira, Cape Verde, Sao Tome and Principe, Canary Islands; in North America: a great part of America, except some of the Antilles, part of the current US and Canada, and a part of Guyana; in Oceania: everything that had been known and belonged to the Europeans. As said at the time, he extended his domain to a straight area "where the sun never sets" outnumbering the conquers of Ghengis Khan, hitherto the most powerful man of all time. As an example, below are the titles that Philip collected during his real life:

By the Grace of God, The Most Illustrious Philip, King of Spain, King of Aragon, King of Castile, Valencia, Mallorca and Sardinia, Count of Barcelona, King of Granada, Lord of Álava, Guipúzcoa and Vizcaya, King of Navarra, King of Toledo, King of England and Ireland (with wife Mary), King of France, Duke of Milan, King of Jerusalem, Duke of Brabant, King of the Two Sicilies, Count of Flanders, Duke of Limbourg, Duke of Luxembourg, Count and Marquis of Namur, Count of Holland and Lord of West Friesland, Count of Zeeland, Duke of Gelre, Lord of the Ommelanden, Hereditary Lord of Utrecht, Count of Drenthe, Lord of Groningen, King of the Indies, King of Portugal and the Algarves and King of Ceylon, Galicia, Seville, Cordoba, Corsica, Murcia, Jáen, the Algarve,

---

[94] António, prior of Crato | Portuguese prior | Britannica.
[95] Terceira Island | island, Portugal | Britannica

Algeciras, Gibraltar, the Canary, Habsburg and the Tyrol, Lord of Biscay and Molina, Duke of Athens, Count of Rossillon and Cerdanya, Marquis of Oristano and Gociano, Archduke of Austria, Duke of Burgundy, and Milan.

With the birth of Charlie and Alex, the four wives started to manage the Baltimore Estate, but were concerned about the Vivone family's property in Portugal. They decided that it would be necessary to pay more attention to it, as there was a growing danger of invasions, given the country's precarious financial situation. However, in the year 1583, Portugal was under the complete dominion of Philip II of Spain and therefore a trip to Lisbon would not be advisable. First, the four wives were English and the relationship between the two countries was not exactly friendly as Spain resented the piracy of England against its possessions and its ships. Second, Philip for religious reasons, had failed to marry Isabel, heir to the throne of England who was a Protestant, since he was essentially Catholic and wanted to convert the world to Catholicism[96]. Third, Isabel decided to help the Netherlands where Philip had sent the Duke of Parma to smother the Dutch rebels, trying to eradicate the country's Protestantism, which was the main reason for his hatred of England. Considering all these factors, at the beginning of 1584, Philip decided that the time had come to invade England.

Therefore, it would not be a suitable time to travel to Portugal due to the total instability of the political and religious situation between the two countries.

In the following year, 1585, the family decided to evaluate its future. At the time, Piatã, Ybyajara, Cauã and Teodoro were fifty-four years old. Silvia was forty-one, Trudy and Sherry forty-three, Elizabeth forty-two. Elza and Bruno were seven, Charlie five and Alex four. The Royal School continued to be an extraordinary success and influenced other schools across the country. The four brothers were successful professionals at the highest level. Therefore, except unpredictable political problems that could arise, there were no major problems on the horizon.

The children followed the teachings of Piatã who showed them how to treat foxes that were still wild animals. Contact with animals was a blessing and

---

[96] Philip II | Biography, Accomplishments, & Facts | Britannica.

positively influenced the growth of the youngsters. On Saturdays and Sundays, the family devoted their time to the pets and the children began to go deeper and deeper into the forest, always accompanied by their parents. On one Sunday, Elza found a hole covered with sticks and leaves beside a tree and asked Piatã what it was.

"Elza, it seems to me that it is a hole where the bunnies live. I must tell you that they are very scary animals. It is difficult to make friends with rabbits because they are afraid of us. In addition, if we take a rabbit home, the foxes may eat it, so it is complicated to join them with the foxes. In any case, let us wait a while to see if a puppy appears that could be tame. Hold this carrot that I brought in case a rabbit appears. Try to stay close to the den and be quiet with the carrot in hand. That's how I managed to make friends with a blue macaw in Brazil."

"Dad, then will you teach me how to talk to the rabbit?" asked Elza. She was seven and already managed to play with the foxes. The others stayed further away.

After half an hour, a beautiful brown puppy appeared, smelling the vegetation at the exit of the den. Elza remained motionless while Piatã watched from about thirty feet away. The rabbit must have thought that Elza was a stone or a piece of wood on the floor and started sniffing the carrot while Elza remained happy and immobile. The rabbit looked at Elza who winked at him which was a mistake. The rabbit ran back into the den.

"Well, said Piatã, now we are going home to get more carrots, but you will have to chop them into small pieces so that the four of you can wait for the rabbits."

Enthusiastic about the opportunity, they ran home and in a brief time they were all lying beside the den, motionless. It did not take even five minutes, two rabbits appeared who began unceremoniously to pinch the pieces of carrot in the children's hands. It was their biggest adventure and even Alex, at the age of four, was perplexed. After the big event, they returned to their parents' laps talking about their rabbit adventure.

"Now the four of you are friends and rabbit tamer. You are to be congratulated because you knew how to stay still, and nobody stressed the animals. Tomorrow if you want, your mothers will be able to accompany you to the forest again."

After twenty days of visits to the rabbit's nest, each of the four children managed to domesticate a rabbit. The pets waited for them daily and devoured the carrots on their hands without any fear, tension, or fright. Soon the children were able to pet the rabbits and take them for a walk in the forest. All this, however, far from home, as they feared the foxes.

Imagine what this episode meant for the children of the Vivone family. It is evident that their love for nature will remain in their minds forever and will certainly pass the experience on to their friends. Isn't it a good start for the formation of loving human beings?

Chapter 45

Another generation of the Vivone family was in bloom. In all these years, they devoted their time exclusively to the education of the children. After graduating from elementary schools and the Royal School, parents found it important to provide everyone with a change of environment. It was the year 1598, and the age of the youngsters was already close to twenty, while the fathers were sixty-seven and the wives approaching fifty-four. Piatã, Teodoro, Cauã and Ybyajara were firmly resolved to retire after a lifetime of work and dedication.

To achieve this goal, the women suggested a trip to Lisbon. The idea was received with enthusiasm, because finally they would all be together on a useful voyage, especially for the wives, as they could improve their Portuguese, something fundamental for the life in the city. In the course they took at the Royal School they learned Italian, French, a little Tupi and obviously improved their native language, English. For the children, Portuguese was also considered important.

Upon arriving in Lisbon at the end of 1598, they learned about the latest episode that occurred in the country since 1585, that is, since the last time they planned a trip to Portugal.

"Just imagine what we found here in our beloved Portugal, said Teodoro: King Henry of Portugal (1512-1580)[97], before his death in 1580, did not decisively designate a successor which opened an opportunity for the Spanish claimant, King Philip II, to take the throne. Consequently, as if by magic, all the lands of Portugal passed to Spain. The Portuguese population was not very satisfied with this situation, but Philip´s strength was extraordinary. In addition, European nations were seriously concerned, believing that he might actually fulfill his dream of world domination."

"In 1588, finally, Philip decided to invade England. To accomplish this goal, he created what he called the Invincible Armada[98], a huge fleet of warships. The king wanted to restore Catholicism in England, normally a

---

[97] Henry | king of Portugal [1512–1580] | Britannica.
[98] Spanish Armada | Definition, Defeat, & Facts | Britannica.

Protestant country. Philip also intended to prevent the British from supporting the rebellion in the Netherlands , which was a domain of Spain and ultimately halt the English captain Francis Drake who continued to plunder Spanish ships who took treasures from America to Spain. Philip organized a troop of nearly thirty thousand men, but first he would have to defeat the English navy."

"The Armada left Spain in May with 130 ships and 27,000 men and came to the English Channel in late July where the Spaniards managed to win a few battles. However, despite having fewer ships, the British fleet possessed a much greater firepower. Commanded by Francis Drake, his cannons were able to reach greater distances, which prevented the Spanish from approaching to attack the English ships."

"Finally, in June 1588, bombarded by the enemies, and suffering the effects of violent storms, the Spanish fleet fled northwards, bypassing Scotland in an attempt to return to Spain. Only sixty ships returned. This overwhelming defeat of the Invincible Armada saved England from the invasion intended by Philip II. In fact, this was the first major sea battle in world history decided by cannons. The reflection of the defeat reduced Spain's power in Europe and changed the strategy of sea battles."

"And what were the consequences of Philip's defeat by the English?" asked Elizabeth.

"Philip took some steps that were very damaging to Portugal. In 1589, he closed the Portuguese ports to the English and, in 1591, to the Dutch. This ban was very damaging to Portugal. As the English and the Dutch could not obtain the goods that the Portuguese imported from the East, the Dutch decided to buy them directly where the decline of the Portuguese colonies was increasing. On the other hand, the English started to attack the Portuguese possessions, such as the Azores and the Republic of Cabo Verde."

"But Philip´s tenacity was extraordinary. Despite the destruction of the Invincible Armada, he did not give up his objective and, in 1596, sent a fleet to Ireland where he lost another forty ships due to violent storms".

"Philip II, an ambitious and inhuman king who crushed everyone with his fierce despotism, died in 1598 of a cancer that caused him a long and painful suffering[99]. In September of the same year, his son took over the kingdom as Philip III of Spain and Philip II of Portugal (1578-1622)[100]."

---

[99] Philip II - Foreign policy | Britannica.
[100] Philip III | king of Spain and Portugal | Britannica

Chapter 46

Conclusion of the First Volume (Years 1200 to 1600)

Classifying leaders as prominent as the kings who led the destinies of their countries is undoubtedly a challenging task. This is also the case when issuing opinions about the behavior of pontiffs and priests of different churches, and heads of state, politicians and nobles who served in the various governments in this period of four hundred years. Based on the descriptions of the main historical periods in which they participated, we were able to classify them as either VIRTUOUS or NON-VIRTUOUS.

A striking feature that characterizes kings and popes in the 12th century and beyond was their hatred of heretics, victims of the Inquisition. We refer not only to Frederick II and Pope Gregory IX (Chapter 1), but to all the pontiffs and monarchs of the time. Those who disagreed with the doctrines of the Catholic Church or with the rules imposed by kings were sacrificed or tortured in the cruelest way possible.

Fifteen Crusades were sent from 1096 to 1316 by the Catholic Church to Palestine with the intention of restoring access by Christian pilgrims to the Holy City (Chapter 2). However, in addition to this humanitarian purpose, they committed a vast number of excesses, the most violent being the Constantinople massacre by the Fourth Crusade in 1204[101].

In the period analyzed in this first volume, it is evident that all the pontiffs of the Catholic Church who supported the punishment of heretics must be qualified as NON-VIRTUOUS. The same can be said about the monarchs who supported these abuses.

However, as explained in Chapter 2, several Catholic priests oppose these massacres perpetrated by the Crusaders and the Catholic Church and admit that people may profess different religions. This category also includes prelates who strictly follow their vocation of kindness and support for the needy and faithfully comply with the rules of morality recommended by Francesco Vivone in his book "Morality and Ethics."

---

[101] Sack of Constantinople | Summary | Britannica.

Below is the classification of the leaders whose acts were discussed in this first volume. The evaluation represents solely our own opinion for which we take full responsibility.

1- Philip VI of France. An episode that involved the dispute of two kings, Philip VI and Edward III was the War of the Hundred Years, an unfortunate episode that cost the lives of thousands of British and French. The war started because of a fight for the throne of France. It would also make no sense for one of the countries to claim that it acted in self-defense because it was attacked (Chapter 9). He was classified as **Non-Virtuous**.

2- Edward III of England. As explained in Chapter 9, in 1337, after the success of a campaign in Scotland, Edward III declared himself rightful heir to the French throne, disregarding the so-called Law Salic, which caused the Hundred Years War. Edward was likewise classified as **Non-Virtuous**.

3- Armagnacs of France. In 1380, one of the groups of the French nobility aimed to seize power. As a result, a civil war broke out causing the death of countless Frenchmen. They were classified as not **Non-Virtuous** (Chapter 15).

4- Burgundians of France. It was the group that also proposed to seize power in France and, like the Armagnacs, were included in the category of **Non-Virtuous** (Chapter 15).

5- Pope Boniface IX of Italy. An absurd and childlike dispute of a slightly different nature occurred between two popes, Boniface IX, Pope of Rome, and Clement VII of the Pontificate of Avignon in France. In this religious crisis, a consequence of the Schism of the Catholic Church, each of the popes promoted the excommunication of the other. The problem remained from 1378 to 1417, that is, 39 years (Chapter 15). Boniface IX was classified as **Non-Virtuous.**

6- Anti-Pope Clement VII of Avignon, France. Described above in item 5, Clement VII was included in the **Non-Virtuous** category.

7- Charles VII of France. A drama shook France in the reign of Charles VII around 1430. It was the life of Joan of Arc, a young French woman who was willing to save France against the English. The ingratitude and abandonment of Charles VII became evident at the end of his life and are the proof of the injustice suffered by Joan of Arc. This behavior showed that Charles deserved to be included in the **Non-Virtuous** category (Chapter 18).

8- Joan of Arc of France. In Chapter 18, more details were presented about the life of Joan of Arc. After fighting heroically for France, she was burned at the stake by the English under the allegation of witchcraft and heresy. This story of human sacrifice made for France and the subsequent abandonment by Charles VII was something unexplainable. Joan of Arc deserved to be qualified as **Virtuous**. She was an unblemished personality.

9- Genghis Khan of Mongolia. Despite being a leader who was born before the year 1200, Genghis Khan was included in the text for his foremost importance as one of the most powerful figures of the world. Genghis Khan lived in the 12th. and 13th. centuries in Mongolia. In addition to his brilliant intelligence, he was also a military genius. However, the emperor was nothing more than a barbarian who allowed his troops to slaughter all his enemies and destroy everything they passed through, being considered a devil from hell and the son of a gray fox. Therefore, he was added to the list of the **Non-Virtuous** (Chapter 19).

10- Kublai Khan of Mongolia. Kublai was the grandson of Genghis Khan. He was emperor of the Yuan Dynasty of China where he lived in the 13th. century. In addition to his eagerness to learn the customs of the West, he was equally relentless with his enemies as Genghis Khan and was therefore included in the category of the **Non-Virtuous** (Chapter 19).

11- Marco Polo of Italy. Another important personality who lived in the 13th. century was Marco Polo. Due to his brilliant intelligence, Marco was received by Emperor Kublai Khan and managed to conduct various international services for him. According to historical information about Marco Polo, there were no acts that could disqualify him in terms of moral principles. Therefore, unless other unknown factors, he may be included in the **Virtuous** list (Chapter 19).

12- Johannes Gutenberg of Germany. This fabulous inventor had a decisive influence in the world of technology. His greatest achievement was certainly the invention of the press around the year 1450, thus inaugurating a new era in the field of culture. From what is known of his work and his honesty, he can be included in the list of the **Virtuous** (Chapter 23).

13- Prince Dom Henry, the Navigator, of Portugal. Another celebrated figure that can be classified as **Virtuous**, according to the information we have had about his life. Dom Henry was responsible for the extraordinary development of science around 1450 and the following years, especially due to his discoveries on the African coast, the application of new navigation instruments and his great wisdom in mathematics and cosmography. It was he who started the great navigation cycle of the Portuguese (Chapter 24).

14- Christopher Columbus of Italy. It is impossible not to mention the name of Christopher Columbus, the discoverer of America, at the end of the 15th. century. Despite his extraordinary courage and his love for new discoveries, the crew summoned Colombo to return to Spain, due to their fear that the trip had been in vain. However, through a phony artifice, he used two different diaries, one showing a smaller distance than what they had already covered, which served to convince the sailors to continue the trip. Such trick unfortunately put him in the category of **Non-Virtuous**. The proof that the concept issued is correct came later, when Columbus imposed terrible suffering to the natives, enslaving them and forcing them to work hard in gold and silver mines (Chapter 28).

15- Pedro Álvares Cabral of Portugal. It is obvious that we could not forget the illustrious Portuguese responsible for the discovery of Brazil. As seen in Chapter 29, Cabral was a man of extraordinary courage who strictly followed the orders of D. Manuel I, king of Portugal. He was rightfully included in the **Virtuous** category.

16- Cristovão Jacques of Portugal. A famous Portuguese navigator, he was regrettably included among the **Non-Virtuous**, due to the brutality with which he treated French prisoners, sending them to Portugal or executing them (Chapters 30 and 31).

17- Jesus Christ of Palestine. It is mandatory to include Jesus Christ in the category of the **Virtuous**. Even if the episodes in his life could be considered debatable by historians, a man who dedicated his life to others and lived with the highest moral principles is worthy of this definition (Chapter 31).

18- Pope Alexander VI and sons, of Spain. In the category of the **Non-Virtuous**, Pope Alexander VI and his entire Borgia family to which he belonged stand out as the exact representation of the human evil. The cruelties perpetrated by them were truly appalling, reaching the point where one of the brothers murdered the other without any hint of regret (Chapter 31).

19- D. Manuel I of Portugal. He lived between 1469 and 1521 and was called "The Fortunate", was a king famous for his achievements in the field of navigation. However, his biggest sin consisted of pleading with the Pope to establish the Inquisition in Portugal. Thus, he had to be included among the **Non-Virtuous** (Chapter 32).

20- John III of Portugal. He was also classified in the category of **Non-Virtuous** for the same reason, namely, the desire to see the Inquisition implemented in the country (Chapter 33).

21- Martim Afonso de Souza of Portugal. He was the first Governor-general of Brazil. In view of his posture as a man of unbreakable character, he deserved to be considered a **Virtuous** leader (Chapter 33).

22- João Ramalho of Portugal. Ramalho sold Indigenous people as slaves and was known for his cruelty with the natives. Despite the services he provided to Martim Afonso de Souza, he was listed in the **Non-Virtuous** category (Chapter 33).

23- Pope Paul III of Italy. Paul III was responsible for implementing the inquisition in Portugal through the so-called Court of the Holy Office (Tribunal do Santo Ofício), installed throughout the country and in Portuguese territories. He was likewise classified as **Non-Virtuous** (Chapter 34).

24- Henry VIII of England. King Henry was a man who managed to have two of his six wives decapitated, an abominable crime for which he was classified as **Non-Virtuous** (Chapter 34).

25- Thomas Cromwell of England. Cromwell was a skilled politician and maneuvered with skill to get what he wanted, but he was not a sordid human being. He was a balanced man, who tried to save the skin of those condemned to death, like Thomas More, punished for refusing to swear in favor of the union of Henry VIII and Ana Boleyn. The references do not contain acts that could classify him negatively. Therefore, he was classified as **Virtuous** (Chapter 34).

26- Martin Luther of Germany. An important figure in the field of religion, Luther was opposed to a part of the ideas adopted by the Catholic Church. With his own religious theories, he managed to convince people to follow his teachings. However, Luther advocated violence, according to his pamphlet "Against the Horde of Peasants who Rob and Murder." Luther said to the princes: *"For a prince and lord must remember in this case that he is God's minister and the servant of his wrath (Romans XIII), to whom the sword is committed for use upon such fellows, and that he sins as greatly against God, if he does not punish and protect and does not fulfil the duties of his office, as does one to whom the sword has not been committed when he commits a murder. If he can punish and does not - even though the punishment consist in the taking of life and the shedding of blood - then he is guilty of all the murder and all the evil which these fellows commit, because, by willful neglect of the divine command, he permits them to practice their wickedness, though he can prevent it, and is in duty bound to do so. Here, then, there is no time for sleeping, no place for patience or mercy. It is the time of the sword, not the day of grace[102]."*

Protestants perpetrated acts of extreme violence, such as what happened during the so-called Sack of Rome. Because of his fanaticism in his way of doing things, Luther was qualified among the **Non-Virtuous** (Chapter 35).

27- Pope Leo X of Italy. His name was Giovanni di Lourenço de Médici. Leo X sold the so-called indulgences, a forgiveness for the sins that people commit, granted for the sole purpose of enriching the church. This dishonest act contributed to classify him as **Non-Virtuous** (Chapter 35).

28- Tomé de Souza of Portugal. Although his work for the benefit of the country was important, in one of his expeditions to find gold, he captured thousands of Native Americans to be sold as slaves. Regrettably, we had to consider him as **Non-Virtuous** (Chapters 37, 38 and 39).

29- Manuel da Nóbrega of Portugal. Due to his dedication and work of catechesis, the Jesuit Manuel da Nóbrega was considered **Virtuous** (Chapter 38).

---

[102] Against the Robbing and Murdering Hordes of Peasants (csufresno.edu).

30- José de Anchieta of the Canary Islands. The same can be said about the Jesuit José de Anchieta, a selfless man, classified as **Virtuous** (Chapters 39 and 40).

31- Mem de Sá of Portugal. Governador-general of Brazil, even though he was an honest man and compliant with the orders received from Portugal, he encouraged the African slave trade to Brazil, which resulted in his classification as **Non-Virtuous** (Chapter 40).

32- Philip II of Spain. Philip was an inhuman and ambitious king. With his obstinacy, he sacrificed the lives of thousands of men in his senseless war, aiming in every way to implant Catholicism in England whose majority of its inhabitants were Protestant. He was classified as **Non-Virtuous** (Chapters 44 and 45).

Below is a table with the above classification.

Classification of Leaders between 1200 and 1600			
Virtuous	**Chapter**	**Non-virtuous**	**Chapter**
Joan of Arc of France	18	Philip VI of France	9
Marco Polo of Italy	19	Edward III of England	9
Johannes Gutenberg of Germany	23	Armagnacs of France	15
D. Henrique, the Navigator of Portugal	24	Burgundians of France	15
Pedro Álvares Cabral of Portugal	29	Pope Boniface IX of Italy	15
Jesus Christ of Palestine	31	Anti-Pope Clement VII, of Avignon, France	15
Martim Afonso de Souza of Portugal	33	Charles VII of France	18
Thomas Cromwell of England	34	Ghengis Khan of Mongolia	19
Manuel da Nóbrega of Portugal	37	Kublai Khan of Mongolia	19
José de Anchieta of the Canary Islands	39 and 40	Christopher Columbus of Italy	28
Mem de Sá of Portugal	40	Christopher Jacques of Portugal	30 and 31
		Pope Alexander VI and Children of Spain	31
		D. Manuel I of Portugal	32
		D. João III of Portugal	33
		João Ramalho of Portugal	33
		Pope Paul III of Italy	34
		Henry VIII of England	34
		Martin Luther of Germany	35
		Pope Leo X of Italy	35
		Philip II of Spain	44 and 45

Only 11 of the main personalities in the first volume were considered **Virtuous**, compared to 20 **Non-Virtuous**.

The evaluation presented in this first volume reflect solely the opinion of the author. All acts and names of the Vivone family are fictitious. The genealogy of the Vivone family as of January 1, 1600, is presented below.

Vivone´s Family Tree in 1600

Francesco Vivone (201-1257) and Larissa Vivone (1201-1258)

Rolando (1232-1310) and Giovanna (1234-1311)

Alfredo (1273-1338)

Salvatore (1273-1338)

Sinibaldo (1232-1303) and Anabela (1236-1316)

Alina (1274-1338)

Bianca (1274-1338)

Godofredo (1232-1312) and Matilda (1240-1313)

Michele (1274-1338) and Robert Valois (1273-1338)

Luigi (1295-1367) and Sigrid Andersen (1305-1369)

Houston (1338- 1404) and Grace Baltimore (1346-1404)

Anderson (1374-1448) and Samira Amal (1390-1461)

Zachary (1416-1493) and Joaquina Querubim (1432-1510)

Clarinha (1467-1541 and Paul Demignon (1461-1540)

Esmeralda (1468-1541 and Eric Demignon (1463-1540)

Gordon (1416-1488) and Margarida de Souza (1438-1510)

Florêncio (1470-1560 and Mayara (1498-1580)

Piatã (1531-   and Sílvia Taylor (1544-

Elza (1578-

Fabiano (1472-1560) and Yjara (1495-1580)

Ybyajara (1531-   and Trudy Watson (1542-

Charlie (1580-

Cauã (1531-   and Sherry Paulson (1542-

Bruno (1578-

Orson (1418-1488) and Manuela Dias (1434-1510)

Bartolomeu (1470-1560) and Angélica de Albuquerque (1495-1580)

Teodoro (1531-   and Elizabeth Evans (1543-

Alex (1581

Cristiano (1472-1553)

Jefferson (1375-1448)

Harold (1338-1404) and Audrey (1346-1404)

Lilian (1376-1448) and Frederic (1390-1455)

Emily (1377-1377)

Demignon´s Family Tree in 1600

Claude (1430-1503) and Gabrielle (1434-1504)

Paul (1461-1540) and Clarinha Vivone (1467-1541)

Jean Pierre (1433-1505) and Jeanette (1436-1497

Eric (1463-1540) and Esmeralda Vivone (1468- 1541)

Hugo (1435-1505)

Olivier (1436- 1500)

Made in the USA
Columbia, SC
21 December 2022

73097562R00124